This Life: A Novel
By Maryann Reid

An Alphanista® Book

Also by Maryann Reid

Available from St. Martin's Press

Sex and the Single Sister
Use Me or Lose Me
Marry Your Baby Daddy
Mrs. Big
Every Man For Herself

ISBN-13: 978-0615968353
ISBN-10: 061596835X

Published by Alphanista® Books LLC

Printed in the United States of America

First Edition: June 2014

For anyone, who has ever wanted to disappear....

Acknowledgments

It's been almost 7 years since I've written one of these. This book denotes my journey back into writing, and it goes without saying that there are many to thank, and they know who they are. My deepest love and gratitude goes to my mother, Veronica Reid, who told me to take this book off my computer and finish it. It had been just a file a year ago from when I first started it in 2007. I am glad I listened. Thank you for your support and always believing.

More gratitude goes to everyone who played a part in reminding me of what I love to do most, and never letting me forget. Part of this book was written in Abu Dhabi, UAE, with the help of an amazing group of women writers. Thank you Angie, Saliha, and Yara. Grateful.

THIS LIFE

Chapter One

February 6
Miami, Florida

Faint whimpers came from the hall closet as Blake stepped out of the bathroom. Nausea churned her gut, and she stood paralyzed by memories of times when she'd made those same sounds. Times when the man she'd loved and trusted enough to marry slapped her to the floor and then...

Please...let it be rats. Or a problem with the plumbing. Anything else...just not that.

She knocked on the closet door. "Is someone in there?"

No answer, although the groans stopped.

Her heart thundered and her hand trembled, but Blake forced herself to grip and turn the knob. Two wide-eyed faces turned toward her as she swung the door wide open.

Sherry Greene, Blake's publicist, had her legs wrapped around the naked hips of NBA star Derrick Fox. Both were panting and covered with sweat.

The three stared at each other for seconds that felt like years to Blake. She felt dizzy for a moment, but then outrage surged through her veins.

"Pull your pants up and get out, Derrick. There isn't an apartment here with your name on it. And, Sherry?" Blake fixed her eyes on Sherry's and lingered there, letting the woman know that Blake had made a decision and nothing could change her mind. "You can get out, too. You're fired."

She tapped speed-dial code "2" on her cell. After barely half a ring her call was answered: "Hi, Ms. Bertrand. What can I do for you?"

"Edith, I've just fired Sherry Greene and told Derrick Fox he's not welcome anymore. Please have security escort them to their cars."

"Right away, Ms. Bertrand." Edith, Blake's right-hand woman, ended the call. Blake knew she'd immediately make another to the security team.

"I thought you was a businesswoman," Derrick complained, zipping his fly as he approached Blake. "For three million and up for a pad, what's it to you if I do the nasty in a hall closet?"

"I don't want tenants who aren't smart enough to know what their bedroom is for." Blake raised her eyes to Derrick's as the power forward for the Chicago Bulls loomed over her. She didn't back down.

"Bitch." Derrick strutted to the door leading out to the courtyard and opened it, shouting over the noise of the party outside, "Yo, Kay-Kay! Say good night, baby, we're outta here."

Through the open door Blake spied Kayla Knight, popular new actress and Derrick Fox's girlfriend of two months, throwing a puzzled glance at her date and making her way through the party crowd to join him. Four security personnel gathered at the door, waiting to see the personas non grata to their cars in the adjacent parking deck.

"Blake, please," Sherry said behind her. "He's so…" As Blake turned to face her, Sherry threw her hands up in a gesture of helplessness. "I just got carried away. I'm sorry. It will never happen again."

"I know it won't." Blake nodded to two of the security guys, who moved to stand one on each side of Sherry. "Thank you, gentlemen." She watched them beckon Sherry to come with them, and Blake turned away as she heard Sherry let out a muffled sob.

***

Back in the bathroom, eyes closed, Blake took a few deep breaths. She opened her eyes and inspected her reflection in the mirror, anxious that the ordeal of chilling memories and the confrontation with Sherry and Derrick might show in her face or posture.

A sigh of relief escaped her lips when she couldn't find any telltale symptoms of the unpleasantness. If she'd gone pale while frightened or red while angry, her bronze skin was back to its usual color. She still carried herself upright and composed, just as she'd done in her modeling days. Her dark eyes looked alert but untroubled. She decided her lipstick could use a touch-up, and gave herself a fresh coat of burgundy before rejoining the party.

Security, Sherry, Derrick, and his date were all gone. Yet as she crossed the empty hallway to the courtyard door, Blake felt as if someone was watching her. She paused at the door and glanced at the security cameras, though she knew they weren't scheduled to be switched on until Monday, when tenants would be allowed to begin moving into the luxury apartments.

"Keep it together, sister," she muttered. She flung the courtyard door open and stepped back out into the crisp night. True cold was a rarity in Miami, its subtropical latitude and proximity to the Atlantic keeping the winters mild. It was cooler than normal tonight, but that only meant the temperature was in the sixties. Some of the men wore long sleeves and some of the women were in jackets or formal wraps. None appeared uncomfortable.

Blake moved to the short table where one of two co-caterers was operating an outdoor bar. Edith stood nearby at the long table spread with appetizers, chatting with the maître d'. Their gazes met, and Edith gave Blake a decisive nod: troublesome persons removed, no drama in the process.

Hiring Edith Wright is still the smartest business decision I've ever made. Blake smiled and waved at her personal assistant, who'd been with her since her time in the world of fashion modeling.

With the Chinese New Year only two weeks away, Blake had chosen that as her decorations theme for the grand pre-opening of The Blake Tower. It lent an exotic ambience to the occasion in Latino Miami.

Paper lanterns hanging from the branches of landscaped trees shed a soft glow throughout the courtyard. Appetizers consisted mainly of Chinese recipes, but also on offer were lamb and lobster skewers, foie gras, and caviar. Chunlian—long, narrow strips of red paper painted with gold Chinese characters—were draped from every balcony and convenient branch. In Chinese culture, red symbolized prosperity and gold symbolized wealth—appropriate, Blake thought, for the opening of an apartment building catering exclusively to the rich and famous.

All around the courtyard the fortunates invited to the party circulated, nibbling hors d'oeuvres and sipping the alcoholic beverages of their choice. Owners of businesses that would occupy the ground floor sat at small tables, explaining to tenants the services they'd offer them. Along with a few other carefully selected vendors, there would be a gourmet grocery store, a high-end fashion boutique with in-house tailoring, a gym and spa, and a jeweler. Tenants could accommodate a number of their most common needs without ever leaving the apartment building.

"Where have you been?" asked Margot, Blake's best friend, dressed in a black, off-the-shoulder knee-length dress.

"You don't want to know," Blake said with sarcasm. "I'm not letting anything get in the way of tonight." Blake smiled across the room.

"Well, you go and do that. I just love seeing you in action. I can catch up on the juicy details later." With that, Margot glided to the bar.

"Good evening, Ms. Yee. You've done superb work tonight," Blake said to the owner of the Chinese restaurant co-catering the party.

"It's an honor to be chosen to serve the admirable Blake Bertrand." Ms. Yee bowed low to Blake, who bowed her head in return.

She next complimented the gourmet caterer on their traditional fare and bar, and then began making the rounds to her guests. Barbara Santers, now retired and rumored to be in the market for a mostly self-contained new primary residence in Miami, was a lifelong idol of Blake's. Her stomach fluttered with nerves as the dignified lady approached her with a broad smile. Local news photographers clustered around to capture the moment, as Blake's respect for Barbara was public knowledge.

"Ms. Bertrand! At last we meet." Barbara Santers opened her arms to offer a hug.

Blake gladly accepted, but couldn't help thinking, *Thank God she'd rather hug than shake hands.* "Please, call me Blake. I'm just so glad you accepted my invitation. I've wanted to meet you ever since I was a little girl." *And now that it's happening, I can hardly believe it. Oh, I hope I don't say something stupid, or trip over my own feet...*

"I'm just sorry circumstances didn't allow us to meet while I still worked in television. You are a brilliant woman, Blake, and you would have made one hell of an interview subject. As it is, I have more than a dozen former colleagues who begged me to ask you to do interviews with them. I'm just not so sure I want them to have what I couldn't." Ms. Santers winked at Blake over her champagne glass as she sipped, and they both laughed.

"Well, I always dreamed of telling my life story to you. I'm not sure I could settle for anyone else." Blake swirled her Grand Marnier Sidecar before taking a sip of it. "But if you decide you want to do a favor for a friend still in the journalism biz, let me know and maybe I'll do it just for you."

"Screw that, maybe I'll make a one-time comeback just to interview you myself! *A Talk With Two B's*, they could call that show." Again they laughed, and clinked glasses to toast each other. Then Santers added, "First and foremost, however, I need to go see your leasing agent. I love Miami, and I think one of your penthouse apartments is exactly what I've been looking for. Talk to you some more later?"

"Anytime!" Blake returned Barbara's small, casual wave, and her idol strolled to the leasing agent's table to sign a rental agreement.

"I see dreams do come true," a welcoming familiar masculine voice said behind Blake.

"Uncle Thorne!" Blake whirled and threw her arms around Thorne Howes, former Santana guitarist and one of her late father's dearest friends. Thorne had a massive soft spot in his heart for women. After Blake's father died, Thorne visited Blake and her mother, Jacinta, as often as he possibly could. Through the years he'd never missed a birthday or holiday, always phoning and sending a gift if he couldn't be there in person. By his side stood his wife, actress and model Michaele Jarvis, who grinned and pulled Blake into a hug of their own.

"You act surprised to see me."

"I am! I thought you'd be busy recording a new album."

"We're on hiatus for the weekend. As soon as I got your invitation, I told them there's no way I'll miss my niece's declaration of independence from her thug of a husband."

In unison the three of them turned to gaze at The Blake Tower, her first solo real estate development in the ten years since she'd married Lang against the advice of her mother and Uncle Thorne. Twenty floors of waterfront elegance, it was also her first project catering solely to the wealthy. Blake Bertrand was a newly free woman with a number of cherished plans, for which she'd need an abundance of money. She knew exactly who to get it from: the super-rich. And, having moved in their circles all her adult life, she knew precisely what they craved in exchange for their plentiful dollars.

"I'd say we should rent an apartment here so we'd have a

second home close to Blake and Jacinta," murmured Michaele, "but I don't think we could afford it, Thorne."

"Don't be silly. If you two want an apartment in The Blake Tower, it's yours." Blake smiled at Michaele, who smiled back before looking at the apartment building again.

"It's magnificent, Blake. Your best work yet," Michaele said.

"Sure is," Uncle Thorne chimed in, his eyes shining. "Your dad would be so proud of you, if he was here."

They made the rounds together, greeting VIPs from not only Miami but across the United States. Manley and Melinda Yates suggested Blake could do some real estate developments in Seattle that could rival New York, London, Paris, and Tokyo in global appeal, and Blake promised to give the idea some thought. *Someday, maybe,* she added in her thoughts. *I have other plans in mind for the next few years.* Oprah Winfrey seized the opportunity to repeat her frequent request that Blake appear on one of her television programs, and perhaps collaborate with her in some charity projects. Blake apologized for having a crammed schedule and promised they'd talk sometime. She renewed old contacts and made new ones, and felt her soon-to-be ex-husband's absence from her side as nothing less than a godsend.

At almost midnight, Blake took the podium set up near the double-door entrance flanked by Ionic columns and colossal statues of ravens, Blake's trademark. Edith rang a bell to attract everyone's attention. When silence reigned in the courtyard, Blake spoke into the microphone:

"Ladies and gentlemen, thank you all for coming. The Blake Tower opens for move-in on Monday. But if you can't wait until then, I've got a leasing agent here to handle preliminary paperwork. Zach, give us a wave so everyone will know where to find you." She paused while her senior leasing agent swung a paper lantern over his head, earning a ripple of appreciative chuckles from the party guests.

One gentleman in the crowd didn't look around for Zach, however. He kept his gaze riveted to Blake's face. She hesitated as she realized that all night he'd been looking at her every time she happened to glance in his direction. He grinned, white teeth in his fine mocha face matching his cream-colored shirt. As the other guests began turning their attention back to Blake, the gentleman lifted one hand in a lazy wave.

From somewhere near the attentive gentleman, a wolf whistle

split the air. Deshawn Thomas, lean and graceful center fielder for the Pittsburgh Pirates, licked his lips at her, not at all bothered to be seen doing so by about fifty of the most influential people in the United States. Blake gave a slight shake of her head. She wanted to tell him his moves for summoning street girls were no use with her, but she didn't want the words she'd choose quoted in tomorrow's news.

Catching her gaze again, her cream-shirted admirer pointed at the vulgar athlete and rolled his eyes. She felt her mouth reward him with a broad smile, almost as if her lips had a mind of their own.

Beside her, Edith cleared her throat, watching Blake with an inquisitive expression on her motherly face. Reminded of her duty, Blake shook off an odd nervous tingling in her gut and spoke into the microphone again:

"As many of you know, next week I have a court date to finalize my official status as a single woman again." Cheers and shouts of congratulations rose from the crowd, photographers and reporters capturing her every move and word. "This is an exciting time in my life, and I have plans that go beyond real estate developments. I've long been called an inspiration to women and girls, especially women and girls of color. In the coming year I will be starting some new projects to benefit women in business. The Blake Tower is grand, but you haven't seen anything yet. Stay tuned!"

She stepped down from the podium to thunderous applause. Before she reached Uncle Thorne and Michaele again, the cream-shirted gentleman moved to intercept her.

"Ms. Bertrand," he said, holding out his hand to shake hers, "I know you're busy, but may I please give you my card and maybe we can meet for lunch sometime?"

Blake frowned at his extended hand. "I'm sorry, but I don't shake hands."

Not only was he not offended, he grinned and playfully slapped his own face. "Doh. I've heard that, but I forgot." He plunged the hand he'd offered her into a pocket of his heather-gray slacks instead, and pulled out a business card. "We both do Miami real estate, and I'd love to talk shop sometime if you'd be willing."

She took the card but didn't look at it. "Who are you?" She was curious to know how he got in the party, but didn't ask in case she'd appear too interested. Besides, she thought, Miami is a small town, and private really means what happens indoors stays there.

"Brett Skeet. I only finished my certification half a year ago, but I've already sold three ball players' homes on Star Island. You're a hero to many of us in real estate, you know. Myself included. I'd enjoy learning from a legend over lunch. Or coffee, whatever."

"I'll have to check my schedule."

"Of course. Just one thing, though, in case your schedule doesn't seem to have any openings."

Blake had half-turned away from him. Now she turned back.

"I've just got to say, your ex-Lang is proof positive that a man can live without brains or balls." Brett Skeet flipped another lazy wave at her and moved off toward the outdoor bar.

For her part, Blake watched him go, and wondered if she should find an opening in her schedule for him. He'd said his one more thing without even a hint of a smile, and he obviously didn't hesitate to go after what he wanted. She couldn't help but respect him for both.

Toward two o'clock in the morning the pre-opening party finally broke up, with some subtle encouragement from Edith and the weary catering and security personnel. Blake, cheerily tipsy and still thrilled to have her Uncle Thorne in town, invited him and Michaele to come home with her and stay the night in one of her empty bedrooms.

"We want to make sure you have a good night's sleep," Uncle Thorne said as he hugged Blake goodnight. "But we'll be over in the afternoon for a visit."

"I'm so glad you're here." Wishing she didn't have to, Blake stepped out of the hug. "Even if it's only for the weekend, it means the world to me."

He ruffled her hair. "You getting yourself free from that son of a bitch you called a husband means the world to me, girl. To your mother, too."

"I know. Let's not talk about him, though." She blew a kiss to them. "I'll see you in the afternoon. Love you both."

Blake turned to go inside the apartment building, stopping when Michaele called, "What's wrong? Did you forget something?"

"No." Blake grinned. "I just need to use the bathroom, that's all. I drank a few too many Grand Marnier Sidecars tonight, I think."

"Yes, I think you did." Uncle Thorne laughed and motioned her to go on. "We'll wait here and walk you to the parking deck."

"You don't have to—"

"We know that," Michaele said, smiling as she leaned against Thorne. "But we want to, so that's that."

Blake opened the door from the courtyard and stumbled a little on her way to the bathroom at the end of the hall. *Lucky I'm wearing flats instead of stilettos. And lucky I've got a chauffeur waiting to drive me home. I'm tore up from the floor up, I do believe.* She plunked herself down on a toilet and let the floodwaters rush out of her.

At first she didn't think anything of the master bathroom door opening, and a pair of feet coming to a stop. Thankfully, the toilet area was private, encased between two walls and a door.

Then the realization penetrated Blake's alcohol-fogged mind. *Michaele wouldn't be wearing Allen Edmonds loafers.*

Icy fear burned in her gut. She knew it wouldn't be, but she asked, begging it to be so, "Uncle Thorne?"

Finished with her business, she swung the door open, and there stood Lang. Her soon-to-be ex-husband. Soot-colored eyes searing twin holes in her soul. "Afraid not, my darling wife."

She stood, knowing herself trapped. Just as she'd been throughout ten years of a marriage made in hell. "What do you want, Lang?"

"You." He shrugged.

"Let me out."

"Sure." He kicked the door open, grabbed her arm, and hauled her out. Then he punched her in the stomach.

Even as he clutched a fistful of her hair and kicked her feet out from under her, part of her couldn't believe this was happening, here and now. On the evening of her return to solo real estate development. Just a week before her divorce was to be finalized.

He kicked her legs, her back, her arms protecting her head. She cried out, begged him to stop.

"Get the fuck away from her, you microscopic dick." It was Uncle Thorne's voice.

"Who's going to make me? Huh?" Lang's expensive dress shoes turned around to face Uncle Thorne's sneakers. "You wouldn't want to hurt your musician's hands, old man."

"See, that's where you're wrong. I'd love to beat the shit out of your punk ass, even if I can never play a guitar again." Uncle Thorne's leather jacket fell to the floor. "Just throw the first punch, so I can honestly say you started it."

"And I'm warning you, he'll have help." Michaele's even, calm voice somehow seemed more threatening than Uncle Thorne's barely restrained fury.

Blake struggled to stand up. Every inch of her ached, screamed protests when she moved. A moan escaped her.

Nobody else made a sound for what seemed an eternity. Finally Lang snorted. "Some other time, maybe, when it's just me and you. I've got no feud with your wife. I don't want to wreck her pretty face."

"Excuses, excuses." Uncle Thorne's sneakers paced toward Blake. "You'd best clear out before I decide I don't care if I go to jail, Lang."

"Fuck for brains." Lang's high-end shoes tapped across the marble tiles, the sound stopping when he reached the carpeted hall.

Uncle Thorne slid one hand under Blake's shoulders, the other under her knees. He grunted as he lifted her. "You're not heavy, you're my niece. But my back isn't young anymore." He smiled at Blake, tears rolling down his cheeks.

Blake managed a smile back at him. She tried to say thanks, but her mouth wouldn't do what her brain told it to.

Thorne looked at Michaele. "Her phone is probably in her purse. Edith should be "1" on her speed dial. We'll spend the night in Blake's place after all. And by the time we leave, she'll have round-the-clock professional bodyguards."

Chapter Two

February 13
Miami, Florida

Her BlackBerry rang at 7:15 A.M., just as Blake finished applying her blue eye shadow. Donna Summer's "She Works Hard for the Money" alerted her that it was her business manager, Charles Douglas, calling.

She skipped the niceties of saying hellos. "I've got to be in court at eight," Blake reminded him.

"I know that, but I've been waiting since closing time yesterday to tell you this. The Wishman family is ready to make a deal."

Her heart galloped in her chest as she strode out of the bathroom and plunked herself on a corner of her bed. "How much are they asking?"

"A billion."

Her galloping heart came to an abrupt halt. "I wouldn't have that much even if Lang gets nothing from me today. What's the FMV?"

"I had to dangle some carrots to get that info for you after business hours yesterday, but here you go. Six hundred million."

Blake winced. She'd have that much only if the divorce order ended up heavily biased in her favor. Otherwise she'd be forced to borrow some money or recruit investment partners if she really wanted to make this deal happen. Which she did. Desperately.

"Offer four hundred mil. Maybe by the time the haggling is all done, we can bring the price close to actual fair market value."

"I'm on it. Good luck today."

"Thanks, Charles. You're the man."

"You've got no idea, even after all these years." Charles clicked off, and Blake shivered with a lovely tingling in her palms and spine.

The Wishman Spears building could really be hers, soon!
Maybe it's a good omen for the day.

***

"All rise," called the bailiff. "The Honorable Judge Eliza Stone, presiding."

Blake stood, as did Carmen M. Morales, the attorney she'd hired to represent her in her divorce. Morales was regarded as the best family law attorney practicing in the Florida counties of Miami, Dade, and Broward.

Lang stood across the aisle, next to his own attorney. Thorne Martin Gruber specialized in representing the wealthy in divorce cases. Usually Gruber practiced in the Tampa area, but for the kind of money commanded by Lang and Blake Bertrand, he'd been willing to travel.

"You may be seated," the bailiff announced when Judge Stone was settled on her bench. Blake, Lang, their attorneys, and the packed courtroom of spectators all sat, rustling skirts and jackets and thumping purses and briefcases.

No journalists were present in the courtroom. This was to be, by Blake's request, a sealed decree of divorce, its exact terms known only to judge, attorneys, and ex-spouses Blake and Lang.

"In the matter of Bertrand versus Bertrand," Judge Stone intoned, "let me start by making an observation. Which is—rarely does anyone get everything they want in a court case." She paused, then added, "Today will be no exception."

Stone plopped a thick stack of paper, obviously numbering hundreds of pages, onto the desk in front of her. "There is simply no way I'm going to read this order of divorce in its entirety. I have provided both parties with a copy of the order, and I hereby enter this copy into the permanent court record. I don't envy you that task." The last statement was an aside to the court reporter, who grimaced as the bailiff picked up the order and handed it over to the reporter for audio recording and written transcription.

"This is the first time I've presided over the divorce of a couple whose holdings jointly total in excess of a billion dollars," Stone continued, "and I hope and pray it will be my last time doing so. Most of my order consists of an itemized division of property, since the two of you couldn't reach agreement in mediation." Stone indulged in one scowl for Lang and another for Blake. "I have been as fair as I possibly can. To sum up, you each asked for everything, and neither of you can have it. Blake Bertrand owned assets of approximately $40 million prior to the marriage, and those she will keep. Everything else was earned during the marriage, and by law you each receive half."

Blake grumbled noises rather than words. Her only comfort was seeing Lang's color go ashen and his hands curl into fists.

"Fortunately there were no children at issue in this marriage, so custody matters are not a concern. Which brings me to a few motions filed by one side or the other, that I need to dispose of." Stone shuffled a much smaller stack of papers, cleared her throat, and held one sheet up for her own reference as she continued.

"It has been requested by petitioner Ms. Blake Bertrand that a gag order be imposed on all present in this place at this time, and that the terms of the divorce order be sealed. This motion is granted."

Morales flashed a smile at Blake. She smiled back at her attorney. This was an important win for them.

"Also requested by petitioner Ms. Blake Bertrand is a restraining order against Mr. Lang Bertrand." Stone lowered the sheet of paper and leveled a stare at Blake. "My understanding is that you allege your husband attacked you only a week ago, at a party you were hosting. Is that correct?"

"Yes, Your Honor," Morales answered for Blake.

"It is also my understanding that you did not phone the police to report the attack. Correct?"

"Your Honor, my client—" began Morales, but Judge Stone cut her off.

"Answer yes or no, please, Counselor."

Morales sucked in an audible breath before replying, "Yes, that's correct, Your Honor."

"I must, therefore, regard the allegation as hearsay. Your photographs and attending physician's reports are accordingly dismissed from evidentiary consideration. However, there have been previous incidents when Petitioner did call law enforcement regarding her husband's attacks on her. On the basis of that history of domestic violence, I hereby grant the motion. Bailiff will please present both parties with a copy of the prepared restraining order, valid for one year from today's date but renewable if circumstances merit it. Lang Bertrand, you are ordered to stay a minimum of five hundred yards away from Blake Bertrand, except if you should decide to dispose of any property awarded to you that was acquired during the marriage. In that case a duly sworn police officer must witness the contact you have, and any proceeds from the disposition of property shall be divided equally."

"Shhhiiiiit," hissed Lang.

"Use such language in my courtroom again, and you'll be spending the night in jail for contempt of court," Judge Stone warned Lang, with a withering glare.

"To continue, a motion has been filed by Respondent asking that Petitioner pay him monthly alimony, unless and until such time as he remarries to a spouse of equal or greater net worth as Petitioner." Renewing the withering glare, Judge Stone informed Lang, "Don't be ridiculous. As of today you're worth almost half a billion dollars of your own assets. Motion denied."

Beside Lang, Gruber actually looked as if he'd just bitten into something sour. Morales winked at Blake, who struggled not to giggle.

"Finally, Petitioner has filed a motion asking that this court order Respondent's last name be changed. My decision regarding this matter requires some explanation."

Absolute silence prevailed in the courtroom. Everyone gave Judge Stone their full attention, waiting with breathless curiosity to hear the outcome.

"When a man and woman marry, it is common for the woman to legally adopt her husband's surname as her own. If the man and woman subsequently divorce, the woman may keep her former husband's last name if she wishes, or as part of the divorce order may change her surname back to her maiden name or even a different name of her choosing. The former husband cannot make that decision for her."

Blake glanced at Morales, whose lips were turned down in a frown of disapproval. *Uh-oh. My attorney doesn't like the sound of this any more than I do.*

"It doesn't happen often, but occasionally when a man and woman marry the man legally adopts the wife's surname as his surname also. I find no reason why a wife should have the power to strip her former husband of her name that he chose to adopt, when a husband does not have the same power with regard to his former wife. Petitioner's motion to order Respondent's surname changed is therefore denied."

She couldn't help herself. "Judge Stone, please—"

The judge rapped her gavel on a wooden block sitting on her desk. "Order in the court!" sang out the bailiff.

"I understand your reasons for filing that motion, Ms. Bertrand, and I sympathize with your disappointment. However, I can't rule any other way than I've done," said Judge Stone. "This court decrees the marriage of Lang and Blake Bertrand dissolved. It is so ordered. There will be a ten-minute recess."

Judge Stone stood and retreated into her chamber, and everyone shuffled out of the courtroom. Morales groped for her purse and briefcase with one hand, tapping away on her iPhone with her other hand. Blake let her breath out slowly, gathering her purse and retrieving her BlackBerry from it.

A text message awaited her, from Morales: <Bathroom before outside. Follow me. Take a stall, sit, breathe until I call your name.>

Damn it, I need to call Charles and ask how negotiations are going with the Wishman family. Blake bit back all the expletives invading her thoughts. *But I'm paying Morales too much to ignore her advice.* She trailed after her attorney, one of several women moving toward the women's bathroom. Here and there a supporter congratulated her on being single again, and she murmured her thanks.

Inside the bathroom, Blake took a stall as Morales had directed her. Morales positioned herself by the window, and Blake could hear her carrying on a series of brief conversations: "*Hola*, Miguel. I'll be back at the office within the hour. Everything set up for the deposition with Señor Ruiz this afternoon? Good, *bueno*." "Nicole? Hi, Carmen here. Listen, I'm still waiting for your... Yes, that's right. I can't really proceed without that. Lunchtime? Sure, that will be fine, just leave it with Miguel." "Good morning, who am I speaking with? Oh, Stephanie, I'm sorry, you sounded different just now. I need to talk to someone in the DA's office..."

While Morales took care of business, Blake summoned up local news on the BlackBerry. Every local television station was broadcasting from the courthouse steps, where Lang and Gruber were answering questions:

"Lang, can you tell us—"

"Mr. Bertrand, please." Lang grinned like a cat that just ate someone's pet hamster.

"My client and I can't comment on specifics of his divorce," Gruber announced, "and by the judge's order neither can anyone else. However, my client's name remains Lang Bertrand, so please address him accordingly."

"Bastards." Blake killed the BlackBerry's Internet connection.

Gradually the bathroom emptied of occupants except for Morales and herself. Her attorney wrapped up her latest phone call, and then said, "Blake? Let's talk."

Blake emerged from the stall and leaned against one of the sinks. She didn't know what to say, so she simply watched Morales expectantly.

Morales examined Blake for a moment. "I thought I told you to take some breaths."

"You did, but I don't understand why."

"Because you're off-balance and need to center yourself." Morales gestured at the mirror over the sink, and Blake looked at her reflection. "See what you're doing?"

Shaking her head, and watching herself do so, Blake replied, "Just waiting for you to explain what this is all about."

"*Mira que cosa tiene la mujer esta.*" Morales gave Blake a quirky grin.

"This isn't *I Love Lucy.*" Blake couldn't help grinning back, though.

Morales pointed to the mirror. "You're touching that scar on your forehead. I know what that means. Do you?"

Blake shrugged her shoulders. "That I should get plastic surgery to remove it?"

"You do that when you feel insecure. Breathe, Blake." Morales took a deep breath and beckoned to Blake to follow her example. They breathed together a few times, and then Morales nodded satisfaction. "That's good. Now listen. I know you wanted to take the Bertrand name away from Lang, but we talked about what you can do if that request was denied. Let him have it. The name Blake is still yours alone. Roll with that."

Again, Blake breathed. She felt like screaming instead. "But the raven—"

"Per Judge Stone's divorce order, neither of you can use the raven logo anymore. Find a symbol that represents Blake to you, and make a new logo from that."

"I hate this."

"I know." Sadness filled Morales's eyes. "Divorce is a kind of death. You've lost something you loved, and you've got to grieve and that never feels good. The good thing, though, is that there's life after divorce. You can resurrect yourself. Make it your mission to bring Blake back to life."

***

Seven hundred million dollars.

At about three o'clock in the afternoon, the Wishman family quoted that amount as their selling price. By half past four Charles still hadn't been able to haggle them down any more. With her post-divorce assets Blake couldn't buy the Wishman Spears building single-handedly, but she felt optimistic that she could probably put up enough collateral to obtain a bank loan for the rest. Or she could recruit one or more investors to put up the remainder.

"Tell them it's a deal. Give them my real estate attorney's name and telephone number, and tell them I can meet with them anytime they choose to close on this." Blake's hand trembled after she ended the BlackBerry's connection with Charles.

Seven hundred million dollars...was one hell of a lot of money, even for Blake. However, for more than a decade she'd dreamed of everything she could do with a building like the Wishman Spears. This was an opportunity she simply couldn't let pass her by.

Only one aspect of seizing this opportunity troubled Blake: she'd be forced to spend a few days away from her mother.

Jacinta Bertrand was a fiercely independent woman. Some mothers of daughters who become wealthy would gladly take up a life of luxury at their offspring's expense. Not Jacinta. Until July 4 of the previous year, she kept her job as a nurse at South Miami Hospital, leased a modest apartment, and did all her own cooking and laundry and shopping. Her only benefit from Blake's success, which she accepted only after the most impassioned argument mother and daughter ever had, was that Blake hired a maid to clean Jacinta's apartment three times per week.

Everything changed when a drunk driver collided head-on with Jacinta's car on her way home from work. Jacinta barely survived, and more than half a year later she still had months of physical therapy ahead of her.

"I wonder if the Wishmans would consider coming to Miami to close the deal. That way I wouldn't have to leave Mom." As the Fisher Island ferry pulled away from its Miami harbor dock, Blake tied on a silk kerchief to keep the wind from slapping her long hair all over her face.

She'd been thinking aloud when she spoke. Matt, the

bodyguard assigned to protect her tonight, answered anyway. "Looks to me like your mother has the best medical care money can buy. I think she'd be all right if you go to New York for a few days."

"I know her nurses are the best. I hired them myself. But she's my mother, not theirs."

Matt slanted a sly grin at Blake. "They're getting paid a lot better to take care of your mother than they'd be to take care of theirs."

Blake rolled her eyes at him, but couldn't help smiling afterward. "Probably true, but I'll feel better if Mom says she doesn't mind."

When the ferry docked at Fisher Island, Blake strolled past two of the Olympic-standard tennis courts, a five-star restaurant, and part of the nine-hole golf course designed by P.B. Dye. Peacocks wandered the island freely, and one of them gave voice to a call as Blake and Matt walked by it.

A peacock's call sounds like a woman screaming, and this was only Matt's second time guarding Blake. Matt nearly jumped out of his skin, and trailed after Blake grumbling inventive profanity the rest of the way to the condo Blake rented for her mother.

"*Hola*, Señora Bertrand," the housekeeper greeted them after Blake rang the doorbell. The housekeeper, Riza, was second-generation Cuban-American, like Jacinta Bertrand. "Your mami has just had her dinner, so the nurses must be bathing her now. Have a seat in the parlor and I'll call you when they're done."

"*Gracias*," said Blake. She led Matt into the parlor, and they sat looking out the large window at the sunset over the Atlantic, until Riza called Blake's name.

"I should only be a few minutes, Matt."

"Take your time." Matt flashed his smartphone at her. "I'll just browse news and sports until you're ready to go home."

Blake nodded and left the bodyguard to entertain himself. She climbed the stairs to the second floor and paused at her mother's open bedroom door. Though it was February, the air conditioning whispered from the ceiling vent. Jacinta liked to sleep in a cold room, burrowed under a thick pile of blankets. A lamp on the bedside table glowed its dimmest setting, which meant the room was dark except for a circle of thin shadows that revealed Jacinta's head resting on her pillow.

"Come on in, *mija*," Jacinta called to Blake. "I promise not to die of a surprise visit from my daughter."

Sitting in one of the bedside chairs, wrapped in a heavy quilt, the night nurse gave Blake an encouraging smile. "It's true, the old dear is tougher than you think she is."

Blake settled into the other bedside chair and took her mother's hand with practiced gentleness. "How was your day, Mami?"

"Like any other day of physical therapy, I suppose." Jacinta shrugged her right shoulder, which was further along in healing than the left. "Brutal. They make me beg for death and then don't give it to me. But then, good physical therapists do that."

They shared a little laugh, and Blake decided her mother was beginning to sound like her old self again. Looking like her old self was still somewhere in the future.

"What about you, girl? How did the divorce hearing go?" Jacinta opened her eyes wider than before and fixed a don't-hold-back stare on Blake.

"There's good news and bad news."

"Let's hear it, good news first."

"I got a restraining order against Lang. Only for one year."

"*Mierda!*" Jacinta rolled her eyes. "You should be given a restraining order for life."

"A year is better than nothing, Mami." Blake patted her mother's hand. "Ready for the bad news?"

"Is anyone ever ready for bad news?"

"My *mami* the philosopher," Blake observed to the night nurse, and they exchanged smiles. Jacinta's spirits were undeniably improving as time went by.

"Well, tell me."

"Lang got to keep Bertrand as his last name."

Jacinta Bertrand exhausted her supply of Spanish curses and had to supplement with a few choice words of English, ending with "Scum-sucking son of an unwashed whore." She rested for a minute, while Blake fought to keep herself from laughing, then Jacinta added, "I only pray your father doesn't know."

"I hope he doesn't know, too." Blake's gaze wandered to the framed photograph of Theo Bertrand next to the bedside lamp. He sat at a candlelit piano, a faraway dreamy expression mellowing his deep-set eyes and angular features. That photograph had been taken during his first public performance of "Nothing But You," a soulful jazz love song he'd composed for Jacinta when they'd still been teenagers. She sighed, then said, "Mami, something else happened today."

Her mother gave Blake's face a searching look. "Something you've wanted, but the timing could be better?"

The night nurse winked across Jacinta's bed at Blake. Jacinta was notorious for making guesses that seemed almost psychic in their inexplicable accuracy.

"Don't look so surprised. You're my only child. I've been reading your thoughts in your face all your life." Jacinta closed her eyes. "Out with it, *mija*. I'm worn out and can't stay awake much longer."

"I've been invited to buy a building in New York City that I've wanted for years and years. I'll ask the owners to come here to sign all the paperwork. But if they aren't willing to do that, will you mind if I go to New York for a few days?"

Cracking one eye open, Jacinta leveled an astonished gaze at Blake. "Sweetie, all day long I'm taking physical therapy. By the end of the day I'm ready to fall asleep the second I get into bed. I'm not able to talk to you for more than a few minutes a day, anyway. You go on to New York and enjoy being free of that donkey's ass you called a husband. I'll be fine."

"Are you sure, *Mami?*"

"In fact..." Jacinta opened both eyes wide again. "Why stay only a few days? You used to love New York, didn't you? Just not the modeling scene?"

"Yes, Mami, but—"

"But nothing! You're lucky enough to afford to travel, and stay weeks or even months anywhere you please. Go enjoy New York for a while. Maybe by the time you come back to Miami, I'll be ready to go out dancing with my girlfriends." Jacinta Bertrand smiled, and a serenity softened her face as she closed her eyes again. "One thing is sure, when I'm recovered I'm going to celebrate the fact I'm still alive. I lived to see my daughter get away from a vicious, brutal bastard who never loved anything but controlling her and spending her money. I thank God for sparing me, Blake, and for sparing you, too. Now kiss me good night and go pack your bags for New York."

Blake stood and leaned down, brushing her lips against her mother's cheek. "Good night, Mami. I love you so much."

"Will you do me one favor before you go?" From the sound of her voice, Jacinta was already half-asleep.

"Anything. You just name it, Mami."

"Put your father's record in the CD player for me, then. Good night, sweetie."

Blake went to the entertainment center lining the wall across from Jacinta's bed. She could have found the CD of the only record her father's jazz band ever made by touch alone—the plastic case had concave spots worn into it where thumb and forefinger had held it so many times over the years. For a moment she studied her father's face again, in the band portrait that comprised the cover art. Theo Bertrand wore a guitar-shaped keyboard strapped over his shoulder, his band mates surrounding him. Raven Glory, the band's name had been.

"In Old French, *Bertrand* means 'glorious raven,'" Theo had told four-year-old Blake, when she'd asked why he gave his band such a weird name.

She plugged the CD into the player and descended the stairs as the first sensuous notes of "Nothing But You" began to play.

Chapter Three

February 23
Miami, Florida to New York, New York

No matter how many times Blake got on an airplane, she always loved the whole experience. Her favorite part was takeoff: the acceleration pushing her back in her seat, the nose of the plane tipping up as the aircraft flirted with peeling away from the ground, the roller-coaster thrill in her gut as the Earth appeared to fall away from her. She always requested a window seat for the best possible view and, until the plane reached an altitude at which scenery details were no longer visible, she sat with her nose pressed against the glass.

"The glorious raven flies again," she murmured.

"Say again?" Matt, one of the three bodyguards assigned to accompany Blake to New York, lifted one earpiece of the headset he'd plugged into his smartphone.

"I just love flying." Blake glanced at him and bent her head, realizing she was as excited as a small child and feeling a bit embarrassed about it.

"Buy a private plane and earn a pilot's license," suggested Suki, another bodyguard newly assigned to Blake, from the seat behind her.

With a shock, Blake realized she'd never considered that idea before, and for a moment she wondered why. Then the obvious answer occurred to her: *Oh, right, Lang never would have let me have that much freedom of movement while we were married. But*—she grinned at the thought—*that's not an obstacle anymore!*

"You know, I think I'll do that." Blake turned half around in her seat and gave Suki a thumbs-up. "Thanks for the suggestion!"

"Eh, you would have thought of it yourself, sooner or later." Suki shrugged. Half a second later she appeared to be deep in meditation.

Blake shivered, a little unnerved by the suddenness of Suki's altered mental state. She turned her gaze to Antonio, her other bodyguard for her stay in New York. The manager of Blitz Security told her he'd chosen to send Matt, Suki, and Antonio to New York with Blake because the three frequently worked together and had such a good rapport that they seemed to communicate without speaking. Antonio glanced from Blake to Suki and back again. He mouthed the words, "She does that."

Antonio then waved one hand in front of Suki's closed eyes. "Don't make me break your hand off your wrist," Suki said sweetly, blank-faced and eyes still closed.

"She could really do that," Matt told Blake. "Suki is a third-degree black belt in combat jujitsu." He paused, then added, "That's what American and British special ops soldiers use."

"If Lang gets close enough to touch you, I'll touch him instead," said Suki, still without facial expression. "He won't enjoy it."

Blake hesitated. *What the hell should I say to that?* "Uh...thank you."

"All in a day's work." Suki raised her hands, palms up, then let them fall to her lap. No other part of her body moved in the slightest.

I can't even see her breathing, Blake realized. She shivered again, and busied herself with her BlackBerry on one knee and her iPad on the other. *The flight stewards can't take drink orders soon enough for me...*

She forgot the spooky introduction to Suki, however, as she discovered a new email from Charles. <Trouble with the Little Haiti bids. Anonymous bidder offering twice your latest. Please advise what you want to do.>

<You've got to be joking,> Blake emailed her reply. <Remind me again what the FMVs for those properties are?>

As she waited for Charles to answer, her BlackBerry alerted her that she had a new text message. From Suki's smartphone, and also sent to Matt and Antonio. <Old man two rows ahead has been eyeing my client ever since we boarded the plane.>

<Right. Anything else?> asked Antonio.

<Not so far,> Suki replied.

<I'm closest, I'll watch him,> Matt tapped out on his smartphone, while Blake sneaked a peek behind her and didn't see Suki holding a phone at all.

That woman makes my skin crawl. I'm glad she's on my side. Blake turned her attention back to her email.

New message from Charles: <330k, 180k, and 117k.>

Blake gazed out the window at the clouds beneath the plane, considering the situation. Her latest bids were 120 percent of the FMVs for the properties. She expected her plans for the three Little Haiti properties to double their value immediately, with their worth increasing as she gradually revitalized the entire community. *I can outbid the anonymous person by a small amount and still turn a profit soon after renovations are completed*, she decided.

<Up my bids to 110 percent of the anonymous bidder's offers,> Blake emailed Charles. As she looked up from her iPad, she observed the old man two rows ahead studying her. He waved, but she didn't wave back.

She plugged the BlackBerry into the nearest of the Delta's first-class power outlets, recharging it while she browsed news using the iPad. Business news websites were rife with gossip that Blake Bertrand was about to buy the Wishman Spears building. Her photograph, as she'd looked the day of her final divorce hearing, was splashed all over the Internet.

"Good morning." A smiling stewardess stopped the drinks cart next to Blake and Matt. "Can I get you a complimentary beverage?"

"I'd love a Grand Marnier Sidecar," Blake answered, returning the smile.

"Nice try." The stewardess laughed. "We've flown together before, Ms. Bertrand. Don't you remember? And we're still not equipped to mix cocktails; but I did tell Delta you asked about it."

Blake faked a heavy sigh. "Well, I had to ask, you know. So...just beer, wine, and spirits still?"

"Yes, ma'am."

"A nice Cab would go down well, I think." Blake nudged Matt, who tugged his headset off and arched his eyebrows. "Want something to drink, Matt?"

Matt shook his head. "I'm not supposed to when I'm on duty."

"You're not on duty until the night shift." Blake winked at him.

"Go ahead," Suki intoned. "She's the boss. Antonio and I can keep watch on Big Eyes up there."

"I'd love a Sam Adams."

"Coming right up." The stewardess rummaged inside the cart for a few seconds, then handed Matt a chilled Sam Adams before pouring a glass of red wine for Blake. "If you need refills, just let a member of the steward team know." She smiled and half-saluted, then pushed the cart along to the next row of customers.

Another stewardess handed Blake a second glass of wine, this one from the menu of drinks that cost extra. It was a Merlot with a heady aroma that made Blake's mouth water. "This comes to you with compliments from the gentleman over there." She gestured to the old man who'd been watching Blake ever since they'd been seated.

This time Blake's sigh was genuine. "Please tell him I said thank you."

"Want me to have a talk with him?" asked Suki.

"Not yet." Blake sipped the Merlot. It was superb, so much so that she wondered what brand it was. "I'll go speak to him. You can intervene if he tries anything, right?"

"Of course."

Blake stood, slid past Matt, and stepped up to the old fellow who'd bought her a glass of expensive red wine. She raised the glass and murmured, "This was very kind of you."

He paused to appreciate how she looked in her form-fitting Chanel suit before he said anything. Then he put out a hand and said, "Glad to do it, Ms. Bertrand, and glad to finally meet you. I'm Stan Walker. Maybe you've heard of me?"

She hadn't, and he obviously didn't know much about her either. *Except that I'm rich and considered beautiful.* "I don't mean to be rude, Mr. Walker, but I never shake hands." Noticing that people in other seats were listening to the conversation, Blake added, "I always caught every bug going around, until my mother advised me to quit shaking hands. She's a nurse. I haven't been sick much since I started following her advice."

"I'll have to remember that. At my age, the old immune system isn't as feisty as it used to be." Walker chuckled. "Anyway, I'm a business journalist. It's been a while since you've agreed to an interview with anyone."

So that's what this is about. "That's true. I stay so busy, it's tough to find time for that anymore." *Busy letting Lang have the spotlight, because if he thought I was stealing attention away from him he'd beat me senseless. Maybe I should schedule an interview soon, just to show him I'm my own woman again?*

"Understandable, that's the way it goes with the best business leaders. I'd love to interview you whenever you've got an hour or two to spare, though." Walker handed Blake his business card. "Maybe write about your plans now that you're footloose and fancy free, eh?" Again his eyes roamed Blake's body.

"Who's your friend, Boss?"

Blake nearly jumped out of her flats. She'd been turned facing her bodyguards all the time, but she didn't see Suki move. Now the woman stood by Blake's side, making no effort to hide the fact that she was memorizing every detail of Walker's appearance.

"Stan Walker, business writer." He held out a hand to shake. Looked Suki over, put his nose a little higher in the air, turned his attention to Blake again.

Suki ignored Walker's hand until he let it drop. Then she inquired, with a voice that almost dripped syrup, "Did you know you literally drool when you talk to a pretty woman?"

Walker's pale face went cherry red. "That's a lie."

His necktie is damp, though, Blake realized, and fought the urge to grin. "I'm sorry, Mr. Walker; Suki here is one of my bodyguards. She's just concerned about your intentions."

"A *woman* bodyguard?" If contempt could kill, Walker's stare would have turned Suki to ashes where she stood.

Suki, for her part, looked as serene as any Buddha statue. "I get by."

"Hmmmpf." Walker lifted the generic tablet that he'd left lying on his ample stomach, and showed Blake a business e-zine's interview with Lang Bertrand. "You should make some time for an interview, in my professional opinion. Your ex is out there stealing all the thunder, while you haven't let out a single rumble."

"I had to fire my publicist just before my divorce was finalized. Since I plan to be in New York for a while, I thought I'd wait and hire someone local, and then I'll do some thundering of my own. Thank you, though, for your professional opinion." Blake nodded to Suki, and they stepped toward their own seats.

"Now *you're* really in luck!" Walker stood and laid a hand on Blake's arm.

She'd barely registered his touch before Suki, eyes fixed on Walker's, gripped his hand and lifted it off Blake's arm. Walker's eyes seemed to double in size.

"Don't touch my boss." Suki dropped Walker's hand.

"I'm sorry. I just forgot myself for a second." Walker looked like a rabbit cornered by a fox.

Suki raised her hands, palms up. "Just don't let it happen again. Next time it will cost you."

Walker turned a big-eyed gaze to Blake. "I apologize, Ms. Bertrand. I really do. I just wanted to tell you I happen to have the best publicist east of Cali. I'd be glad to write her name and phone number on the back of my business card for you."

Dazed by the exchange between Walker and Suki, Blake had to clear her throat before she could speak again. She handed the card back to Walker and managed, with a bit of a squeak, "Sure."

Walker pulled his fountain pen out of his shirt pocket and hastily scribbled on the back of his business card, and thrust the card back into Blake's still-outstretched hand. "Be seeing you," he blurted as he sat down again.

Blake settled back into her seat and tucked the card into her purse without ever looking at it. *My return to New York is certainly off to an entertaining start,* she reflected.

***

"And then, sweet as pie, Suki asked the dude if he knows he literally drools when he talks to a pretty woman." Matt laughed into his smartphone. He lay sprawled on the sofa in the living room of Blake's new East Thirty-sixth Street penthouse apartment, chatting with his girlfriend back home in Miami. "I don't know, babe. Raised by wolves is my theory."

Blake listened to Matt's end of the conversation as she unpacked. She didn't have any choice, unless she asked him to take his phone call outside the apartment. He wasn't being offensive, and he'd be going to bed soon, so she endured feeling like an eavesdropper.

That, and an opinionated outsider. Blake wanted to urge Matt to break up with his girlfriend and find someone closer to his own age. He was only twenty-two, and his lady Miranda was thirty-eight. They were about the same ages that Blake and Lang had been when they'd married. With the wisdom of hindsight, Blake now realized that hooking up with someone significantly older herself had been disastrous. *But Matt and Miranda are not me and Lang*, Blake reminded herself.

She looked around the master bedroom, trying to decide what to unpack next. Essentials, such as beds, sofa, a pair of recliners, dining table and chairs, and the flat-screen television, had been set up by the moving company Edith had hired to pack and deliver some of Blake's most valued possessions to the penthouse, after Blake signed the lease and took her trio of bodyguards out for a late lunch.

Other items, such as her father's turntable record player and collection of vinyl albums, sat in their labeled boxes waiting for Blake to position them. Blake decided she wanted the turntable centered under the single window that filled most of one wall. She dragged its shipping box to that spot and lifted it out with the utmost of care.

"I didn't know anyone owned those anymore." Suki's voice drifted from the bedroom door.

"People who are nostalgic do." Blake hefted one of the twin speakers, almost as tall as her own five feet nine inches.

"Can I help you with that, or anything?" Without waiting for an answer, Suki hurried to Blake's side and helped her settle the speaker in a corner. Together they extracted its mate from the shipping box and placed it in the other corner.

Next to the turntable itself Blake set up the rack she kept the vinyl albums in. One at a time, with gentle handling, Blake began stacking the albums in the rack.

Suki examined the cover art of each album as Blake pulled them from their separate shipping container, a sturdy plastic case generously stuffed with protective padding to prevent damage to the contents. "I know some of these. Jelly Roll Morton, Duke Ellington, Louis Armstrong, Ella Fitzgerald, Dizzy Gillespie, the Marsalis clan. Oh, and Amy Winehouse, best female jazz singer since Ella..." Her voice trailed off.

Blake paused and studied Suki as she hadn't before. "You're a jazz fan?"

"I'm more into classical and Eastern, but I also like some old jazz and Latin music."

Smiling, Blake went back to stacking albums in the rack. "My dad would really like you, if he were still alive."

"He was a jazz composer and band leader himself, wasn't he?"

"Yeah." Finished with that task, Blake pressed the power button on the turntable and put a Louis Armstrong record on to play.

They both stood silent for a minute or so, simply listening to the title track that opened Armstrong's "What a Wonderful World" album. Satchmo's raspy voice filled the room, and Blake's eyes watered as she remembered her father singing the song to her at bedtime, in a near-flawless imitation of Armstrong's voice.

"Why didn't you go into music, like your father? Instead of modeling and then real estate development?"

Blake gazed out the gigantic window at the frantic activity of Manhattan, far below. "I lack the talent." She shrugged, then added, "I can barely carry a tune when I sing, and I can't play piano without tripping over my own fingers. What most people don't know is, by going into real estate investment I still followed in his footsteps. He spent a few years earning money by doing that, to finance promotion of his band."

"Really? I had no idea." For the first time, Blake could see real emotion in Suki's face. The woman was impressed. "He'd be proud of you, I bet."

"For that, yes. If he agreed with my mother, though, he would have hated my marriage to Lang." Blake shut her eyes and savored the rest of the title track, reopening them only when that song ended and Satchmo plunged into "Cabaret." "Not that it's his fault, but if Dad hadn't died my marriage to Lang never would have happened."

They looked at each other as Blake wondered whether Suki could be trusted to respect her privacy. Suki didn't ask for an explanation or hazard any guesses, and that alone made her different from almost everyone else Blake knew.

"My mother eventually remarried, after Dad was reported dead. It was my stepfather who got me started modeling, when I was still a little girl." Memories tried to pry their way into Blake's consciousness, remembrances of those terrifying first childhood excursions to New York to audition for modeling agencies. Disappointing her stepfather wasn't an option.

A bodyguard doesn't need to know about all that. Blake took in the view of Manhattan as she continued, "When I wanted to raise money to get into real estate investing, modeling was the only way I knew how to earn large sums of money fast. And that's how I met Lang. Through modeling."

Suddenly Blake felt totally drained of energy. She sat on the edge of her bed and watched the record spin round and round on the turntable. "Right here," she whispered. "In Manhattan."

Suki went to the door, out of Blake's sight, then murmured a suggestion. "Get some rest, Boss. I think you're going to need your strength."

"Good idea." Blake stretched out, fully clothed on top of the covers. She closed her eyes, and Satchmo's crooning was like a lullaby as darkness enfolded her.

***

Blake arrived with Antonio at the law offices of Coleman, Mitchell, Gomez, & Park at half past noon, half an hour early for the Wishman Spears closing. She wasn't surprised to discover the conference room empty when she checked in, because it was her habit to be first on the scene for every business transaction. Blake liked to scope out the site and position herself for maximum effect.

They'd barely chosen where to sit when they were joined by her friend and frequent investment partner, Thomas Mills, along with the two other real estate speculators helping Blake finance the Wishman Spears purchase. Before they sat down, Thomas hugged her and introduced her to the speculators, whom she'd heard of but never worked with before.

"Margot thanks you for asking me to be part of this," Thomas said with a grin splitting his distinguished dark face as he settled in at the conference table.

Blake thought about that for a moment, but couldn't guess the reason. "Why is that?"

"She's been nagging me to take her on another vacation in New York for years. When I told her I'd be helping you buy the Wishman Spears, she immediately started packing."

They were still sharing a laugh when Rich Kaufmunn, her Miami real estate attorney, arrived a few minutes later in the company of Susan Golden and Peter Britell, the attorneys from Venable LLP's New York office assisting with her purchase of the Wishman Spears. "Afternoon, Blake," Rich said as he seated himself to her right. "I hope your flight was more comfortable than mine. I swear airlines keep cramming seats closer together."

"You don't think it's your expanding waistline?" she teased, prompting Golden and Britell to exchange glances.

"My wife would tell me if she had to start replacing all my pants with a larger size. She hates to shop."

Two paralegals carried in a tray with a pitcher of ice water, pot of steaming coffee, cream, sugar, glasses, and mugs. "Can we get you anything else? We've got sodas, herbal teas, fruit juices. And if anyone is hungry we've got some cinnamon buns."

Everyone said thanks and promised they were fine, just in time for the Wishman patriarch and his grandson to arrive and make it necessary for the pair of paralegals to repeat themselves.

Blake wondered why they didn't just post a double-sided sign in the center of the long table, listing the available refreshments. *Too much like a restaurant menu, I suppose.*

At precisely one o'clock in walked Ernesto Nunez and his anorexic-looking redhead paralegal, who were assisting senior partner Joe Mitchell in representing the Wishman family. Nunez greeted everyone while his slip of a paralegal handed out copies of the closing papers, so that they all could follow along.

"To review, the terms of this agreement are—" Nunez tried to begin, but Blake interrupted:

"We should wait for Mitchell."

"I'm afraid Mr. Mitchell can't be here." Nunez squirmed in his seat as he continued, "But he looked everything over this morning, and he said—"

"*Why* can't he be here?" Blake demanded, folding her hands together on the table and leaning toward the nervous associate.

"Something came up." The redhead was fighting a noble battle to refrain from smirking, but it was a battle she quickly lost.

"I see." Blake turned to Kaufmunn, Golden, and Britell. "Would someone on my legal team please get Mitchell on the phone for me?"

Kaufmunn fished his no-frills cell phone out of his jacket pocket, grinning. "You're making this whole trip worthwhile for an old man, Blake."

Golden and Britell swapped glances again, and the latter cleared his throat and murmured, "It's your choice, Ms. Bertrand, but if Mitchell is satisfied that everything is in order, there shouldn't be any jeopardy if we proceed without him."

"True, it's my choice. And I choose to leave no room for error." Blake heard a woman's voice answer Kaufmunn's call, and he put his phone on speaker so that everyone could hear what was said.

"Good afternoon, ma'am. I'm Rich Kaufmunn, one of the attorneys representing Ms. Blake Bertrand in her acquisition of the Wishman Spears building. My client needs to speak with Joe Mitchell right away, please."

After a moment's hesitation, the woman's voice replied, "Mr. Mitchell asked not to be disturbed this afternoon."

"Has he forgotten I'm in the building?" Blake inquired. "Tell him he can get on the phone, or I can climb the damn stairs to his office, but either way he's going to talk to me."

"Please hold," the woman squeaked, and put the call on hold

for half a minute.

"Mitchell, here." He sounded breathless.

"Get in here, fast, or you can explain to your clients how you cost them seven hundred million dollars today," Blake snapped.

"I'm sorry, Ms. Bertrand, but I really—"

"You really what? Prefer to bang your paralegal instead of attending the closing?" Ignoring the gasps of Lawrence Wishman and Nunez and the snickerings of the grandson, the redhead, and Kaufmunn, Blake continued, "I'm not a fool, Mitchell. I've been around enough to know bedroom eyes when I see them, and that's what you and your paralegal were giving each other the whole time I met with you yesterday. But you are lead counsel for the Wishmans. It's your fucking *job* to be present for the closing, reviewing the terms and assuring your clients that they're getting a fair deal from me. If you were *my* lead counsel, you'd be fired. As it is, I'll give you ten minutes to drag your skanky ass into this conference room, or else you're going to lose your clients a fortune. Understand?"

After a moment Mitchell blurted, "I'll be there in a few minutes." The dial tone rasped from Kaufmunn's phone.

Ms. Golden was living up to her name, positively aglow with enjoyment. "Is doing business with you always this entertaining, Ms. Bertrand?"

"I hope not," Blake answered. She reached for the coffeepot and filled a mug to half an inch below the rim, and as she added a dollop of cream, she said, "If I'm usually entertaining, I'm not being taken seriously. That's what I expect first and foremost in business. Everyone else had better be serious about business, because I certainly am."

"Even so," Kaufmunn murmured to Golden, "people underestimate Ms. Bertrand just often enough to keep a real estate attorney from perishing of boredom."

"It would be a privilege and a pleasure to assist you with any other real estate business you do in New York," Golden informed Blake.

"I'll keep it in mind."

Six minutes after he hung up his office phone, Joe Mitchell dashed into the conference room. His hair was dripping wet and he reeked of soap. Blake scrutinized him from head to toe, shook her head, and faced Nunez.

"*Now* you can begin."

Chapter Four

March 2
New York, New York

"I'm sorry, Ms. Bertrand, but I'm not accepting new clients right now."

"Well, thank you for your time." Blake thumbed the End Call button and put a strike through Brooklyn-based publicist Marsha Grayson's name.

Prior to the Wishman Spears closing, Edith had compiled a list of the Northeast's top-rated publicists and sent it to Blake via priority mail. Edith was out of town for a family emergency for the day, and it was up to Blake to get it done. Frankly, she didn't mind, because she believed in first impressions, even over the phone. She could tell from the first few seconds of meeting most people if she'd like them, and this was no different. Blake had waited until after the weekend to start contacting them, letting business circles grow excited about her newest property and eager to learn her plans for it. She expected that, within a couple of hours of making phone calls on Monday morning, she'd have appointments with several candidates thrilled by the prospect of becoming her new publicist.

Instead, she'd now called every name and number on Edith's list, and had made not a single appointment. Only one name was left—the one recommended by the fellow on the flight from Miami to New York. She understood that the woman was widely regarded as the best of the best, but what sort of person agrees to represent a drunken old lecher? Blake shook her head. *No, Ms. Vickie Sharp, I won't be contacting you unless I can't find any alternative.*

"But what the hell alternatives are out there?" She padded into the kitchen, thirsty after making nearly twenty phone calls in two hours.

"Sorry, what did you say?" Antonio looked up from the daily crossword of *The New York Times*. He was a riddle to Blake: The man had an Ivy League MBA in Economics, so why in the world was he working as a bodyguard?

"I thought after buying the Wishman Spears I'd have no trouble finding a new publicist." Blake poured herself a tall glass of pomegranate juice and took a sip. *I'll be damned. The man even does the crossword in ink. His brain is wasted in his line of work.* "But all I'm getting is a bunch of excuses."

"Weird." He laid the crossword aside and leveled a speculative gaze at Blake. "How many publicists have you called?"

"Seventeen."

Before saying anything else, Antonio picked up his mug of coffee and drank it dry. His eyes never left Blake's. She thought she could almost *hear* him analyzing the problem.

"You've been sabotaged. I'd bet a month's pay on that, if I were a gambling man."

"Sabotaged? How?" Blake took a seat across the table from Antonio.

"Now that, I couldn't say, not without doing some investigation. I'm cross-trained for that, but it's not really my thing. Want me to call the office, ask them to put someone on finding out why you're out in the cold with the publicist crowd?"

Blake shook her head. "No. When you put it like that, I'm fairly certain about what's happened. I want to make sure, though, so I'm going to get dressed, and then we're taking a cab to chat with the last publicist who refused to meet with me."

The car that Blake hired parked in the cramped lot behind a renovated brownstone mere minutes before 11 A.M., when early lunchers would slip out of their offices to go in search of food. Antonio inspected the street-front side of the building while Blake negotiated with the taxi driver to wait for them.

"She didn't turn you down because she can't use the work," Antonio remarked to Blake, scrutinizing the windows over the top of his Ray-Bans. He pointed to a residue of grime accumulated on the glass. "Looks like she hasn't spent money on a window washer for a while. Windows of the office next door are sparkling, though." He motioned at the other building.

"Well, let's go ask Ms. Marsha what's going on." Blake pushed open the swinging glass door, and a little bell tinkled to herald their arrival.

A mousy receptionist darted out of the first door on the right in the hallway. "Good morning! Do you have an appointment?"

"I do now," Blake said. "Which one is Ms. Grayson's office?"

"I can't let you—"

"Relax, you're not. I'm bigger than you, and my bodyguard is bigger than both of us together. When I push past you and he follows me, you never stood a chance of stopping us."

The receptionist's mouth dropped open and worked like a guppy's. Blake strolled by her without even needing to give her a "back off" look, and Antonio trailed after her. Judging by the plaques hanging on the doors, this building accommodated multiple businesses. Ironically, first on the left was a private investigator. Blake grimaced, fighting a temptation to hire him to investigate his neighbor's finances. She kept her eyes on the prize, however, and opened the second door on the left, on which a large sign proclaimed Grayson Relations.

Although the exterior of the building suffered from some neglect, Grayson's office reflected well on her. It was decorated in shabby chic, and Blake recognized one of the French designer names as one of her own favorites. Behind a refurbished rolltop desk sat the willowy brunette who must be Marsha Grayson.

"Good morning," said Grayson, throwing a puzzled glance at the door. Antonio seemed to fill every inch of the aperture. He grinned and waved at Grayson, who turned her attention to Blake. "I'm afraid I don't know you. If you need to hire a publicist, I'd be glad to speak with you, but I'm expecting an eleven o'clock appointment with a client. Would you be able to come back—"

"No, because you already refused to talk to me, and you're probably about to do that again. I need to know why." Blake settled into one of the three plush chairs fronting the desk. "I'm Blake Bertrand."

"Oh." Grayson didn't seem to know what to do with her hands.

"You are one of seventeen publicists who said no to a meeting with me, when I called to arrange one. I just want to know who is responsible, my ex-husband or my ex-publicist."

"Oh," Grayson said again, and studied the floor as if she'd never seen it before.

They sat unspeaking, Blake watching Grayson, who no doubt tried to think of a way to get rid of her without telling her anything. A minute ticked by, then another.

Blake pulled her wallet out of her purse, slid out a hundred-dollar bill, and held it out to Grayson. "How about I hire you for sixty seconds. Not even that. However long it takes you to say either Lang Bertrand or Sherry Greene."

Grayson lifted her gaze to the crisp slip of currency. "She tells everyone you're a monster to work with," she said at last, taking the hundred. "That you expect celebrities to greet you everywhere you go, that you fight every penny of expenses, that you have temper tantrums if you're not front-page news at least once a month, that you try not to give raises..." Her voice trailed off and she glanced at the wall clock. "Please go now. I've got a client coming in any minute."

Blake stood and nodded in response to Antonio's quizzical gaze. "That's all I needed to know. You have a good life, Ms. Grayson."

Outside the brownstone, Antonio slid his Ray-Bans back on and asked, "Any of that actually true?"

"Twist a claim enough and anything is true, I suppose. I wouldn't let Sherry Greene charge her clothes and hairstyles and such to her expense account for reimbursement, because I don't get to charge my wardrobe to buyers when I resell a property. I got angry when she offered to invite celebrities to an event I was hosting and later I learned none of them showed up because they never actually got an invitation. Everything she said has some tiny basis in truth. She just blew it all out of proportion when she gossiped to other publicists."

He opened the taxi door for her, and she climbed in. When he was seated next to her and the cab merged with traffic, Antonio asked, "So what will you do now?"

Blake shook her head. "I haven't worked that out yet."

***

March 3
New York, New York

Blake still hadn't worked out her publicist problems when her BlackBerry played a verse of "Sophisticated Lady" at nine o'clock the next morning, alerting her that her best friend was calling. "Margot! I thought I'd hear from you before now. Thomas told me at the Wishman Spears closing that you're in New York with him."

"Oh, honey, I thought you'd be busy setting up press conferences and that sort of thing. I didn't want to take up too much of your time." Margot's voice always made Blake think of how sunshine would sound, if human ears could hear it.

"As it turns out, I'm not. I can't seem to find a new publicist to represent me."

"What? That makes no sense. You're all over the business news these past few days, and some of the mainstream news too. It's easy money for a publicist to go to work for you right now."

Blake nodded to Antonio, sitting at the kitchen table with her. He was drinking coffee and doing the crossword as usual, while Blake ate an orange and a bagel with cream cheese. She opened the sliding glass door onto the terrace, with its grand view of the Empire State Building.

"I know, but I'm told nobody wants to work for a miserly shrew, which is what my former publicist says I am." It was a chilly morning, and her breath came out in cottony puffs. She enjoyed the nip in the air, however. Although not as fond of cold as her mother, Blake did relish temperatures in the forty-five to sixty-five range. *Which are rare in Miami*, she reflected with a wry smile. *Maybe I should move north one day*.

"That Sherry Greene. I never understood why you tolerated her as long as you did. She got full-time pay for part-time work, and never appreciated how lucky she was. And her taste in clothes!" Margot clucked her tongue before finishing, "Ghetto fabulous."

Blake laughed full-throated for the first time in months. "Margot, you do my soul good. How much longer will you be in the city?"

"Well, that's why I'm calling. Today is our last day. Our flight back to Miami leaves early in the morning. I was hoping we could get together for lunch today, if you don't have any other plans."

"Even if I did, I'd reschedule them for you. Do you have a restaurant in mind?"

"No, Thomas doesn't bring me to New York nearly often enough to know what's here. You choose. I'll pay."

"The Four Seasons at noon? Does that sound good?"

"Girl, that sounds better than good. I still have fond memories of that place from however many centuries ago Thomas last brought me to New York." In the background, Thomas groaned.

Blake laughed again, seeing clearly understanding the theatrics her best friend's husband was putting on. "I'll see you in the Grill Room."

"See you there and then!" Margot ended the connection, and Blake went inside to dress for the occasion.

In the mood to walk, Blake opted for a layered strategy. She wore slim Armani slacks and blouse with Gucci ballet flats, plus a hip-length Gucci leather jacket to keep out the cold. Antonio dressed like the Ivy League business grad he was, in a blue suit and striped red power necktie. They waved good-bye to the doorman at eleven and kept a leisurely pace, detouring somewhat as they neared their destination so that Blake could show Antonio the Rockefeller Plaza, Radio City Music Hall, and Saks.

Even though they arrived early, as usual for Blake, Margot Mills was already at the Four Seasons. She was enjoying a cocktail, and she'd taken the liberty of ordering a Grand Marnier Sidecar for Blake. They hugged each other tight, and Blake introduced Antonio.

"Would you ladies like me to sit out of hearing range?" he asked them, after shaking Margot's hand.

"Certainly not!" gushed Margot. "I haven't laid eyes on such a handsome young man since Thomas and I first met."

"Good thing he's not here to see you ogling my bodyguard," Blake teased.

"Oh, Thomas and I agreed a long time ago that being on a diet doesn't mean we can't look at the menu."

They all requested warm spinach salad for an appetizer, and for their main courses Margot ordered the Veal Four Seasons, Blake the Dover Sole, and—after a wince—Antonio the Sirloin Burger. "I can't believe any burger is worth nearly forty dollars," Antonio muttered as their waiter walked away.

"Everything here is excellent," Margot promised him. "And don't worry. If I can't afford it, your boss can." She winked at Blake and the two laughed like schoolgirls.

"Now, I've been doing some thinking about you being without a publicist," Margot confided after she finished off her highball. "You're getting publicity right now from the Wishman Spears purchase, even without someone setting up press conferences and such for you. Just keep that ball rolling, girl. Start a new project that everyone would be interested in, and reporters will spread the word for you."

"Interesting idea," Blake said, meditating over her Sidecar. "I've been planning to get more involved in charity, even start one of my own. Maybe I should get started on that."

"Perfect! And I even know a celebrity who might agree to be a spokeswoman for your charity." Margot leaned in close to Blake, and spoke barely above a whisper. "Thomas and I vacationed in Jamaica for New Year's, you know, and guess who else was there then?"

Blake shook her head. "Too many possibilities, Margot. I have no idea."

"Lanre, that's who!"

"I know she was a shining star of R&B for a couple of years," Blake said, jabbing her fork into her salad without truly paying attention to it. "But I haven't heard anything about her for quite a while."

"True, she said she had creative differences with her record label and ended up breaking her contract with them. Now she's got material for a new album and plans to make a comeback. It seems to me you'd be helping her as much as she'd be helping you. Should make for a loyal and enthusiastic spokesperson, don't you think?"

"Maybe." *Half a generation has gone by, or at least that's how it feels. Will anyone in the younger end of the age range I want to reach even know who Lanre is?*

"Well, here, I'll write down her phone number for you. Use it or not, as you see fit. But if you want my advice, I think you should use it." Margot tore a page off the pad of Post-it notes she kept in her purse, scribbled a number she looked up in her cell phone's contacts list, and handed it to Blake.

Blake looked at it before sticking it inside her wallet. "What about you, Margot? How are you keeping yourself entertained these days, whenever Thomas is away on business?"

For the first time since Blake walked into the Grill Room, Margot didn't seem to know what to say. She signaled their waiter to come to their table, and ordered another highball. "Every day is different," she said at last.

She said it to her highball, not to Blake.

***

March 19
New York, New York

Though Blake hated waiting while attention to her Wishman Spears purchase faded, Lanre wasn't available for a New York meeting until two-and-a-half weeks after Blake's lunch with Margot. She put the intervening time to use as best she could, interviewing contractors for her Wishman renovation plans and consulting with attorneys who specialized in forming and administering charitable organizations. Finally the day came when Lanre was in the city to spend a few days in a recording studio and perform at two local clubs.

Lanre suggested that she and Blake talk over brunch the morning after her arrival in New York. She requested they meet at Madiba, a Brooklyn restaurant specializing in South African cuisine. Blake and Suki, with whom Antonio had traded shifts so that he could see a dentist, were waiting outside the restaurant when the doors opened at eleven o'clock.

At half past, when Lanre still hadn't shown up, Blake tried to call her but only reached voicemail. *I get the feeling this isn't going to work out.* With a strained smile, Blake said to Suki, "As long as we're here, we may as well eat."

"I've never tried South African food before. Got any idea what's good, Boss?"

"Your guess is as good as mine." Blake studied the menu, and was trying to decide between a safe lamb curry or an adventurous boerewors roll when at last a stern-faced, middle-aged brown-skinned woman marched up to Blake's table, with Lanre slouching behind her.

"Blake Bertrand?" demanded the older woman, oblivious to Suki's appraising stare.

"I am," Blake agreed, looking past the woman at Lanre. The singer appeared to be in the throes of a wicked hangover.

"Let's get down to business, then." The woman impatiently waved Lanre into a chair, and plunked her own ample hiney onto another. "How much are you offering to pay my daughter to hype this charity of yours?"

"I haven't decided on a specific amount yet." Again Blake gazed at Lanre, bewildered by the younger woman's total silence. *I've had some hangovers in my time, but I could still speak if I needed to. What's up with this girl?*

"Well, that's something we've got to know up front. My daughter is going to be extremely busy in the next few months, working her way back to the top of the R&B charts. Her time is valuable, and any time spent away from advancing her music career must be well compensated. Isn't that right, Lan?"

The older woman looked at the younger, who apparently found the tabletop fascinating. "Uh," Lanre said after a moment. An achingly long second later, she added, "huh."

"Please excuse me for a few minutes," Blake said, keeping her voice quiet as a courtesy to the afflicted singer. "I really need to visit the bathroom."

"Where my boss goes, I follow," Suki informed the two, and accompanied Blake to the ladies' room.

Blake retrieved her wallet from her purse and found the business card on which the old fellow from the Miami-to-NY flight had written the name of his own publicist. She keyed the number into her BlackBerry, listened as the other end rang twice, and breathed a sigh of relief when a silky woman's voice answered, "Vickie Sharp PR, this is Vickie speaking."

"A client of yours gave you a glowing recommendation, and I need a good publicist as soon as possible," Blake answered. "I'm Blake Bertrand. Please tell me we can meet sometime in the next few days!"

Chapter Five

March 20
New York, New York

When Blake emerged from a morning spent consulting with attorney Susan Golden about zoning restrictions on the Wishman Spears building that she'd need amended before proceeding with her plans, she powered on her BlackBerry and immediately regretted it. An email from Charles was waiting for her. Its subject line: <Trouble in Little Haiti.>

"Damn it all." She opened the message, took a deep breath, and let the bad news sink in.

<Your anonymous rival bought up the Dessalines, and has outbid you for two other properties you wanted. Amounts exceed maximums you're willing to pay.>

"That doesn't make sense." Blake frowned at her BlackBerry, as if the device were to blame for the disappointing news.

"What doesn't make sense?" Antonio stood between Blake and the curb, watching for the taxi the law firm had called for them.

"I've been trying to buy three properties in Little Haiti. They have low market values, but based on their locations and history and other factors I could use them to remake the neighborhood as one of the most desirable places to live and work in the United States. I've been dreaming about it for years, almost as long as I dreamed of renovating the Wishman Spears. Up here," Blake tapped her forehead, "I've got plans for the whole neighborhood for the next ten years, but I need those three properties. Some idiot bidding anonymously is offering so much for them that they couldn't possibly break even for at least five years."

"Can you afford to wait longer than five years to break even?"

"Of course. I can outbid my rival for all three and still not pay more than two million dollars total. That's only a drop in my bucket." Blake shook her head. "I won't do it, though, because that drop may make the difference in affording another deal I want to do later. It makes no sense to overpay by more than a certain margin, even if you can afford it. You just limit your future opportunities if you do that."

Antonio nodded as the taxi stopped at the law firm's driveway. He opened the door for Blake, waited for her to scoot over to the far seat, and folded his large frame by her side in the backseat. "More sabotage is what it sounds like to me," he said as the taxi merged with traffic.

Blake considered that through a few blocks of travel. "This does sound like something Lang would do. He has little business savvy, but a lot of mean spirit."

"So what are you going to do about it?"

"Let him have Little Haiti. I hate it, but I can't ruin myself financially just because my ex wants to play competitive games." She opened a new message to Charles and typed:

<Abandon Little Haiti. Quietly look for bargains in other parts of Miami that need new life.>

When they were back in Blake's penthouse apartment, she went into her bedroom and shut and locked the door. After putting some Duke Ellington on the turntable, she tapped "3" on her BlackBerry's speed-dial.

"Johnny Capps Surveillance," a man's voice answered.

"Hi, Johnny, Blake here." She plunked herself down on a corner of her bed.

"Well, hi, Blake! Listen, I don't have anything new to report about your boy, but I could snap some more pictures."

Her fingers tightened on the BlackBerry for a moment, the face of "her boy" springing unbidden to mind and paining her heart. "I'd love that, but I'm actually calling you about something else."

"Oh yeah? What can I do for you?"

"I'm going to email you addresses of three Miami properties I just tried to buy, but an anonymous bidder kept raising their price until I had to give up. I want to know who the anonymous bidder was."

"Lang, probably."

"That's what I think too, but I want to know for sure." Blake stood and moved back to the turntable, looking out the huge window.

"I'll get right on it. Talk to you soon." Johnny clicked the call off.

She couldn't help herself. Blake pulled the Raven Glory album out of the rack and stood for a while studying every detail of her father's long, slim face.

Then she shook the vinyl record out of its cover and, with it, several photographs. Each showed a boy whose features resembled Blake's father.

And Blake's mother.

And Blake herself.

***

It was almost lunchtime, and Blake couldn't stop thinking about her lost hopes for Little Haiti. She wanted to think about something else, something still in her power to have a positive influence on. Wanting and doing were two different things, however.

Damn you, Lang. You know how to push my buttons even from hundreds of miles away, don't you?

Suki wandered into the living room, perspiring from her all-morning jujitsu practice and still in martial arts uniform. "Hi, Boss. After I shower I think I'm going to run out and get some lunch. I'm thinking—"

The sudden silence got Blake's attention as the words hadn't. "Hi, Suki. Sorry, I was thinking."

"I could see that. Matter of fact, you looked like you were thinking of breaking someone's bones."

Blake grimaced. "He'd deserve it, but I don't have it in me to do that."

"Oh. Him." Suki swiped one loose sleeve over her forehead to mop up some of the dampness. "Listen, Boss, do you ever go to the gym?"

"Yeah. I mean, I did until my mom's accident. Since then…"

"…you're afraid of running into Lang," Suki finished, after Blake stopped in mid- sentence.

"Am I that obvious?"

Suki regarded Blake without expression or sound, until Blake squirmed under her bodyguard's gaze. "This isn't the first time any of us have protected a battered woman," Suki said at last. "And we all three agree you've got a hell of a lot more in you than you realize."

With what she knew must be a weak smile, Blake murmured, "Thanks."

"Time to start realizing it, though. Get changed into workout clothes, Boss. We'll grab a light lunch, and then we're going to whichever gym is your favorite. I'm going to teach you some basic self-defense moves." Suki strode into the bathroom adjoining her bedroom, and seconds later Blake heard the shower.

Suited up in a body-skimming Armani jumpsuit that made Suki arch an eyebrow, Blake and her deadliest bodyguard directed their taxi to take them to a corner café for soup and salad to go. From there they cruised over to the Reebok Sports Club.

Together they went through an hour's worth of warm-up and fitness training. Then Suki led Blake into the boxing studio, and they climbed into an available ring.

For two hours Suki taught Blake two blocks, a kick, and two punches that she said were the most useful moves in combat jujitsu. Over and over Suki commanded Blake to practice each maneuver, and gradually Suki refined Blake's posture and delivery. Blake noticed a crowd gathering to observe, but Suki kept her too busy to fret about how she must look to the bystanders.

"Exam time," Suki said, just when Blake felt so exhausted she didn't think she could lift either hand above her waist again and her legs felt too wobbly to hold her up much longer.

"Please tell me that's a joke," Blake groaned.

"I teach self-defense to women and girls, part-time. One woman who'd been taking my classes for only three weeks was attacked just outside her home," Suki told Blake, folding her arms across her chest and leveling a stern stare at her boss. "She and her attacker traded blows before he finally gave up and ran away. He was a determined motherfucker. What I'm teaching you can save your life from determined motherfuckers. So use it!"

With that Suki lashed out a punch aimed for Blake's throat. Blake had no time to think, no time to fear. Her left hand swept up in the first block Suki had taught her. A yelp escaped her lips as the bodyguard's fist smacked into her wrist—if she'd done it correctly the blow would have impacted the side of her hand.

"Sorry," Blake gasped.

"Why? You stopped me from smashing your windpipe. Again!" Suki struck out at Blake's abdomen, and Blake's right hand flipped the bodyguard's forearm aside and opened her up for the kick Blake had learned. Suki blocked it, of course, but she grinned and exclaimed, "Perfect!"

A round of applause went up from their audience. Blake felt

heat rush into her cheeks. For a minute she'd forgotten people were watching them.

"Okay, we'll stop now," Suki said. "I'll call a taxi. But I want you to practice those moves for half an hour tonight. Tomorrow we're going to practice them some more, and I'm going to teach you a couple of new tricks."

Blake, bent over with hands braced on knees, muttered, "Fuck me..."

"Don't mind if I do." A man's voice, somehow familiar.

She found the strength to turn around. At one corner of the boxing ring stood a fine-looking specimen, watching her with bright teeth showing in a broad smile and mocha skin still glowing from recent exertion. Blake remembered meeting him at the pre-opening party a week before her divorce was finalized. What she didn't remember was his name.

"Um, hi."

"You forgot my name?" He clasped at his heart, eyes going wide in theatrical injury. "Oh, woman, you may as well kill me where I stand. It couldn't hurt worse than this."

Blake laughed, even as she glanced at Suki, who was just ending her call for a taxi. "How about you just remind me, and then I can let you live?"

"I suppose that will do. Brett Skeet. You don't shake hands, but do you high-five when you've put on a kick-ass show?" He lifted a hand, ready if she was willing.

"I hope a smile is good enough?" She smiled hugely at Brett. Suki moved to Blake's side and glanced from her boss to the gentleman she didn't know, then back again. The bodyguard took one step back to have them both in view and within reach, but said nothing and stood blank-faced.

"Listen, if you want to wait until you're back in Miami I'll understand. But if you'd be willing to do that lunch and shoptalk while we're both in New York, name a time and place and it's on me."

Blake studied his fine face for a moment, then blurted, "How about dinner tonight?"

"If I'd known you had that much energy left, we'd still be practicing," intoned Suki.

Chapter Six

March 20
New York, New York

At 8 P.M. Blake arrived with Matt at the Vault, a former bank and gentleman's club located on the Lower East Side that had been remade into a festive trilevel supper club with dance floors. She'd agonized about what to wear, uncertain whether to view this as a business dinner or as a first date. Finally she'd settled on a knee-length, one-shoulder glittery black Calvin Klein dress, along with her Gucci ballet flats.

Matt was wearing a black suit and, under protest, a crimson necktie.

"This is why I like working third shift," Matt grumbled, tugging at the tie. "I can usually dress for comfort instead of style, and the client doesn't care because they're asleep."

"You'll survive," Blake promised him. She spoke to the hostess just inside the door. "Excuse me, but has a gentleman by the name of Brett Skeet already reserved a table?"

"No, ma'am. Shall I find a table for you and your escort, and note that Brett Skeet will be joining you?"

"Yes, please. My name is Blake Bertrand." Blake shrugged out of her coat and draped it over her arm while the hostess snapped her fingers for a waiter and told him to prep a table for three.

"I thought you looked familiar," the hostess added, when the waiter hurried away in search of a table. "It's a pleasure to have you at the Vault, Ms. Bertrand. If you need anything at all, please don't hesitate to come to me."

"Thank you." Blake smiled her appreciation at the hostess, but the smile faded when she noticed Matt tugging at his tie yet again. "Stop that, Matt. It's all crooked now."

She was straightening Matt's tie when Brett's voice, which reminded her of Duke Ellington's smoothest jazz pieces, sounded behind her: "Only one woman in the world can look as good sweating and worn out as she does in a little black dress, and that's Blake Bertrand."

Blake felt her face grow hot again. *I wouldn't have thought any man could still make me blush, but this man sure has proved me wrong.* "Hi, Brett. We just requested a table."

Brett was examining Matt. "Who is this?"

"Matt Guidry. One of Ms. Bertrand's bodyguards." Matt put out a hand and shook Brett's.

"One of, you say," Brett commented, but rather than Matt he looked at Blake.

She caught herself about to touch the scar on her forehead hidden by her long bangs. Putting her hand back down, Blake took a deep breath and explained, in a hushed voice almost lost in the dance music playing farther inside the Vault, "My ex-husband beat me up a week before our divorce was finalized."

Brett let that sink in before asking, "At the party where I met you?"

She nodded. Words wouldn't come. A chill crept down her spine.

"I should have stayed." Brett's words held a hint of a growl, and his shoulders were tense, as if Lang Bertrand stood before him, available to be punched. "I'm tempted to catch the next flight back to Miami and beat his sorry ass right into the ground."

He sounds like Uncle Thorne. Blake almost felt like smiling.

"Hey, relax, man. Nobody's going to do that to Ms. Bertrand again. That's what me and my coworkers are here for." Matt clapped Brett on the back, and Blake watched Brett gradually calm down again.

Their waiter returned then and introduced himself. "Good evening, I'm Tim, I'll be your waiter tonight. I've got a great table ready for you, just follow me."

Tim led the way upstairs to the second level, where live rock music was being performed by new superstar Amanda Brown and her band. Blake recognized Brown from the third season of the television show *The Voice.* Margot had raved about the former backup singer for Adele until Blake watched the show herself for the second half of the season, simply to hear the talent her best friend couldn't stop talking about. *Just wait until Margot hears that I got lucky enough to see her favorite new rock singer giving a concert at a nightclub!*

They had a front-row seat, and got to hear Brown's chart-topping single "Distances" as they looked at the menu. Brett and Matt both decided on prime rib, french fries, and coleslaw, and Blake opted for a Vietnamese beef salad.

While they waited for their food, Matt turned to Brett and asked, "So you met Ms. Bertrand back in Miami? What brings you to New York?"

Brett laughed. "You've got yourself a thorough bodyguard, Blake."

She smiled, but Brett's comment troubled her a little. *He's talking to me like Matt isn't here. Like he's "the help," someone who should do their job and be ignored.* "I was going to ask the same question, Brett. You said you were off to a great start in Miami real estate. How did you end up here?"

"Oh, I grew up in Harlem." Brett leaned back in his chair, perfectly at ease. "I did get off to a great start—so great I earned a vacation already. So I've come home to visit family and friends for a couple of weeks."

Blake looked Brett over. He was dressed all in Prada. *You've got to do well to afford that.* She smiled again. "Well, congratulations."

"Thanks! I've been wondering—everybody is wondering—what plans are you making for the Wishman Spears?" He leaned in for a confidential talk, and Blake shared an outline of her ideas.

Meanwhile Matt tapped away on his smartphone, seemingly okay with being left out of the conversation. Blake glanced at him often, not really happy with how Brett behaved toward the bodyguard. Matt looked up once and gave her a thumbs-up, so she trusted that he was comfortable.

Their food arrived, and apparently all three of them were ravenous, because they barely spoke a word as they ate. Amanda Brown was rocking the house, her fans and Vault regulars enthusiastically breaking it down on the dance floors. "This is the best night I've had in a long time," Blake said, thinking out loud.

"Let's make it even better." Brett stood up, finished eating except for a few fries. "Come on, let's dance."

Matt looked up from his plate, watching them. Blake asked him, "Will it make your job too hard if I dance with Brett?"

"Nah. I've worked dances, concerts, sports championships, you name it. Go have fun." Matt gave her a thumbs-up again.

She let Brett lead her to the center of the dance floor. He was quick and elegant on his feet, had a great sense of rhythm, and sensuous moves like no man Blake had ever known. Trying to keep up with him soon tuckered her out, especially after the rough afternoon of self-defense training she'd done with Suki. Her muscles ached in protest, but her hormones screamed for her to impress Brett or die trying.

Blake lost all sense of time. She slipped away from Brett when she noticed how late it was getting, and didn't want Amanda to leave without getting to her. Amanda Brown took the microphone and announced, "Ladies and gentlemen, it's been a pleasure to sing for you tonight at the Vault! Please put your hands together for my amazing band. On lead guitar—"

"I've got to try to meet her," Blake managed to say, breathing hard. She rushed back to their table, where Matt sat tapping on his smartphone again. "Matt, come on, let's find the back door the band will exit through. My best friend is a huge fan of Amanda Brown. I'm going to get her autograph for her."

Matt shook his head. "Sometimes you forget who you are, don't you, Ms. Bertrand? You don't have to lurk outside any back door." He beckoned their waiter, passing by on his way to another table, and said, "Hey, Tim, Ms. Bertrand here would like to ask Amanda Brown for an autograph. Can you ask for a meeting?"

"Sure! I've got to go downstairs to the kitchen anyway. I'll ask the boss." Their waiter scurried away to the staircase.

Blake slumped into her seat at their table, catching her breath while they waited. Amanda Brown and her band had left the stage, and the roadies were packing up amplifiers and microphones and the drum set and all. Somewhere out of sight, a DJ took over musical entertainment duties and put some contemporary disco on for the crowd to dance to.

A mustached gentleman in slacks and blazer followed Tim back to their table. "Ms. Bertrand, hi, I'm Amanda Brown's manager. She said she'd be glad to sign an autograph for you. Just come with me."

"I've got to go with her," Matt informed Brett. Blake heard a firmness in the bodyguard's voice that she hadn't before. "Hold our table for us. We won't be long."

Matt fell into step behind Blake, who fell into step behind Amanda Brown's manager. They left Brett sitting with a stunned expression on his face, and Blake couldn't help giggling a little.

Amanda Brown was waiting at the door to the dressing room, her face lit by a glowing smile. "Girl, congratulations on your freedom!" She surprised Blake with a hug.

"Thank you so much!" Blake grinned. "And congratulations on your success! From backup singer to superstar in three years is quite an accomplishment."

"Not as much as surviving everything you've been through, and I bet the world doesn't know half of that. Who should I write this to?" Someone behind Amanda handed her a pad of Vault stationery and a fountain pen.

"My best friend's name is Margot Mills, spelled M-A-R-G-O-T." Blake watched, with a feeling like she was floating, while Amanda wrote a note in a flowing hand.

To Blake's surprise, Amanda flipped the top sheet of the pad back and wrote on the next page, as well. *Wow, this is turning out to be a long autograph. Margot is going to be so thrilled! She'll look like a kid at Christmas!*

Amanda tugged the top two sheets loose from the pad and handed them to Blake, and surprised her again with another hug. "I wish I could sneak back out there and have a drink and talk, but we've got to get on the road to our next tour stop. Say hi to your friend from me next time you see her, though!"

"I will, and thank you again!" Blake waved, and Amanda waved back before retreating into the dressing room again to change clothes. With Matt behind her, Blake weaved her way through dancers back to the table they shared with Brett.

Brett was talking on what looked like an Android smartphone until Blake and Matt sat down at the table. Then, "Listen, Blake is back, I've gotta go," Brett said, and clicked the End Call button. He grinned at Blake and asked, "So how is Ms. Brown?"

"She's such a sweet woman!" Blake knew she was gushing, but she couldn't help herself. "Margot is right to love her, she's got a personality as beautiful as her voice." About to fold the note Amanda Brown had written to Margot, Blake found herself reading it.

"To Margot Mills: One of my inspirations is a quote from Goethe, which says, 'Whatever you can do, or dream you can, begin it. Boldness has genius, power, and magic in it.' I wish you the boldness to dream big and the power and magic to make your dreams come true. All my best, Amanda Brown."

"All that fits easily on one page," Blake murmured. "What in the world did she write on the second page?" She looked, and found an Amanda Brown autograph of her own.

"I'm glad we met, Blake Bertrand. I remember when you were one of the world's top models. I thought if your father's music had a body, it would look just like you. Keep changing the world one neighborhood at a time, and keep being beautiful. You're an inspiration to all your sisters! Best always, Amanda Brown."

Blake found herself trying not to cry. Carefully, she folded the two sheets of paper and slipped them into an inner pocket of her purse for safety.

"You okay?" Brett was leaning in close to see Blake's eyes, his own gone soft with concern for her.

"Oh. Yes. She just wrote such a sweet note to me, that's all." Blake smiled, her cheeks feeling warm again under Brett's intense gaze. "Do you want dessert?"

"I do, but not anything they serve here." Brett grinned at her, and now his eyes were filled with mischief.

"Bad boy." They laughed, while Matt briefly looked from one to the other before returning his attention to his smartphone.

She waved their waiter back to their table the next time she spotted him, and started to pay for dinner. Brett pushed a credit card of his own into Tim's hands. "No, ma'am. I said this would be my treat, remember?"

After their meal was paid for, Blake finally thought to check the time. "It's almost one in the morning!"

"Sorry about that. At least it's the weekend." Brett stood up and held Blake's coat for her. "Let's take you home. Why don't we walk?"

"Long walk," Matt muttered.

"Gives us more time to talk." Brett said that to Blake, still acting as if Matt weren't around.

"I'm exhausted. How about a compromise? We'll call a cab, get out a few blocks away from my apartment, and walk the rest of the way." Blake glanced at Matt, who nodded approval of her suggestion.

"Well, sometimes a guy has to take what a lady is willing to give." Brett offered Blake his arm, and with arms linked they descended the stairs and stepped out onto the street.

And found that it was snowing, big fluffy flakes of the kind little children dream of seeing on Christmas Day. Like a little child, Brett turned his face up to the sky and caught a snowflake on his tongue.

That tongue, long and agile, made Blake feel warm all over.

Brett looked at her and grinned. He'd meant his gesture to speak to Blake's hormones, and he'd succeeded, and he knew it.

Matt phoned for a taxi, while Brett caught more snowflakes and Blake laughingly joined him. She felt sorry when the taxi arrived for them, but the warmth and the sense of security of sitting between two big, well-muscled men was almost sinfully delicious. They got out of the cab five blocks away from Blake's apartment, and Brett put an arm around her waist and held her close as they walked.

By the time the doorman welcomed Blake home, there was no question to be asked. She waited for Brett to come in, and he did.

Standing between her bed and the window that filled most of the wall overlooking the street, Brett helped Blake out of her clothing, one garment at a time. Blake unbuttoned his shirt with her teeth, making sure he knew that she, too, had skills. Her hand moved as if it had a mind of its own to his hot, hard crotch, but he gently brushed her away.

"No, let me." He slid down his pants first, standing framed against the city lights. His best friend was trying to escape from his briefs, and Brett slipped those off too, his dick high and...mighty. Blake's lower lips thrilled with anticipation.

He made her wait for it, kissing her breathless and nibbling her ears and nipples. She dug her fingernails into his ass cheeks, making him gasp and slide himself between her legs. Blake moaned, feeling sudden wetness down below and a need so strong it hurt.

"Please," she begged him, and he lifted her in his arms and stretched her out on top of the bed covers. Without preamble he spread her legs and brushed his tongue over her mound, once, twice, then wiggled it between the folds around her clit and licked that once before suddenly sucking her hard.

"Christ," she groaned, her hips thrusting with a will of their own. He seized her hips and pressed them still, then rose and kissed her quiet as he slid his buddy inside her.

If he hadn't been kissing her, she would have awakened the whole apartment building.

Chapter Seven

March 26
New York, New York

Suki peeked into Blake's bedroom and announced, "We've got a taxi on the way, Boss. Are you about ready to roll?"

Blake stood looking at her black leather Gucci carry-on, consulting a list she'd made in a file on her phone. "Got everything," she answered. She zipped the carry-on shut, locked it, and started rolling it through the living room.

That was when her BlackBerry played Peter Gabriel's "Big Time" to announce a phone call from Vickie Sharp, Blake's new publicist. "Go watch for the cab," Blake told Suki. "I'll keep this short, I promise."

"Blake, I've got such good news for you!" Vickie piped in Blake's ear as soon as she pressed the Talk button.

"Well, no matter how good it is, make it quick. I've got a taxi coming to take me to the airport."

"You're leaving New York? But I need you tomorrow. I just talked to some television producers looking for a host for a new reality show, and you're exactly what they need."

"That does sound interesting, and I'll be glad to talk to them anytime after this weekend, but I've got to go now."

"I've already scheduled a meeting for tomorrow morning!"

"Reschedule it. You should have checked with me first, anyway. I often have appointments with lawyers, brokers, other business contacts. Talk to you when I get back."

"But that might be too late! They want to hire someone immediately!"

"I've got to go," Blake reminded Vickie, and clicked End Call.

She found Brett standing between her and the door. "You still haven't explained why you've got to go back to Miami for the weekend," he said, well-muscled arms folded across his bare chest.

Antonio, relaxing on the sofa and watching *Criminal Minds* on the large flat-screen TV, arched an eyebrow. By now Blake knew him well enough to know that meant he was listening to the conversation a few steps away from him, though his gaze stayed fixed on the show.

"I've got something personal to take care of back home." She rolled the carry-on in her trail, out the open door.

Brett followed her. "Is something wrong with your mom?"

"No."

"Then what's happening?"

"I seem to remember saying it's personal, Brett." She turned around to face him. He didn't seem aware of the fact, but Antonio stood behind Brett, monitoring the situation.

I'm relieved to see Antonio watching over me. What does that say about my relationship with Brett? She bowed her head, torn and reluctant to think about any of this, especially now.

"I get it. You don't trust me." Brett's eyes narrowed. Even though Antonio couldn't possibly see that, he reacted to Brett's tone of voice by moving a step closer, ready for action.

"We've only known each other a few days, Brett. You don't know everything about me, and I don't know everything about you. Give it time." She turned around again and pulled her carry-on toward the elevator.

"Take me with you."

"Not this time, Brett."

"But why?"

"What about the word 'personal' don't you understand, dude?" asked Antonio.

As Blake pressed the elevator button for the ground floor and the doors started to slide shut, Antonio and Brett faced each other in the hallway, looking on the verge of a fistfight. *What have I got myself into?* She contemplated that question as the elevator began its descent.

Chapter Eight

March 26
Miami, Florida

L ang climbed out of the steaming Jacuzzi and stretched himself from toes to uplifted fingers, free for the moment from aching joints. He motioned to Gabby to follow him, and she did, making sure to bring the shot glasses and half-empty vodka bottle with her. They dripped from the enclosed patio to the den and dropped themselves onto the sofa, unconcerned by the work the water stains would make for the maid team.

"Pour me another shot," he grumbled, leaning over the coffee table. A mirror lay ready, where he'd left it earlier. He tapped a small quantity of cocaine out of a clear plastic baggie onto the mirror's surface. He used his MasterCard to cut the powder into two smaller piles, which he shaped into two lines about the width of a drinking straw and the length of the credit card itself.

With one end of a tightly rolled hundred-dollar bill inserted in his right nostril and his left index finger pinching his left nostril shut, he sniffed his way up one line of coke. He paused when the line was gone to breathe gently out of his mouth, then snorted hard to draw the powder all the way up into his nose.

"Ahhhh." He felt a mild sensation of lightness, as if a breeze could carry him away. "Fuck yeah, this is good stuff."

"Hey, I want some!"

"Just wait your goddamn turn. I pay for this stuff, I decide when you get some." He transferred the rolled hundred to his left nostril, pinched his right nostril shut, and repeated the process with the other line.

Now he felt like he was floating, and only two things could make him feel even better. He put out a hand for the vodka shot Gabby had poured for him and gulped it down in a single swallow. Then he lay back and spread his legs. "Suck me."

"I want some coke first."

"Well, you're not getting any until you suck my dick."

Gabby hesitated, and Lang knew she was thinking of grabbing the baggie and prepping a couple of lines for herself. He also knew she remembered what happened the last time she defied him. She finally cupped him in one hand and slid his hardening prick into her warm, wet mouth and suckled him.

"Oh yeah. Take me, cunt. Harder."

She did as he told her, sucking him with more force. He reached down and grabbed fistfuls of her hair and pulled as she sucked, until finally he arched his back and shot his jism down her throat. She coughed a little, just once, but licked her lips and swallowed as he'd taught her.

"You're getting pretty good at that now," he said, when he was no longer panting for breath.

"Thanks." After a few seconds, the blonde actress asked, careful not to whine, "Please, can I have some coke now?"

"I guess you earned a little reward." He sat up and tipped a tiny bit more powder onto the mirror's surface and shaped a single line, of the same dimensions as each of the two he'd snorted.

"Just one line?"

"I can dump it back in the bag, or snort it myself."

"I'm sorry. Please. Thank you. Lang, please..."

As he handed her the hundred, his iPhone rang. He glanced at the caller ID, and his heart raced. Snatching up the phone and the baggie, he said, "I'll be back in a few," and shut himself inside his study.

"What's up, Sal?" Lang dropped into his favorite recliner, put up the footrest, and made himself comfortable.

"Blake just boarded a flight back to Miami."

That made him sit straight up, the act making him wince from the strain in his abs. "When does her plane get in?"

"About ten tonight."

"Well. I think we should welcome the bitch home." He felt a tingling excitement shiver up his spine at the thought.

"That isn't really the sort of thing Donato sent us here to do."

"Fuck Donato," Lang growled. "Listen, I want you and Lucio to follow her. You know what her car looks like. She has a chauffeur, so this will be tough to pull off. But the first chance you get, I want you to slash her tires."

"Won't the driver put up a fight?"

"I doubt it. He's an old man. But if he gives you trouble, rough him up a little."

"Okay. But if Donato hears about this—"

"Don't be a moron. Make sure he doesn't." Lang clicked the call off and sat back, grinning up at the ceiling.

"Maybe there's a god in heaven after all. Here's my chance to teach the bitch a lesson she'll never forget."

Chapter Nine

March 28
Tampa, Florida

Henry Walden, Blake's chauffeur since a 9/11 back injury forced him to give up his career as a New York firefighter, parked the rental car in the Poe Garage with half hour to spare before the Florida All State Band concert would begin. Instead of his usual suit and tie, he was dressed in jeans, sweater, and a jaunty beret. Blake and Suki were likewise dressed to blend in: Suki in jeans and blouse, and Blake in slacks and sweater.

Suki didn't wait for Henry to open the door for her. As soon as the car stopped moving, Suki popped out of the backseat and turned in a slow circle, inspecting every detail of their surroundings.

"I thought you were trained to blend in," Henry teased. Chauffeur and bodyguard had taken an instant liking to each other, chattering like old friends throughout the drive from Miami to Tampa.

Who would have guessed Suki can be really friendly? Blake smiled as Henry opened the door for her.

"I think you should come inside with us," Suki said to Henry, ignoring his little joke.

Here and there, cars were pulling into parking spaces. Thirty- and forty-something couples climbed out of most, usually with one or more teenagers or young children. Some cars yielded senior citizens, probably grandparents of children performing in the afternoon's concert.

Blake found herself watching them all with a jealousy so intense it pained her heart. *I should have kept Lionel, and never married Lang. My son and I should be a family...*

Suki ceased examining the area, half-turning so that she could see Blake and Henry and yet still keep watch on activity in the garage. "I don't know what it is, but something isn't right. Come inside the Straz, Henry."

"I'll be fine staying with the car. I do it all the time," Henry replied, his voice mellow. "My grandkids got me this fancy phone. I sit in or near the car, goofing off on Facebook…"

"You shouldn't do that this time," Suki insisted.

"What's wrong, Suki?" Blake slung her purse strap over her shoulder, anxious to go inside the Straz and lay claim to a seat as close to the stage as possible.

"Like I said, I don't know." Suki frowned as a couple walked by, their toddler shrieking to enjoy the echoes in the garage.

"We only have two tickets," Blake reminded Suki.

"Then take Henry in, and I'll stay here."

Henry shook his head. "No, you've got to stay with Miss Bertrand. She's the one who needs protection. I don't have an enemy in the world, thank God."

"But—"

"Suki, we need to go in." Blake glanced at the time on her BlackBerry: twenty minutes until the concert would start. All the best seats might already be taken. "Henry, keep your eyes open. If there's any chance of trouble, run inside the Straz and text Suki, okay?"

"Yes, Miss Bertrand." Henry shut the rear doors of the car as Blake hurried to the covered walkway leading from the Poe Garage to the Straz Center. Suki hesitated for a moment, looking at Henry with worry etched into her facial features. Then the bodyguard trotted to catch up with Blake and stayed by her side the rest of the way.

All the seats in the first five rows were occupied, but they managed to get seats near the center of the sixth row, and those weren't bad. Blake's tummy flip-flopped as if it were she, not her son, due on stage in fifteen minutes. Suki sat tapping text messages into her Android smartphone. *Probably to Henry. She's really very worried about him. I wonder if I made a mistake…*

Then the lights dimmed, and the band moved onstage and took their seats. Blake couldn't see Lionel's face well, but she knew he was the taller and lankier of the three French horn players. A student conductor took the shadowed podium, and a spotlight flashed on to illuminate a balding man in a blue suit.

"Ladies and gentleman, the state of Florida has tens of thousands of talented young musicians. Only the best of the best, however, are selected for All State Band. Every young man and woman on this stage with me today was chosen from hundreds or even thousands who play the same instrument."

The speaker paused for breath and approval, and the audience clapped their hands in enthusiastic reception of the praise he was bestowing on their children and grandchildren. Blake clapped her hands so hard that her palms stung, and she felt warm tears brimming in her eyes.

"Professionals would spend weeks rehearsing the pieces of music you're about to hear. These kids had only one week to master them, and I think you'll agree they did, in fact, master them. I'm honored to present to you this year's Florida All State Band!"

With that, the bald man scurried off the stage, the lights brightened again, and the tuxedoed student conductor bowed to the audience before turning his attention to the band. He tapped his baton on the podium, and in unison the musicians readied their instruments. A crisp wave, and the stringed instruments offered up the pondering first notes of Dvorak's "New World Symphony." The first clarinet sounded a question, and Blake's son Lionel suggested the first French horn's answer, which the flutes and piccolos then discussed briefly before the whole band started arguing.

Blake felt as if her chest would burst, she was so filled with pride. She sat hypnotized as the band completed the first movement. They then launched into Gunther Schuller's "Diptych for Brass Quintet and Concert Band," the opening phrases of which sounded like perfect music for the soundtrack of a horror movie.

From the end of that piece the band swung into a rendition of Gershwin's "Rhapsody in Blue" that at last got Blake's tears flowing. *My dad would have loved every note of the jazzy piece.*

Next came "I Dreamed a Dream," from *Les Misérables*. And then, to Blake's surprise and delight, Lionel stood and moved to the front of the stage for a performance as a soloist.

Her son made the French horn sing the romantic lyrical phrases of "I Dreamed a Dream," with as much soul as any world-famous instrumentalist. When the piece ended with Lionel's horn murmuring the last sad line all alone, Blake found herself on her feet, cheering as well as clapping fit to knock her hands off her wrists. She was not the only one.

She sat again as Lionel returned to his seat, and noticed Suki diverting her intense gaze from the stage back to Blake. The bodyguard studied Blake's face as if picking her out of a police lineup.

"Is there a problem?" Blake asked Suki, swallowing tears and trying to sound stern.

"Not that I know of, Boss." Suki's face took on its accustomed blankness, and she continued texting Henry or whomever else she might be in contact with as the band struck up Sousa's "Stars and Stripes Forever," their grand finale. After the last soaring triumphant note, in unison the band members and their conductor bowed to the audience, who gave them a standing ovation that lasted long after the kids had left the stage.

Blake was still applauding when Suki clasped her hand and hissed in her ear, "We've got to go now, Boss."

"But I—" She yearned to go find Lionel and hug him so tight he'd have trouble breathing, tell him how talented he was, how he was so like his grandfather. *But he doesn't know me*, she reminded herself, and suddenly it was Blake who couldn't breathe.

Suki either didn't notice, or didn't care. "*Now*, Boss." She dragged Blake with her, pushing other audience members out of their way, and by the time they reached the covered walkway to the garage they were moving at a full-on run.

"What's the—" Blake gasped out, but then Suki started hauling her up three flights of stairs.

"Henry missed check-in," Suki rapped. She didn't break stride, and she wasn't breathing any harder than if they'd been moving at a lazy walk.

On the fourth level Suki pulled Blake, still at a run, directly to the rental car. At first Blake thought Henry must be napping, his head bowed over his chest.

Then she realized his gray hair was red with blood.

"Crouch behind me and dial nine-one-one," Suki snapped at Blake.

Down on her knees, struggling to see the BlackBerry's keypad through her tears, Blake noticed the car's tires were slashed. Suki must have seen it too, because the last thing Blake heard before the emergency dispatcher spoke to her was Suki snarling, "Goddamn it, the tires should have been enough. He's just a nice old man..."

Chapter Ten

Not long ago, the Marquee nightclub was the sort of place Brett Skeet could only dream about what the inside might be like. Tonight, with cash withdrawn from the business Visa that Blake left with him in case any expenses related to the Wishman Spears came up while she was in Florida, Brett was in with the in crowd. The doorman giving priority admittance to VIPs was happy to promote Brett to that status for the night.

Just inside the door Brett halted and looked around, impressed with the decor. Blue light illuminated the whole club, and hanging over the central dance floor was a double-helix strobe light. Pictures and patterns of light projected onto all four walls were reminiscent of Japanese anime. Surrounding the dance floor were padded benches fronted by small candlelit tables. There was a single long, sleek oak bar, but an absence of bar stools ensured that all patrons would have easy access to the bartenders. Staircases led up to railed catwalks where exhibitionist dancers could put on a show for their fellow customers.

Brett claimed a table, because as a VIP he was entitled to table service. Seeing the badge the doorman had given him, a perky little blonde bartender hurried to his table and chirped, "What will you have tonight, sir?"

"Give me a Cherry Bitch." He struggled to refrain from grinning.

"I'll be back in a few minutes with that for you, sir." The perky blonde dashed back to the bar and assembled ingredients: black currant tea, gin, lime juice, apple juice, syrup, fresh cherries. Brett listened to the music and people-watched, and in about ten minutes the bartender brought him an iced glass of liquid sin.

Some of the most flamboyant customers were already on the catwalks, shimmying for all to see. A tall, curvy redhead with hair down to her waist was doing a fair imitation of Shakira's belly-dancing moves, and she kept throwing glances at Brett. He raised his glass to her and grinned. She beckoned to him to join her, but he shook his head and ran his tongue along the rim of the glass, keeping his gaze fixed on her. Watching her watching him.

She danced down the stairs and approached him, glancing from her own rolling hips to Brett and back again. He drained his glass when she reached his table. When she put out her hands for his, he let her coax him out of his seat and onto the dance floor.

Her hips undulating against him were as intoxicating as a thousand Cherry Bitch cocktails. She smelled of liquor and sweat and a sweet smokiness he belatedly recognized as marijuana. Turning her back to him, she commenced grinding her firm buttocks into his crotch. He yearned to lay her out on the dance floor and explore every inch of her in full view of everyone, but the Marquee wasn't that kind of club.

Instead he danced with her, his hip-hop moves somehow blending with her own exotic, sinuous motions. They were soon the center of attention, many of their fellow customers gathering around to watch them. Dance song after dance song they shook and stamped and weaved together, two strangers bound by a glue of sexual chemistry.

At long last, his muscles jittery from exertion, he clasped her hand in his and led her back to his table. "I've got to have a drink and catch my breath. You're too much woman for any man to handle all night without a break, girl."

She laughed, and he waved the perky bartender back to wait on them. He ordered another Cherry Bitch and she, intrigued, decided to try one herself. While they waited for their drinks, he gasped between breaths, "I'm Brett, by the way."

"Savannah," she told him, and held out her hand to shake his. Instead he kissed hers, giving each fingertip a teasing little suckle. She giggled and moaned, both at the same time.

They danced and drank until the Marquee's closing time. Out on the sidewalk she told him, "I don't want this night to end."

"Me either." *That bitch Blake is happy to let me run errands for her, but she won't take me on trips with her or even tell me why she's going away. Probably fucking some dude she knows in Miami. Well, two can play that game.*

Savannah stood on her tiptoes and grabbed his head to pull his lips against hers. They kissed on the sidewalk as though their lives depended on the eroticism of their performance, and when at last they stepped apart she whispered, "My place or yours?"

"Mine." He hailed a passing taxi, and they felt each other up in the backseat all the way to Blake's apartment.

Inside, Matt sat cross-legged on the sofa, watching late-night television. He wore only a pair of jeans, and Savannah eyed his well-defined abs and biceps with obvious appreciation.

"Who's this?" Matt asked, eyeing the redhead with a different sentiment entirely.

"A guest," said Brett, and escorted Savannah inside,
Matt put his hands up. "Hate to be the cock blocker, but that ain't happening."

Brett stuck his chest out in defiance. "Or you'll do what?"
Savannah looked on in amusement.

"I'll tell Blake," Matt said coolly.

Brett turned to Savannah and spoke in a forced, formal tone. "We'll have to reschedule our meeting another time. Sorry about the inconvenience."
Matt rolled his eyes.

Savannah spun around on heels, flipped her finger to both men, and marched to the elevator.

Brett walked in and Matt went back to watching television.

***

March 28
Tampa, Florida

Blake sat in the surgery waiting room, watching the minutes crawl by on the wall clock. Suki paced like a caged tiger, and occasionally growled like one too.

Edith must have Henry's wife on a plane by now. What the hell am I going to tell her?

At that moment Blake's BlackBerry rocked out a chorus of "Big Time." Vickie, her new publicist, was calling. Blake considered letting it go to voicemail, but she didn't really have anything else to do except wait for the surgeon to come out and announce Henry's prognosis.

"This is Blake," she said, her words seeming to crawl like the wall clock's minute hand.

"I know who I called," snapped Vickie. "What I don't know is what the hell you were thinking."

"If you're going to swear at me, I can just hang up on you."

"Seems to me you already have. It's all over the news that you went to some high school band concert today, and—"

"What?"

"You heard me. Don't try to change the subject."

"I'm not. Are you telling me I was in the news by name? Blake Bertrand?"

"What other name would you be called in the news? The—"

"I flew to Miami using a false name and ID."

That got Vickie's attention. For at least five merciful seconds the line was utterly silent.

"Why?"

"It doesn't matter."

"Well, I'll tell you something that *does* matter. The producers of that reality TV show who wanted you as their host are going to hear about this, that you blew them off to go to a stupid fucking school band concert. You don't even have a niece or nephew, let alone a child of your own. It's going to be a miracle if they still want you when they hear about this."

"That's fine."

"Oh, no it isn't! Listen, Blake, I've always said there's no such thing as bad publicity. But I think you just proved me wrong. When being in the news means you're unpredictable and disrespectful, that's bad, and the best publicist in the world can't save you from that kind of reputation."

"I'm not asking you to do anything about this. I'll talk to you when I get back to New York."

She pressed the End Call button, and watched the crawling of the wall clock's minute hand.

Chapter Eleven

March 31
New York, New York

At about the same time the Delta began descending for its landing, Blake received a text message from Connor Stafford, the New York–based project director she'd hired to supervise her Wishman Spears operations: <Sorry to do this to you right now, Ms. Bertrand, but I've got to ask you to come to my office today. We've got a problem to discuss.>

"Oh, that's just fantastic," Blake muttered.

Suki, trying to get a nap during the flight because she hadn't slept since they found Henry beaten nearly to death, cracked one eye open. "What's gone wrong this time, Boss?"

"I know you're exhausted, but I've got to run a business errand before we go back to my apartment."

"Hoo-fucking-ray," Suki agreed, and opened her other eye and breezed down the aisle to visit the bathroom before passengers were instructed to buckle their seat belts. While her bodyguard answered nature's call, Blake phoned for a taxi to meet them at the airport.

Connor Stafford's office was located in Queens. Their cabdriver was a wily lifelong resident of New York, however, and delivered them to the office in half the time Blake would normally expect. She paid him to wait, hoping for an equally speedy trip home.

More than anything else in the world, at the moment, I want a long hot soak in the bathtub and some soothing jazz. I may even go to bed after my bath and sleep through dinnertime, through the night, and barely wake up in time for a late brunch.

She was expected, so the receptionist waved her back to her boss's office immediately. Blake knocked on the door, eased it open, and found Connor on a phone call. She took a seat in one of the two chairs across from his desk, and Suki slumped into the other.

"I'm going to need to call you back," he said after a moment. "I've got something urgent to tend to. Talk to you again before I close up shop for the day." He placed the phone on its cradle and announced, without preliminary greetings, "We've got a zoning fight on our hands, Blake."

"But we were expecting that, weren't we?" She wished the chair wasn't so comfortable. Her eyes were trying to close against her will.

"Yes, but you know it's no good to delay addressing this sort of thing. A public meeting has been scheduled, and already there's almost twenty 'concerned citizens' signed up to speak against your plans for the Wishman. They complain that traffic is certain to more than double in the area."

"I'm sure it will, but the influx of new business—"

"It's not me you've got to convince, it's local residents. You or your architect or both will need to attend the meeting and give a presentation on why the economic benefits outweigh the traffic inconveniences."

"Forgive me for complaining, Connor, but I don't see why there's a problem that required me to come here today. All you had to do was get me signed up to speak at the meeting."

"That's exactly why I needed to talk to you. Don't you usually leave these things up to Charles? Some guy Brett Skeet said he was in charge of any fee payments or signatures that might be needed during your absence."

"Yes. Charles is in California meeting with investors. Brett volunteered to handle this."

"Well, that's fine, except that I tried all weekend and all yesterday to get him on the phone. He never accepted or returned my calls."

A heat began to rise in Blake's gut. "When is the deadline to sign up to speak at the meeting?"

"Four o'clock this afternoon."

She glanced at the time on her BlackBerry's display. It was half past two already. "I'm so sorry, Suki, but—"

"We need to run another errand." Suki pushed the words out even as she pushed herself out of the chair and onto her feet.

"I apologize, Connor," Blake said before she followed Suki out of the office.

Chapter Twelve

March 31
New York, New York

It was a few minutes after five o'clock when Blake and Suki finally arrived at Blake's penthouse apartment. Suki immediately proceeded to run the shower in the bathroom adjoining her bedroom, but Blake still had one item of business to attend to before her hot soak in the bathtub and an early bedtime.

Unfortunately, Brett Skeet was nowhere to be found. His luggage still sat next to her bedroom closet, but the man himself was missing.

She sat on the bed and texted him as she kicked off her ballet flats. <I'm back. Where are you?>

As she undressed, she expected to hear the chorus of The Police's "Message in a Bottle" signaling that she'd received a text. Her BlackBerry lay silent on the bed covers, however, as she stripped out of her black Versace slacks and ruffled blue blouse.

She dialed his number, gazing out the huge window at New York's rush-hour traffic ten stories below. Her call went to his voicemail.

"Brett, I need to discuss something important with you. Please call me back."

Finally she trudged into the bathroom, mixed the hot and cold water to exactly the temperature she wanted, and let the tub begin to fill. She dribbled some luxury bubble bath into the water under the faucet's flow.

Might as well brush my teeth, since I'm planning to skip dinner and just go to bed. She wet her toothbrush at the sink, and glimpsed something out of the corner of one eye. A splash of scarlet red protruding slightly from behind the toilet.

Blake crouched down and reached for the spot of color that didn't belong on the bathroom's slate gray floor. It was fabric. She pinched it between thumb and forefinger and held it up for inspection.

A bra. Two cup sizes larger than Blake wore.

She laid the foreign garment out on the sink counter and shut her eyes.

***

"Get out of my face!"

That was Brett's voice, coming from just outside Blake's closed bedroom door. Blake fumbled in the dark for her BlackBerry, which she'd placed on the bedside table just before she crawled under the covers and promptly fell asleep. She accidentally knocked something off the table, but judging by the sound it wasn't her phone. With another grope she found the BlackBerry, tapped a key to light its display, and checked the time:

11:40 P.M.

Matt was speaking now, but Blake couldn't make out his words. She heard Brett clearly, however, when he snarled, "Touch me again and I'll knock you on your ass, white boy."

Blake slid out of bed and opened the door. Matt and Brett, confronting each other, both turned their heads to look at her. She slept nude, and hadn't taken the time to put on her bathrobe before going to break up the fight.

"I apologize for not having any clothes on, but both of you need to chill." She moved over so that most of her body was hidden by the door. "Now, tell me what this is about, one at a time. Matt first."

"Your *friend* here"—Matt loaded the word friend with so much contempt that Brett actually took a step backward—"brought a guest here for the weekend. I told him to tell you or I would."

"I already know about that," Blake told them, her voice hushed and even.

Matt and Brett both stood staring at her, slack-jawed. After a few seconds Brett realized it was his turn to speak and he'd better convince Blake that Matt was lying.

So, with great passion but no originality, Brett shouted, "He's lying!"

"I'll be back in a second." Blake turned around, groped her way into the bathroom, snatched up the bra too large for her, and returned to the door and dangled it in Brett's face. "This is too big for me. I'm a C cup, this is a DD. So, if it isn't mine and you didn't entertain another woman in my apartment, I take it you're a cross-dresser?"

Matt howled laughter, waking Antonio and Suki. They appeared in the other two bedroom doors, bleary-eyed and baffled. Blake pushed the bra into Brett's hand and said, "You can return that to your friend. It would be polite. Now get your luggage out of my bedroom and your whoring ass out of my apartment."

She turned around to go crawl back into bed, but Brett called to her, "Wait."

Without looking back, Blake asked, "What do you want?"

"You said I'd get my turn to explain."

"Go on, then."

"Please, Blake. Let me talk to you in private."

"Want me to show him out, Boss?" Suki called to her.

"Not yet. Brett, this had better be good." She turned the knob to put the bedside lamp on its dimmest setting, sat on the bed, and pulled the covers up to her shoulders.

Brett stepped inside and looked her over with hungry eyes. Blake stared back at him. Stay strong, girl, she reminded herself. *No matter how sweet he can be, the shit he did while I was away is just unacceptable.*

When Brett still hadn't spoken several seconds later, Blake told him, "If this is your idea of explaining, you need to grab your luggage and get out, like I said before."

"I'm sorry. Your body makes a man's head go empty." He slide-stepped to the bed and sat on one corner, his gaze on the swell of Blake's breasts under the covers.

"True or not, that doesn't explain why you spent the weekend fucking another woman in a bed that I paid for, or why you didn't answer Connor Stafford's phone calls after I asked you to monitor developments with the Wishman Spears building while I was away."

He rubbed her foot through the covers. "I was hurt."

"Don't touch me."

Brett moved his hand to his lap. His eyes rested on her bare shoulders.

"What do you mean, you were hurt?"

"I'm crazy for you, Blake. You wouldn't take me with you to Florida, and you wouldn't even tell me why you were going there. I couldn't stop thinking you must be fucking some other man. It killed me to think that, and all I wanted was to make you hurt as bad as I did." He dropped his gaze to his hands on his knees. "I know I was wrong. I heard about your chauffeur. I'm sorry. I've wandered the city all day trying to think what to say to you, but there's nothing I can say that makes up for what I did."

God, he looks like a little boy whose favorite teacher just scolded him in front of his whole class. Stay strong, Blake! Finally she said, "That's for damn sure."

"Please just give me another chance. I swear I'll never doubt you again, Blake, and I'll do everything I can to make you happy." He raised his eyes, brimming with tears, to hers.

She watched his face, trying to read whether he meant it or was only trying to hang on to a meal ticket. *Lang was hanging on to a meal ticket. He beat the hell out of me so I'd be afraid of what he'd do if I tried to leave him. Brett isn't as bad as Lang*, she reassured herself.

"All right." She caught herself touching the scar on her forehead, and moved her hand just before Brett swept her up in a joyous hug. "Ugh, but you can't sleep here tonight."

"I'll check in at the Trump Tower."

As Brett stood up, he noticed something on the floor and picked it up: one of the pair of six-inch, black velvet Alexander McQueen platform heels Blake kept on the bedside table, under a framed photograph of herself wearing them years ago at a business convention with Lang.

Blake put out her hand for the shoe and said, "I'll take that, thanks."

"I don't understand why you keep a pair of stilettos on the bedside table, anyway. Why don't you wear them anymore? And if you don't want to wear them, why not throw them away?"

She breathed a long sigh. "That's personal, Brett."

Like air blasting out of a punctured balloon. "Okay, fine," he said, and left.

Blake set the shoe next to its mate and stared at the photograph for a few seconds. "Never again," she whispered to herself. Then she slid out of bed again, pulled on her bathrobe, and stepped out to talk to her bodyguards.

"I'm giving him one more chance," she told Matt, Suki, and Antonio, all three seated on the sofa waiting to learn the outcome of her private talk with Brett.

None of the three bodyguards said a word. They stared at her with mutinous expressions, until finally Suki flowed onto her feet in the eerily graceful way she had about her. "I'm still worn out, so

I'm going back to bed. Good night again, all." She drifted back into her dark bedroom and shut the door.

"I better go back to bed too," murmured Antonio. "I'm back on duty in a few hours." He vanished into the bedroom he used by night and Matt used by day.

Matt folded his arms across his chest and shook his head as he kept his gaze on Blake. "With all due respect, Ms. Bertrand, I think you've lost your mind. Miranda would have my skin for a rug if I did the kind of shit that dude did."

What do I say to that?

She didn't know, but felt like she needed a good hard scrub in the shower.

Chapter Thirteen

April 1
New York, New York

Blake woke up just before sunrise, her throat feeling like someone poured kerosene down it and applied a lit match. The rest of her felt as though she'd been hit by a train, which then backed up over her and finally ran over her again. She dragged herself out of bed and stumbled into the living room, where Matt sat watching a black-and-white movie on TV.

He looked up at her and did a double take. "Whoa, Ms. Bertrand. You don't look so good."

She tried to smile but didn't have the energy. Instead, she collapsed on one of the recliners and said, "I feel how I look."

"You want me to take you to an emergency room?"

"No." Blake shivered as she suddenly felt like she'd been dropped naked in the Arctic. "But maybe a clinic with walk-in hours..."

"I'll find one."

She must have fallen asleep or passed out then, because she wasn't aware of anything else until Antonio scooped her up in his arms and carried her out of the apartment. Matt held the door open for him and then hurried ahead to the elevator.

Matt pressed the elevator's button to keep the doors open. Blake looked at Matt and managed to squeak out, "Tell Edith...to take care...of business...for...me."

Matt punched the button to close the elevator doors. Then, as they started to slide shut, her cell phone range. It was Brett. She turned it off.

She drifted in and out of consciousness, but she did hear the doctor tell Matt and Antonio that Blake was among the flu season's last victims. "We can give her something to short-circuit the virus, but that just means she'll be sick for a week instead of two or three. Lots of rest, plenty of fluids..."

That bitch he had in my bed must've had some nasty ass cold. I fucking hate germs.

***

She wasn't aware of much until Sunday afternoon, when she finally woke up no longer feeling like she was dying and wishing she could hurry up and be done with it. Not surprisingly, Brett was nowhere, but she imagined he wasn't too far. His luggage still sat by the closet door.

First things first, however. Her grumbling stomach insisted she feed it.

Blake slipped into her bathrobe and slippers and padded into the kitchen, where Suki was finishing her lunch. Take-away pad thai, it appeared to be, and it smelled delicious.

"Feeling any better, Boss?"

"Ravenous! You didn't happen to get enough of that stuff for me to have some too, did you?"

Suki grinned. "I got enough for three bodyguards, but I can go back out and pick up some more for Matt. Have a seat." She got out a clean plate and dished out a couple of large spoonfuls. "Let's see how you do with that much, to start with. It's been a few days since you've had anything but chicken broth."

Blake demolished the food while Suki brewed some ginger tea for both of them. She stirred in some honey and handed Blake a mug. Blake sipped the hot liquid and relished how it eased her residual sore throat and stuffy sinuses.

"Oh, this is heavenly. Thanks, Suki."

"You're welcome." The bodyguard watched her drink the tea for a minute or two, then asked, "Do you feel like you'll be awake for a little while?"

"I think so. Why?"

"The guys and I need to talk to you, Boss."

"Am I recovered enough for this?"

Suki appeared to give that some thought before saying, "From what I've learned about you, there are things you don't want to talk about, no matter how you feel. But, Boss, you've hired Antonio, Matt, and me to protect you. We can do that better if we know more about who might want to hurt you, and why. Make sense?"

Blake stared at her now-empty tea mug and wished for

something much stronger. "I don't like it, but I understand."

"Atta girl, Boss." Suki went to the kitchen door and called, "Yo, Antonio, the boss is awake and I told her we need to talk to her. Grab Matt, will you?" Suki took her seat again, and a couple of minutes later Antonio and a bleary-eyed Matt joined them.

"Well, where shall we start?" Antonio looked at Suki.

"How about we start by giving props to our boss? Not many women with her name and face recognition could have a child and keep it a total secret for more than a decade." Suki raised her tea mug to Blake in a salute, then finished off the beverage.

Blake slumped in her chair. Obviously, this was going to be a difficult conversation. "Yes. I have a son."

"His name is Lionel, you gave him up for adoption at birth, and he played French horn in the All State Band concert we attended," said Suki.

"Why is this something we need to talk about?" Blake wished, again, for a more potent beverage than tea.

"Because anyone who wants to hurt you might just think they'll cause you more pain by harming someone you love, than by harming you personally." Antonio fixed his gaze on Blake's face. Matt and Suki followed his example.

"That's not possible." *Or is it? How many other people wondered why I went to that concert, and have found the truth? Christ, if I've put my son in danger...* "Nobody knows Lionel is my son, except me. I'm so careful..." Blake's voice trailed off as her chest ached with doubts.

"It's not just possible, Boss, it's a certainty. Whoever beat Henry up, it wasn't a mugging, and it wasn't a grudge against him. Our agency has been checking that out." Suki snapped her fingers in front of Blake's nose. "Wake up, Boss. Someone knows you don't just give the man a job; you care about what happens to him. Everyone else you care about is in danger, too."

"Your mom," said Matt.

Blake remembered Matt waiting downstairs while she told her mother about her chance to buy the Wishman Spears. "I've got Mom living in an exclusive island community. She should be safe there."

"Not from a trained killer, she isn't. Or even someone without training who is good at planning." Suki shook her head. "Any of us three could get to her. We've all dealt with other people who could do the same."

"Anyone who finds out about Lionel could get to him, too. It would be easy," said Antonio.

"Or Edith," added Suki.

"Or your friend Margot," Antonio suggested.

"Your 'uncle' Thorne and his wife," Matt said.

"*Stop.*" The tea mug slipped from Blake's grasp and cracked into a bunch of pieces on the marble floor. "I get it. But what do I do about it?" She covered her face with her hands. *I feel so helpless. Damn it.*

"You start by telling us everyone who might want to hurt you, and why." Antonio tapped the keyboard of his smartphone. "I'm taking notes. Go."

"Well, there's my ex-husband, Lang." Blake kept her hands over her face. *I really don't want to talk about this. But what if someone I care about gets hurt or killed because I kept everything to myself?*

Antonio nodded. "Ten years of marriage, several phone calls to the police about domestic violence. Always him violent to you. Now the question is, why?"

"He's just that way."

"No offense, Boss, but that's bullshit." Suki stood up. "Every man who beats up women has a reason for doing it. They grew up seeing dad slap mom around and think it's normal, or their big sisters made them wear dresses and made fun of them, or some other lame excuse. It all comes down to control. They need the women in their life to fear and obey them, or they don't feel like men. They beat respect out of women because it's easier than earning it."

Suki rambled in the refrigerator while Antonio nodded and said, quietly, "My dad beat up my mom. If I had a nickel for every time I heard him yell at her to do what he told her and like it..."

"But I don't know! If there's some reason why Lang is angry at women...I don't know what it is."

"I'm gonna have to call bullshit on you again, Boss. You're too smart and too careful, even after what your stepfather did to you. Deep down, you probably have an idea why Lang beat you up." Suki plunked down four ice-filled glasses, a two-liter bottle of Coca-Cola, and a bottle of Jack Daniel's. "Have some liquid courage, and we'll join you."

"Jack and Coke is what we drink after a job that's been a real hair-raiser," Matt confided to Blake as Suki poured the drinks.

Blake accepted the glass handed to her, and took a swallow. It momentarily burned her throat, which was still a little raw, but then she felt a warm glow spreading from her middle. To her own surprise, she wasn't upset when she asked, "How did you know about my stepfather?"

Matt shrugged. "You started modeling as a kid. Everyone knows that. And everyone knows you, uh, acted out. In ways abused girls tend to act out."

"Then you turned around. Dropped out of modeling at sixteen. Got back into it at eighteen, and you were totally different. You kept out of trouble and didn't take any shit from anyone anymore," said Antonio.

"Until Lang." Suki locked gazes with Blake, peering over the rim of her glass. "Start there. How you met him. Why you hooked up with him. And judging by Lionel's age, there's a story there too, close to when you got tangled up with Lang."

"It was my mom who turned me around." Blake forced herself to continue meeting Suki's gaze. *She's a woman. And she teaches self-defense classes for women and girls, she said. If anyone can understand, it's probably Suki.* "One day, when I was sixteen, she caught my stepdad about to rape me after beating me with his belt. It wasn't the first time he did that. I hated him and never felt safe with him."

Blake paused for another swallow of Jack and Coke, and smiled at the drink as she remembered Jacinta coming to her rescue. "You should have seen my mom that day. She was amazing. She stood in the door of my bedroom looking ten feet tall, and I still remember word for word what she said to that bastard Jim: 'I'm a nurse. I know many ways to kill you and make it look like natural causes. If I ever see your face again, I'll assume you're trying to get your hands on Blake, and I will see you dead. Understand?'"

"Well done, Mrs. Bertrand," Antonio said with a smile. Suki broke out into solemn applause, and Matt joined her.

"She wanted me to see a counselor, but I didn't want to talk to anyone about it. I just wanted to forget about him, feel safe again, and finish high school and get into real estate like my real dad did for a while." Blake stopped as the three bodyguards exchanged swift, knowing glances. "What?"

"That explains why you cracked under Lang's pressure," said Suki. "You didn't recover from your stepfather's abuse, you just buried it."

"And so it stayed there, making you vulnerable to another asshole like him." There was a sadness in Antonio's eyes that made Blake want to get up and go hug him. Or maybe it was the Jack and Coke, or missing Brett.

"Where is Brett?" Blake shook her head, puzzled that she hadn't asked sooner.

Matt rolled his eyes. "He's out 'taking care of business' for you. We want to talk about him, too, but let's finish up with Lang first."

Blake nodded, thinking, *Best to get this over with.* "How I met him. That was fifteen years ago. I was nineteen, and I'd been back in modeling for almost two years. I was a global sensation. Armani asked me to do a television commercial for one of their new fragrances, and the contract was worth a lot of money. I was saving up to get started in real estate development, so I was happy to take the offer. They cast Lang to be the handsome, distinguished man who caught a whiff of my perfume, and nothing could stop him from meeting me. Well, after the commercial was filmed Lang asked me out on a date, and when I kept saying no, he started sending me little gifts. My friends in the modeling business kept telling me to give him a chance. So I finally did."

"What happened?" Suki leaned forward, her eyes studying every detail of Blake's face. *Watching for any sign I might be lying*, Blake realized.

"It was wonderful," Blake said, and it was the truth. "He treated me to a fancy dinner and a Broadway play. We talked about his career as an actor, and he was so sad about his fading popularity. I told him I was planning to get out of modeling, and start investing in real estate like my dad did for a few years. He was really interested, and he encouraged me. He said he needed to find something else to do, too, and joked that maybe he'd be begging me for a job soon."

Suki shot a glance at Matt and Antonio. "Uh-oh." The two men nodded agreement.

"I don't understand." Blake frowned. She was usually so quick-witted. Either the lingering effects of flu or the Jack and Coke were messing with her head.

"That was a red flag, if you'd only known it," Antonio said, still looking terribly sad. "Most men don't like the idea of a woman telling them what to do. He wasn't making a joke or respecting your business ability, he was seeing how you'd react to the idea of being his boss."

"How *did* you react?" asked Matt.

Blake struggled to remember. "Lang is...quite a few years older than me." She wanted to glance at Matt, see what he thought of this revelation, since he was dating an older woman. With all her willpower, she forced herself to keep looking at Suki instead. "Being with him felt more like being with an older brother than a young stud in a rush to get laid."

"Older brother," Suki said, her voice gentle and quiet, "or father?"

Her chest hurt when she thought about it. "God..."

Antonio reached across the table and laid a comforting hand on her arm. "Keep going. You can do this, and it's helping us help you."

She nodded and hurried on. "I wasn't really attracted to him, but I kept seeing him because he was just so good to me. Then he found out I was still dating other guys, and he slapped my face so hard I had a bruise for almost a week." Blake grimaced. "I had to reschedule one photo shoot and wear heavy makeup for another. He tried to apologize, but I wouldn't talk to him anymore. And I told him so."

"That decision didn't stick, though," Matt said. "Why?"

"Because a few months after I broke things off with Lang, I was raped." She drank the rest of her Jack and Coke, needing a few seconds to brace herself to talk about that. "I worked late, and when I got home my apartment was completely dark. Someone was there...waiting for me. It was dark. I couldn't see him. He grabbed me from behind, and uh..." Blake paused with a flash of the brutal moment he raped her before her eyes. "And I got pregnant. I thought about getting an abortion, but I couldn't help thinking I'd be executing a baby for its father's crime. But I couldn't be the baby's mother, either, because I was afraid I'd hate it for the way it came into my life. So I booked several months at an expensive spa in Switzerland that guarantees total privacy."

Antonio nodded. "You told the world you had a bad case of mono, but really you were giving birth in secret."

"Yeah." Blake suddenly realized she was touching the scar on her forehead, and tucked her hand inside her bathrobe pocket. "When I'd arranged the adoption and got myself back in the same physical shape I had before I got pregnant, I came back to the

United States. Lang hired some guy to visit me dressed as a teddy bear and read me a letter that Lang had written to me. He said he was a changed man, that when he heard about my illness he realized he needed to get help for his anger and drug problems. The teddy bear had copies of Lang's payments to the rehab place he went to. He said he'd never cared about anyone as much as he cared about me, and begged me for another chance."

"So you gave him one?" Matt sounded stunned, even though Blake's ten-year marriage proved she'd given Lang another chance eventually. Blake smiled. *It's not hard to see what Miranda must see in him. He's such a sweet kid.*

"Not at first. I told him I'd try being friends with him, and maybe, if I really believed he'd changed, just maybe we'd try dating each other again. I also told him I planned to see other men, unless I became convinced Lang is the love of my life. He said he looked forward to winning me over." Blake handed her empty glass to Suki, who had motioned for her to pass it over for a refill.

"Well, we know he succeeded, because you ended up marrying him," said Antonio. "How long did it take for him to start beating you up?"

"That started as soon as we came home from our honeymoon. We'd bought a house before our wedding, and after our honeymoon we moved in. When we finished unpacking, Lang told me he wanted me to clean the house naked except for a pair of high-heeled shoes." She paused for a sip of her Jack and Coke refill, then said, feeling heat rise in her cheeks, "I thought it was a sex thing. He followed me around, watching me, and I thought he was just waiting until he was turned on and ready to fuck. I wasn't really trying to do a great job of cleaning, because I thought we'd hire a maid. We could afford one without any problem. But then he asked me if I really thought the master bathroom was clean, and he punched me in the stomach. In high heels, I never had a chance of staying on my feet. I fell and hit my head on the corner of the sink counter...and got this scar."

"You asked about Brett, Boss, and we said we want to talk about him too," said Suki. "We were going to ask you about the high heels you keep by your bed, because Brett has been asking about them."

Blake felt like someone had knocked her on the head with a sledgehammer. "Who has he been asking?"

Matt tapped a few keys on his smartphone and turned the display so that Blake could see it. He was showing her a picture he'd taken with the phone's camera, and the picture was of a phone's list of made calls. She recognized numbers: Vickie's, Edith's, Charles's, even the house phone of her mother's island condo.

"Everyone he thought might know the answers to his questions, and whose phone number he could get from your phone while you were sick, Boss," said Suki. "He could have grabbed it when I was in the shower. It's the only time that phone would be out of my sight."

"To be fair," Antonio said quietly, "we don't know why he's been asking personal questions about you. But with his history, we're worried his intentions may not be good."

"I want to go back to bed." Blake wished she hadn't woken up yet. She felt weary in her bones and torn up in her heart.

"One more question, Boss." Suki laid a hand on Blake's shoulder. Even though Suki seemed to be barely touching her, Blake found she couldn't stand up. "Is there anyone else who might have a grudge against you?"

Blake searched her memory for a few seconds. "The publicist I had before I hired Vickie. Remember we found out she's been talking crap about me to other publicists, Antonio?"

He nodded. "We'll do a background check on her, try to find out if she's someone who'd do even worse."

"Thanks for trusting us, Ms. Bertrand." Matt stood up and helped Blake to her feet. "I'll help you back to bed, and Suki will help you out of your bathrobe if you want her to."

"Never mind the robe." Blake leaned against Matt, and thought again that it wasn't any wonder Miranda was crazy about this younger man. "I just want to get under the covers and sleep for another week."

Chapter Fourteen

April 6
New York, New York

When Blake next woke up, it was to the familiar tune of "Message in a Bottle" coming from her BlackBerry. She picked it up and found that she'd just received a text message from Vickie: <Call me as soon as you're feeling able to go to a meeting.>

Am I feeling that much better yet? Blake lay in bed for a few minutes, contemplating that question. Her throat felt fine, she no longer hurt all over, and her sinuses were mostly clear. She felt worn out, but another day or two of rest would probably solve that problem.

Two shopping bags sat next to Brett's luggage; he'd stayed a few more nights at the hotel to give her space. Evidently he'd come and gone again while she slept. She wondered what he'd been buying, and whose money he had used to do it.

Blake crawled out of bed, still in her bathrobe, and stepped into her slippers. Her stomach grumbled for more food as she shuffled into the kitchen, and she pressed the speed-dial number for Vickie as she tried to decide what kind of cereal she wanted.

"Hi there, Blake," Vickie said after only one ring. "Your assistant called and told me you got hit by the flu. I'm glad you're feeling well enough to call me back, though, because I've got good news for you."

"What's that?"

Honey Smacks would be yummy.

"Remember the new reality TV show I told you about, and the producers wanted to talk to you about being the host of the show?"

"Yeah." She moved the BlackBerry to her other ear, freeing her dominant hand to pour Honey Smacks into a bowl. Even so, her arm trembled with exhaustion, and she spilled some.

"Well, they phoned me again and said they still think you're perfect for the job. Mind you, I'm sure that means they talked to some other business tycoons and decided nobody else has as much charisma as you do. But what's important is that you still have the opportunity."

"That's nice." Blake wrestled with the milk, trying to hold her arm steadier than she'd managed with the cereal. She only dribbled a little onto the table when she lifted the carton away from the bowl.

"How soon do you think you'd be able to meet with them? They'd really like to talk to you as soon as possible."

"I'm still sort of weak, but otherwise okay. Maybe Wednesday. Or Thursday, if they think the meeting will take longer than an hour." She cleaned up her spills with a paper towel and realized she still hadn't gotten out a spoon.

"I'll ask them how long they anticipate the meeting lasting, and schedule it accordingly. But...Blake?"

"Mmmm-hmmm?" Blake spooned Honey Smacks into her mouth without even sitting down yet. They were as delicious as she remembered, the flavors of honey and milk all swirling around her tongue.

"Don't blow them off again. Not even if you relapse. If anything goes wrong this time, they'll probably settle for someone with less personality and more greed for their money."

She dropped her spoon into the bowl and resisted the urge to cuss out her publicist. "I'll meet with them, Vickie, but you need to understand something. I'm good at making money, but I don't love money for its own sake. Money is only as valuable as the good uses it's put to."

"Well, *you* need to understand something, too, Blake. You've got a right to your opinion, and maybe that opinion serves you well in real estate. But now you're getting into other projects, and you need your face in the public view to build support for your goals. *Everyone* you need to help you with that—reporters, celebrities, marketers, everyone—does love money for its own sake. You'd better learn to help them get what *they* want, if you want them to help you get the things you want."

Vickie clicked the call off, and Blake sat brooding over her cereal. "It's just like the late great Gilda Radner used to say," she told the frog on the cereal box. "It's always something—if it isn't one thing, it's another."

The frog on the box grinned, confident that by the time she

finished eating his cereal she'd feel much better. "Frogs aren't exactly known for their brain power," she told him. "Why would frogs have anything to do with honey, anyway?"

She didn't know, and the frog fortunately didn't answer her question. But the cereal did cheer her up some.

Chapter Fifteen

Thursday was the day Vickie scheduled the meeting between Blake and the television producers who wanted to hire her to host their new reality show. Late Wednesday afternoon, however, script problems with a show they were already producing forced them to reschedule. Blake was secretly relieved. She still didn't have her normal high energy back, and she welcomed the chance to stay in her apartment and rest.

Brett, on the contrary, had other ideas. He pranced through her apartment door Thursday afternoon with a pair of tickets in hand.

"Pack your bags, babe. I have a surprise for you. We're going to Las Vegas for a long weekend!" He leaned over Blake, sitting on the sofa and watching *Cold Case* with Antonio, and planted a noisy kiss on her cheek.

She winced. "Can you get a refund or change the travel dates? I really don't feel like traveling."

"And even if she did, you'd need to buy three tickets, genius," said Antonio. "At least one of her bodyguards has to go with her wherever she goes."

"No you don't." Brett glared at Antonio. "I can keep Blake safe, myself."

Antonio's lips twitched, and then he broke into gut-busting laughter. Brett threw a punch at him, and Antonio swatted his fist away, all without ceasing to cackle.

For her part, Blake was disgusted. "Brett, I'm not going to Vegas. And I think you should grab your bags and go back to your family."

"What, why?" Brett shifted his attention from Antonio to Blake. "I don't understand. I've been taking care of business for you while you were sick, and—"

"Really? Edith and Charles handled most of my business. I see from the bags that your business is shopping lately?"

"I got a few new clothes. I've got to look good for you when I'm representing your business."

"Yeah. I suppose the *assistant* to Blake Bertrand does need to be a sharp-dressed man, as ZZ Top would say." Blake stared at Brett until he hung his head.

She had let Brett do a couple of light errands for her but she would have loved it if he could prove he was capable of more. She thought the shopping—with what looked like his own money—was a good effort to look the part.

"Okay, so I stretched the truth a little when I talked to a couple of people. But if I told them I'm just the guy you're fucking, they wouldn't take me seriously. It's hard to do business that way."

That's actually a good point. Blake studied Brett's face, wondering if her bodyguards were wrong about him and if she was wrong to let them influence her. "Why do you want to go to Vegas, anyway?"

"I still feel bad about how I acted while you were in Florida." Brett laid a hand on Blake's hair and stroked it as he continued, "I just want to take you away for the weekend and spoil you. We already spent several days apart. Nothing wrong with that, is there?"

"I guess not." She smiled at him in spite of herself, and ignored the sudden sound of Antonio clearing his throat. "I tell you what—if there's one more seat available on the departure and return flights, I'll pay for it. I do need to bring one of the bodyguards, but after feeling like death for a week I'd really enjoy some spoiling."

Brett leaned down and kissed her again, this time on the lips. He ran the tip of his tongue between her lips before he pulled away, grinning. "Thanks, babe. I'm going to show you a great time, I promise."

He showed Antonio his middle finger as he stepped into Blake's bedroom to phone the airline. Blake glanced an apology at Antonio, who shrugged and muttered, "Little punk."

***

April 10
Las Vegas, Nevada

Brett had booked them into the five-star Red Rock Casino, Resort & Spa, located near the base of Red Rock Canyon. They had a spectacular view of the canyon, and after sleeping until noon they ordered room service and had a generous lunch of grilled T-bone steaks, baked potatoes, steamed asparagus, and buttered yeast rolls with a rich red wine to wash it all down. After lunch they soaked in a hot tub for a while, got massages, and finally went swimming in the pool before showering and getting dressed to go out for dinner.

Throughout it all, Suki watched over them, blank-faced and silent. Blake had a hunch that Suki would like to corner Brett alone somewhere and ask him some pointed questions.

Much to Blake's surprise, Brett dressed for dinner in a tuxedo. He looked so handsome and sexy that she couldn't complain.

Brett could complain about Blake's choice of clothing, however. She was slipping into a skirt and blouse when he looked her over and said, "I wish you'd wear something fancier. This is a special occasion. Our first weekend getaway together. Let's make it something we'll never forget."

She fought the urge to sigh. *He's going to a lot of trouble to spoil me. If he wants me to dress more formal for dinner tonight, that's the least I can do to thank him.* "Any ideas?"

He considered the clothes she'd packed, and chose a mid-thigh-length white lace cutout dress, and a pair of white ballet flats. "This would look magnificent on you."

"Okay." She got changed while he watched, and felt herself blush when he approved the final result with an admiring whistle. *He's not a bad guy, really. Maybe I should introduce him to Mom and Uncle Thorne sometime soon...see what they think.*

She expected a taxi to be waiting to take them into the city for dinner, but instead Brett ushered Blake into a waiting limousine. Suki arched an eyebrow at Blake as she climbed inside with them, but still said nothing.

Blake, by contrast, had plenty to say when the limo parked at the Little White Wedding Chapel. "This had better be a joke, Brett."

"It isn't." He hopped out of the limo, got down on one knee, and said, "Blake Bertrand, I want to spend the rest of my life with you. Marry me."

"Oh, hell no. Get back in this car, Brett. We're leaving."

"I've made a reservation. Everything is ready. It will only take a few minutes."

"I don't give a freshly dropped shit. We are not getting

married."

"But, Blake, I love you!"

Wedding chapel staff were drifting outside, no doubt wondering why the happy couple were lingering at the limo instead of racing inside to say their vows. A plump, balding man in minister's clothing glanced away from the limo to look meaningfully at his wristwatch, then continued staring at them again.

"This is unpleasant to say, and worse to hear, but it's the truth—I don't love you, Brett. We still barely know each other."

"And whose fault is that? Every time I try to get closer to you, you just push me away."

"Brett, get in the goddamn car or I'm going to leave you here."

"You can't. I hired the limo. The driver takes orders from me, not you."

Blake pulled her wallet out of her purse, slid out a thousand dollars in hundred-dollar bills, and waved it so that the driver could see it in his rearview mirror. "I don't know how much he's paying you, but I can pay you more. I'm worth half a billion."

"Where do you want me to take you, ma'am?"

Brett scrambled onto his feet and climbed back inside the limo, slamming the door shut. He said not a word, and wouldn't look at Blake. That suited Blake fine.

"Back to the Red Rock. I'll get something from room service." She leveled a cool stare at Brett. "After I rent a separate room for the rest of the weekend, that is."

For the first time since they boarded the plane from New York to Las Vegas, Suki spoke for a purpose other than ordering a meal. "You could share my room and save yourself some money, Boss."

If looks could kill, Brett would have annihilated several miles of Las Vegas on the way back to the hotel.

Chapter Sixteen

Their taxi from the airport dropped off Blake, Brett, and Suki at Blake's apartment just a few minutes before 10 P.M. In silence they lugged their bags inside, though Blake nodded to the doorman when he welcomed them home. As soon as Matt opened the apartment door in response to Blake's knocking, Blake turned to Brett and said, "I want you to go now."

He still wouldn't look at her, and that didn't bother her. "Where the hell am I supposed to go at this time of night?"

"You said you've got family and friends in Harlem, right?" put in Matt.

"They'll all be in bed by now."

"Oh, someone must love you enough to wake up and let you in their house," Suki said, practically purring. "Now, just put those bags down, and go get the rest of your luggage from my boss's room, and I'll walk you back out to the taxi."

"I can do that," Matt offered to Suki, though they both kept watch on Brett. "You must be tired."

"Not too tired for this," Suki promised him. "But our friend here hasn't moved, so maybe he needs a little help."

"With pleasure." Matt clapped a firm hand on Brett's shoulder and hauled him inside the apartment.

Blake wanted to take a hot tub bath and go to bed, but she thought it might be best if she stayed out of her bedroom until Matt and Brett finished collecting Brett's luggage. She dropped her suitcase by the sofa, went into the kitchen, and heated water for some herbal tea.

As she stirred some honey into a steaming mug of chamomile tea, she heard Suki say, sounding positively gleeful, "There, we're all ready. Come on, I'll give you some advice about women while we're in the elevator."

I wonder if Suki's advice about women leaves bruises. Blake sipped her tea and wondered if she cared. She was about to fetch her suitcase from the living room, but Matt was already carrying it into her bedroom for her.

Matt hesitated before leaving Blake's bedroom. "I know you're probably hurting, Ms. Bertrand, but that guy was no good for you. Now he's gone, maybe you'll meet a real man."

She managed a smile. "If I meet a real man while I've got you, Suki, and Antonio guarding me, I'll know that's what he is, because you three will tell me."

"You better believe it." Matt grinned. "Good night, Ms. Bertrand. Pleasant dreams." He shut her bedroom door for her on his way out.

As the bathtub filled with hot water, Blake stripped naked, and decided she wanted some jazz while she soaked. She went to the turntable and put the late, great Amy Winehouse's album *Back to Black* on to play.

A little while later, as Blake drank her tea in a luxuriously hot bubble bath, the ghost of Amy Winehouse sang mournfully that "Love Is a Losing Game."

"Girl, you were so right about that," Blake agreed, with the restless spirit crooning from the turntable. "But I've learned my lesson. I'm done with all that."

***

April 13
New York, New York

At 9 A.M., Blake found herself, Antonio, and Vickie at Caffe Reggio. Sitting across the table from them were Vanessa Reeves and Jerome Harper, a team of television producers still new to the business but widely regarded as one of the most promising players in the TV producer game since Rob Reiner.

Vanessa was an imposing long-haired redhead, tall and slender but obviously athletic. She reminded Blake of the legends of the Amazons. By coincidence, she arrived wearing a Chanel suit identical to the one Blake wore. "Great minds thinking alike. That's a good omen," Vanessa joked, holding out a hand to shake Blake's.

"I'm really sorry, but I don't shake hands, because I get sick easily." *My life would be so much easier if we got rid of that custom,* Blake considered, not for the first time.

"Oh yes, and you just got over the flu. It's better if Jerome and I don't risk catching that, anyway." Vanessa smiled, which immediately put Blake at ease.

Jerome was African American and almost the same height as Vanessa, but he reminded Blake of the nerdy kid Steve Urkel from the '90s sitcom *Family Matters*. He was spindly, wore granny glasses, and dressed like he must be colorblind, and Blake reckoned he must ping gaydars for hundreds of miles around. This guy must be the brains of the team. He certainly didn't win contracts for the team based on his sense of style. She liked him immediately.

They ordered breakfast, commented on the signs that spring was coming to New York, and made casual inquiries about each other's work: Blake's plans for the Wishman Spears and her new charity, and Reeves and Harper's two current hit shows on NBC. Work discussions transitioned smoothly into the reason for their meeting after their food and beverages were delivered.

"Now, speaking of your shows on NBC, Vickie tells me you're planning a reality show you'd like me to host?" Blake paused between bites of pancake to pose the question.

"Blake, you'd be perfect!" gushed Vanessa, her face glowing with enthusiasm. "You're glamorous, and you're a true rags-to-riches American success story, and you're one of the smartest businesswomen on the planet. People love you. If you'll host this show, it will guarantee top ratings!"

"That's all very flattering." Blake turned a quizzical gaze to Jerome. "But what is the show about?"

"We're calling it *The Takeover*," Jerome explained, gesturing his fork with fluid wrist movements. "Contestants will be aspiring entrepreneurs. As the season progresses, they'll have to complete projects such as formulating a mission statement for a business, researching the competition's products and marketing strategies, developing a new goods or service and planning for its promotion, recruiting investment partners, various problems that real entrepreneurs must solve to be successful. You, as host, will evaluate how well each contestant completed the latest project, and whoever performed worst is eliminated."

I could really make a useful contribution by doing this, Blake considered. So many people dream of owning their own business but don't have the courage, and people who are already successful don't help them because they don't have the time. This show could give them the courage and platform they need.

"I'm definitely interested," Blake told them.

"Excellent!" Vanessa sat back, relaxing in her triumph. "We'll fax you and Vickie a copy of our standard contract, and—"

"Hold on. I have some terms and conditions for you." Blake finished off her coffee while the inevitable protests erupted.

"For God's sake, Blake, their standard contract is one of the most generous in the industry," Vickie scolded, under her breath. "Don't be a diva."

Meanwhile, as Vickie criticized Blake, Vanessa turned on the charm. "Of course we'll be glad to consider any requests you've got for us, Ms.—"

"These aren't requests. They're requirements." Although Blake didn't raise her voice in the slightest, a hush fell over the whole restaurant.

Vanessa took to ripping her napkin in tiny shreds while looking out the window at the distant park as though nothing really important were happening inside the restaurant. Jerome squirmed like a small boy who needs to go to the bathroom but for some reason is unwilling. Vickie slanted miffed glances at Blake.

As for Blake herself, she calmly beckoned Alyssa, their waitress, to come and refill the coffee cups at their table. Alyssa, pale and shy, poured coffee, squeaked an inquiry as to whether they needed anything else, and scurried away to the kitchen.

"This isn't a showdown in a Western saloon," Blake said into the silence, just before sipping her coffee.

Embarrassed, the other diners found something—anything—to talk about among themselves. Blake waited, watching a street dancer perform on the corner. She had what these people wanted. All she had to do was wait for them to realize they wanted her enough to make a few concessions that weren't standard procedure for them.

"Well." Vanessa brushed the napkin shreds aside and leveled her gaze at Blake. "Let's hear these requirements of yours."

"It's simple, really. I'm starting an organization called Mentors & Protégés that gives the average person a chance to hang out with and learn from a millionaire for a day. I'm talking to a few celebrity spokespersons like Jennifer Gutiérrez, Victoria Leck, Manley Yates, and Mark Summers." Blake paused, letting Vanessa and Jerome absorb Blake's impressive public relations coup. "My first requirement is that your show air, free of charge, advertising for the charity."

"That's going to take some negotiating with the network." Jerome's squirming got worse.

"You do that all the time already. This is just one more item of business for you to discuss with them." Blake kept her eyes on Vanessa's, recognizing the woman as the fierce guardian of the gate that Blake needed to get through. Jerome clearly supplied brilliant ideas and left the tough work of turning dreams into realities to others, primarily Vanessa.

"All right, I'll see to it. What else?"

"This part will be painless, I promise. I have plenty of money, and I'm always earning more. Whatever salary we agree to, it's to be automatically donated to Mentors & Protégés. Put it in my contract."

Vanessa let out a sigh of relief. "Consider it done."

"One last requirement."

"And what is that?"

"NBC will donate a small part of its profits to my Mentors & Protégés organization.

"You're out of your mind, Blake Bertrand!" Vanessa was so agitated that spittle flew from her mouth. Blake handed her a fresh napkin and mimed dabbing at her lips. After a few seconds of outrage mingled with puzzlement, Vanessa took the hint and wiped saliva off her face.

"I'm no such thing," Blake said, once again into a total silence. "I've done my research, you see, and NBC can easily afford to expand its charitable contributions with no noticeable decrease in overall profitability. Half a percent would make a real difference, and it's so small an amount to NBC that it won't even deprive any executives or stockholders of their yearly new car."

Antonio, wearing his Ray-Bans, was an enigma to the producers and publicist. Blake, however, noticed the slight curl of his lips that meant he was amused at seeing Blake make the rules, even in an industry completely new to her.

Vanessa looked at Jerome. Jerome looked at his plate and squirmed. Vickie looked like she'd bitten into something sour.

"Will there be anything else?" Vanessa finally whispered.

Blake pretended to consider the question before answering, "No. That's all."

"It's a deal."

Chapter Seventeen

April 13
New York, New York

After lunch, Blake sat down at her desk to start putting together her presentation for the public hearing about the Wishman Spears zoning changes she was requesting. She faced a tight schedule in the next two weeks. The public hearing was scheduled for Friday, and most of the following week she was scheduled to film the first commercials for *The Takeover*.

Fierce knocking on her apartment door made her literally jump in her chair. "Something, or someone, better be on fire," she muttered to herself as she deleted the gibberish she'd accidentally typed into her Docs2Go file.

Suki leaned her head inside Blake's open door. "Not yet, Boss, but you might be in the mood to light someone up in a few minutes. Your Wishman Spears project director is here to see you, and says he's got bad news for you. The man is nearly breathing fire himself."

"Oh, great." Blake took a deep breath to brace herself. "Show him in."

Connor Stafford loomed behind Suki and stalked into Blake's bedroom the moment the bodyguard moved aside for him. "You promised me this wouldn't happen again, Blake! That little no-good assistant of yours has fucked everything up for a year, and there's not a damn thing we can do about it!"

"Edith?" Blake asked, astonished.

"No, that Brett person," Connor fired at her.

"He's not my assistant, and he's completely out of my life now," Blake updated her project director.

"Well, I suppose that's good, but it's too little too late. I'm telling you, he's screwed us all for twelve solid fucking months." Connor looked like he was searching for something he could break, flexing his fingers as he paced Blake's room.

"Exactly what did he do?"

"Look, I know you couldn't help getting sick. But those applications for zoning amendments were due by 4 P.M. on Wednesday, April 8. That little shit said he's a licensed Realtor and knew exactly how to fill in the forms and append supporting documentation. He amended Charles's changes, and said he would take care of it. Well...he didn't."

This can't really be happening. After finally wising up and leaving Lang, how could I have made such a bad mistake with a man again? Blake massaged the scar on her forehead, realized what she was doing, and kept doing it anyway. "Are you telling me he never filed the applications at all? Or that he filed them, but with mistakes?"

"He filed them with a mistake, but not one we can correct by filing more paperwork. None of the required supporting documents were appended, Blake. Those have got to be submitted with the applications, or the applications are automatically denied. By city ordinance, we can't reapply for twelve months."

I'm going to have to tell Thomas Mills and the other investors. They're expecting me to make the Wishman Spears profitable within two years, and Brett just cost me a year. Oh, God, how do I tell them something like that?

"You're sure?" Blake felt as if she might become nauseated.

"Certain." Connor ran a hand through his thinning hair. "I didn't tell you this sooner because I've already talked to the lawyers we're working with. Not a damn thing we can do now, except wait a year and reapply. And get it done right next time."

She nodded slowly. "I guess I've got bad news to deliver to some people now. When should I plan on getting back to work on this project with you?"

He hesitated, then said, "Check with me in ten months. It will be at least that long before there's anything useful I can be doing with this now."

"Okay. I'm very sorry about this, Connor."

"Yeah." He stalked out of her bedroom and out of her apartment, and Blake understood that Brett Skeet had damaged her professional reputation as even Lang never had.

***

April 24
Miami, Florida

Lang and Gabby were exhausted from hours of drugs and sex, and now they lay intertwined on the sofa in the den, watching the eleven o'clock news. *Gabby is no Blake*, Lang found himself thinking, *but she's better than nothing.*

What he craved, though, was either possession of Blake or destruction of her. Restless, he kept brooding on how to achieve one or the other.

He'd expected a reaction from her when he kept outbidding her for Miami properties she'd long wanted to buy and revitalize. But there hadn't been a peep from the bitch when he sabotaged her Miami real estate development plans.

Blake's secret trip to that hokey school band concert had been a gift to Lang. He'd laughed and cheered, watching news reports on television about the mysterious attack on the great Blake Bertrand's chauffeur. At long last, having a couple of Mafia henchmen at his command had really been useful for him.

The chauffeur had recently been released from the hospital, though, and Lang was hungry to make Blake suffer again. But he had no idea how to make that happen. It was like his early days, and late days too, as an actor with a cocaine habit and not enough acting jobs to indulge as much as he'd like. He needed a fix, but how to pay for it?

"Say, babe, isn't that your ex-wife?" Gabby fluttered a hand at the television.

Lang turned his head and paid real attention. A commercial was showing, and sure enough, Blake was in it. So was J-Lo. They were talking about some new charity Blake was going to open in a few weeks. NBC had already agreed to be a contributor, and Blake's salary for the reality show she'd just been hired to host would also be directly donated to the cause.

What? Blake is going to host a reality show?

He sat up, almost dumping Gabby onto the floor. *Entrepreneurs... Goddammit, it would make Blake crazy if I got on her show as a contestant, but that fucking restraining order kills that idea...*

"You could warn a girl before you knock them off the sofa." Gabby wrinkled her nose, a look that was not at all cute on her. She sat cross-legged on the opposite end of the sofa, staring sulkily at the baggie that was full of coke earlier in the day but now lay empty on the coffee table.

That restraining order couldn't keep Gabby from being on

Blake's show, though...

"Hey, Gabby?"

"Yeah?"

"Have you ever thought about being an entrepreneur?"

She turned her glazed eyes on him and asked, "I don't know, what's a under...usher...umber-bum-pure?"

I'll make this work somehow, damn it.

Chapter Eighteen

May 1
New York, New York

With Antonio at her side, Blake stood on the sidewalk in front of her apartment building. They were waiting for the taxi she'd phoned to take her to the airport. On impulse, she'd booked a flight to Miami for the weekend.

She hadn't seen her mother since February. Jacinta Bertrand seemed in good spirits whenever they talked on the phone, but Blake wanted to see for herself how her mother's recovery from her injuries was progressing.

Moreover, she wanted to visit her chauffeur, Henry. He'd been released from the hospital a week and a half ago, but he too was still recovering from his injuries. *From a beating he got for being my chauffeur,* Blake reminded herself, and shivered. *Who but Lang would do something like that? But I can't prove it, and neither can Miami's police, so the son of a bitch is going to get away with it...*

In addition to all of that, she yearned for a quiet weekend on Fisher Island. New York's frantic pace had enthralled her when she was eighteen, but she'd been discovering in the past few weeks that in her mid-thirties, she enjoyed a more mellow way of life. *I love the cooler climate up north, but if I ever move I'll need to find a more relaxed city to live in.*

"Blake? Blake Bertrand? Girl, is that you?"

That voice was familiar, but she didn't immediately remember who it belonged to. She looked around and saw a petite, achingly pretty, short-haired blonde crossing the street toward her. The woman looked very much like Audrey Hepburn, but with an almost-bald hairstyle reminiscent of Sinead O'Connor.

It was the resemblance to Audrey Hepburn that clued Blake to the woman's identity. Robin Love had been a new model herself when Blake returned to the business as an eighteen-year-old after her two years of absence. Back then, Robin had worn her hair much longer, halfway down her back. She'd been Blake's best friend until Blake fled to Switzerland to give birth in secret. When Blake returned to the United States, Robin was no longer working in the modeling business and Blake had no idea how to contact her.

"Robin Love. I haven't heard from you since before I got married." Blake hugged Robin and then faced Antonio, who was keeping alert watch on Blake's old friend. "Antonio, Robin and I were models together, a long time ago. Robin, this is Antonio, one of my bodyguards."

"Bodyguards! Girl, does real estate bring out as many weirdos as modeling did?"

They laughed together, and it was as if the lost years fell away. Robin had always been fun to be around, and Blake's common sense had probably kept her overly adventurous friend out of trouble a few times. *Possibly even the morgue*, Blake suspected, looking back on all their wild old times.

A taxi rolled to a stop, exactly in line with the apartment building's door. Antonio sidled over to the cab and chatted with the driver, trying to buy Blake a little more time with Robin.

"Listen, I'm on my way to the airport, Robin, but I don't want to wait a decade and more to talk to you again. Can I give you my cell phone number? You could give me a call anytime after Sunday night, and I'll treat you to lunch and we'll get caught up with each other. Say it's a plan!"

"It's a plan." Robin grinned, and readied her smartphone to add Blake's number to the contacts list.

***

May 2
Miami, Florida

Just as Blake was finishing breakfast with her mother, her BlackBerry rang out the Dire Straits song "Money for Nothing." That meant Thomas Mills was calling. Blake excused herself from the table and shut herself alone inside her mother's parlor. She suspected this was going to be an unpleasant conversation.

"Hi, Thomas," Blake said, sitting by the window and watching peacocks strut around her mother's lawn and the empty street.

"Blake, I've been talking with the other two investors I found to help you buy the Wishman Spears," boomed Thomas, "and we're all three mighty pissed about how you dropped the ball with this property."

I'd be pissed too, if someone wasted a year of my time and millions of my dollars because they were thinking with their hormones instead of with their brain. Blake pressed her forehead against the cool glass of the window and wondered what she could possibly do to remedy this problem.

"Thomas, I can't blame you and the others for being angry. I admit it, I made a mistake. But I give you my word, I'm going to repay your investment in the time promised."

"We don't see how that's possible, Blake. You were supposed to make the Wishman Spears profitable in two years. That's possible, but now it's going to be a year before you can touch the place. Can you make it profitable in only one year?"

"I'll find a way."

"I've known you a long time, Blake. Only other mistake I've seen you make is when you married Lang. You're a damn clever businesswoman, and if anyone can make the Wishman pay with only a year to renovate and market, you're the person who can do it. But the other investors don't know you like I do. They want to see firm, detailed plans showing how you're going to salvage this deal."

An icy panic gnawed Blake's gut. "How soon do they want to see these firm, detailed plans for profitability?"

"You've got sixty days."

Two months. If I can't come up with something in that time, nobody can. "What do they want to do if, by chance, I can't meet the deadline?"

"We'll call in our loans."

Oh...shit. I can't pay out hundreds of millions of dollars, not with everything I own backing the Wishman purchase. "Like I said. I'll find a way."

"Good luck." Thomas clicked the call off.

"I am so completely fucked," Blake muttered to the peacocks outside.

Chapter Nineteen

May 7
Chicago, Illinois

Thunderous applause rewarded Blake when she finished delivering her speech and stepped down from the podium. No sooner had she filed for divorce than NeoBuild, the world's largest real estate trade show, invited her to be their keynote speaker for their latest convention. She'd been looking forward to the event ever since accepting the invitation. It would emphasize her independence from Lang, and moreover it would be an excellent opportunity to hear industry gossip.

Matt stood, having sat behind her while she was speaking, and moved to her side. He looked around as he asked, "What's next on your schedule, Ms. Bertrand?"

"I've got a luncheon lined up with several of New York's leading real estate developers," she answered, consulting her BlackBerry. "There's a panel discussion I've got to participate in this afternoon, and tonight I thought I'd research some possibilities for making the Wishman profitable in only a year."

"How do you plan to do the research?"

She winced. "Nothing is new under the sun, they say. There's got to be a similar problem that somebody has solved. I just haven't thought of the research terms that will find it yet."

Matt fell into step behind Blake as she followed the map included with her convention program brochure. They found the conference room where in two hours the panel discussion would be held. A few people had already claimed seats in the audience, to Blake's astonishment.

The luncheon was catered by world-famous Chicago restaurant Charlie Trotter's. Blake and Matt slowly stuffed themselves while the conversation ranged over a number of New York real estate topics. Finally, with a half hour to go before the panel discussion was scheduled to begin, Blake thanked the Realtors who cohosted the meal, and she and Matt made their way back to the conference room.

Already the room was nearly packed to capacity. Blake looked for the panel seat with her name on the place setting, but was interrupted when a voice well known to her called, "Blake! Ms. Bertrand, I really need to talk to you."

She turned around, her shoulders stiffening as she faced Sherry Greene, her ex-publicist. "We really don't have anything to discuss, Sherry."

"Please." Sherry folded her hands together as if she was about to pray. "Blake—"

"Ms. Bertrand, to you," Blake said.

"Sure. I'm sorry." Sherry's face turned pink with embarrassment. Everyone in the room was silent, listening to the confrontation. "Ms. Bertrand, please let me come back to work for you."

"No." Blake turned back to the conference table.

"Ms. Bertrand, you're the best employer I've ever worked for, and I know I made a mistake, but I've learned my lesson, and—"

Blake whirled around, nearly colliding with Matt. "I can't believe my ears, Sherry. Me, the best employer you've ever had? The way I heard it, I was a monster to you. Expecting celebrities to follow me around, fighting you about reimbursing your expenses, not willing to give you any pay raises. And that's all on a good day. Wasn't that what you said about me to other publicists?"

"I know I shouldn't have done that. I was just angry you didn't give me a second chance, but now I understand that's my own fault—"

"Yes, it was."

"Please, Ms. Bertrand. I'll do anything to work for you again." Incredibly, Sherry got down on her knees.

Blake stared at the woman, wondering if what Sherry meant by "anything" was what it sounded like.

"Anything," Sherry repeated. Looking into Blake's eyes, seen only by Blake and Matt, Sherry positioned her praying hands to give her breasts a boost.

Same ole Sherry. "I said no, and I *meant* it." Blake returned to her search for her seat, found it, and moved around the table to sit down.

Sherry bowed her head to the floor for a few seconds, her shoulders shaking. Then she scrambled onto her feet and fled from the room, shedding copious tears.

"I never would've guessed real estate could be so entertaining," Matt muttered as he pulled a chair behind Blake and sat down.

***

Lang had followed the confrontation between Blake and her ex-publicist with rapt attention, imagining a variety of exciting possibilities. When Sherry ran out of the conference room, Lang seized Gabby's hand and dragged her with him as he jogged after the weeping woman.

Sherry raced into the nearest women's bathroom, and Lang turned to issue orders to Gabby. "Go in there and tell that woman Lang Bertrand wants to talk to her."

"I don't know if I oughtta do that, babe. She looked really upset."

"That's why I want you to bring her out here to talk to me."

"But I don't want to talk to anybody when I'm upset, so why would she?"

He gripped her arm so hard that she yelped. "Don't fucking argue with me! There's not much time before the panel discussion starts. Go in there and bring her out."

Gabby scurried into the women's bathroom. A couple of minutes later, she returned with Sherry Greene at her heels.

Lang put out a hand and shook Sherry's. "You remember me, I hope, Sherry?"

"Of course, Mr. Bertrand." Sherry slanted a puzzled glance at Gabby, but the clueless blonde was no help.

"Call me Lang. I'm not a bitch like my ex-wife." He smiled at her, his soot-colored eyes glinting. "Speaking of Blake, though, I'm planning some unpleasant surprises for her. I thought you might be interested in helping, especially if I put you on my payroll."

Sherry flicked a worried look in the direction of the conference room, as if afraid Blake could hear their hushed conversation from a distance. "How much will you pay me?"

"Well, how much did you earn as Blake's publicist?"

"A hundred fifty thousand per year."

"I'll double that."

Sherry's wide mouth curled up in a grin. "I'll do anything."

***

It was standing room only in the conference room as the panel discussion got started. Blake was in the middle of answering the first question directed to her, about the criteria she used to decide if a particular property should be bought up during a struggling economy, when a latecomer intently studying his program brochure edged his way into the room.

She paused, ice forming in her gut. *That height, that build, that posture... It can't be him.*

"Ms. Bertrand? Are you okay?" asked the moderator.

Blake nodded, taking a quick deep breath. "Sorry, folks, I thought I saw somebody I used to know."

Someone in the audience sang out, "But you didn't have to cut me off!" reminding them all of the Gotye song Blake had quoted unintentionally. They all enjoyed a good laugh before Blake continued answering the question. For the rest of the panel discussion, however, Blake noticed Matt watching the people in the back of the room.

When the time allotted for the panel discussion ended, the audience applauded the panel members and people began making their way out of the conference room. Matt tapped Blake's shoulder and asked, "Is there a way out of here other than the door we all came in through?"

"Not that I know of," Blake whispered. "Is something wrong?"

"I think someone is in violation of a restraining order," said Matt. "Stay behind me." He led the way toward the door, Blake following him close.

Lang stood up, having taken a seat when people began exiting the room. He motioned to a blonde to stand up with him, and said, "Gabby, I don't believe you've ever met my ex-wife, have you? Blake, Gabby here is my girlfriend."

"Yeah, but speaking of your ex-wife, a judge ordered you to stay a minimum of three hundred yards away from her," said Matt, "and right now you're not even 30 inches away from her. I suggest you get yourself gone, and fast."

"Relax, Mr. Bodyguard." Lang sneered at Matt as he took a folded business envelope out of his jacket pocket and handed it over for inspection. "If you care to take a look, you'll see I registered for this convention back in August. *Before* it was announced that my charming former missus would be keynote speaker."

Matt handed the envelope back to Lang without bothering to look at whatever was inside. "Why not cancel your registration and get a refund?"

"Because I have a right to stay in the business I've worked in for the past ten years, even if I don't work with Blake anymore. I think the judge would agree getting a divorce shouldn't force a man out of business."

"I'm going to have to notify convention security and the local police. They can talk to the judge. But no matter what they say, I'm warning you to stay out of any room Ms. Bertrand is in, and don't try to talk to her." Matt put a protective arm around Blake and started to guide her out of the room.

"What a shame. I just bought the Jenny Tower that Blake has wanted for quite a few years. Bought some properties in Little Haiti she's had an eye on, too. Sure you don't want to work together again, Blake?" Lang leaned casually in the conference room door, his face wearing a smug grin.

"No, you paid three times more than those properties are worth. Deal with your mistakes yourself," said Blake.

"Just ignore him, Ms. Bertrand," Matt advised, and he kept himself between Blake and Lang as Blake left the room.

"You can't avoid me forever," Lang called after them.

"I can damn sure try," Blake muttered, moving at a trot to keep up with Matt's long strides.

Chapter Twenty

June 3
New York, New York

Blake arrived a few minutes early at 30 Rockefeller Plaza with Antonio, her stomach fluttery with nervousness. Until she'd filmed the promotional ads for *The Takeover*, her only experience with filming was more than a decade ago, when she'd done the perfume commercials. This reality show was a much more complex job. Instead of a few hours of rehearsal and filming to produce sixty seconds of advertising, this job meant several full-time days each week to produce each one-hour episode.

"I hope I'm ready for this," she thought aloud.

"You'll be great," Antonio reassured her. "The producers hired you for good reasons. You're a rare combination of business savvy and star quality. All you've got to do is be yourself."

She smiled thanks at him as a flustered-looking young woman trotted toward them. "Ms. Bertrand? I'm Olivia, I've been assigned to do your makeup. We'd better get started. Filming starts in an hour."

Olivia led Blake and Antonio into a dressing room, where she kept dabbing foundation, blush, eye shadow, and so forth on Blake's face and then shining a stage light on her to judge the results. Antonio entertained himself by reading a detective novel. Blake wished she could read the news on her BlackBerry, but Olivia needed Blake to keep her head up.

A few minutes before 10 A.M., Olivia set Blake free to join the cast and crew. What had been a bare stage when Blake arrived was now furnished like the den of a British mansion. The lights, microphones, and cameras were set up and preproduction tests were in progress.

Vanessa Reeves and Jerome Harper, the executive producers, noticed Blake's stage entrance. Jerome spoke to a woman whose back was turned to the door Blake and Antonio had just come from, and brought the woman to meet her. Blake thought the woman looked familiar, but she couldn't remember who she was.

"Ms. Bertrand, have you ever met Joy Vardash? She'll be the master of ceremonies for *The Takeover*." Vanessa introduced Blake and the young woman.

"No, we haven't met before, but I'm glad to collaborate with a fellow businesswoman who's made her mark in the fashion business on this project." Blake smiled and nodded to Joy, who smiled back and complimented Blake on her stunning pinstriped Chanel business suit.

"Joy will introduce the concept to the audience first, then bring you onstage and invite you to say a few words about yourself. So you might want to be thinking of a short biography to share with viewers," Jerome advised. "After that, she'll call the contestants onstage one at a time, and each of them will tell you—and viewers—a little about themselves."

"I wish someone had warned me about the bio a few days ago," Blake muttered. "Nice to meet you, Joy, but I've got some fast thinking to do."

"So have I. Reality TV doesn't have a script." Joy grinned. "I'll see you again in a few minutes with the cameras rolling, Blake."

Blake moved to the far end of the stage, away from everyone else except Antonio, and brainstormed aloud what she could say about herself: "I'm thirty-four, divorced, self-made businesswoman..."

"This isn't a dating show." Antonio lowered his Ray-Bans and grinned. "Your age and marital status don't matter. Just give your business credentials."

"Antonio, you're a lifesaver."

"Only if someone under my protection is threatened, but you're welcome." He slid the Ray-Bans back into place.

"Right. So. After I graduated from high school, I worked as a model for a few years, because I knew I could make a lot of money fast. I used that money to buy and renovate important properties—"

"Don't forget the handsome actor husband who brought in your first celebrity customers," said a voice Blake recognized instantly and hated with unspeakable passion.

While she'd been meeting Joy, Blake's back had been turned to the rows of seats where the audience would sit. Ushers had quickly and efficiently led the spectators into the theater, and now that Blake turned around, she faced a packed house. In the very front row was the owner of the only voice in the world that made her skin crawl.

"Goddammit, Lang, you can't keep following me around wherever I go. Remember the restraining order?" Blake looked around for NBC's security personnel. "Security!"

His mouth turned down in misery, the senior security guard shuffled over to talk to Blake. "Nothing we can do, Ms. Bertrand. Judge granted an exception to the restraining order for the duration of filming of this show, so he can attend tapings and other related events."

Blake felt her jaw drop, and for a moment words failed her. Finally she managed a weak, "Why?"

Vanessa clapped her hands for everyone's attention. "Places, everyone! Filming starts in sixty seconds!"

"Don't worry, you'll find out soon," Lang called after Blake as she moved to wait in the wings for Joy to call her onto the set.

She forced herself to look anywhere but at Lang, while Joy explained that twelve contestants would be mentored personally by Blake as they completed an entrepreneurial task each week, and each week the contestant whose performance was poorest would be eliminated by Blake herself. Whoever won would receive a million dollars of startup capital for a business of their own.

"Now let's meet the brilliant businesswoman who will be coaching our contestants on how to create thriving businesses of their own. Ladies and gentlemen, put your hands together for the Blake Bertrand!" said Joy, and she applauded along with the audience as Blake strolled onto the set and took her seat at the head of a long table. Holding a microphone toward Blake, Joy added, "Just in case anyone has been living in a cave for the past few years, tell us a little about yourself, Blake."

Blake hadn't finished planning a bio, but she improvised one as best she could. After reciting her experience as a model and using those earnings to buy her first properties for development, she added simply, "I went on to become a millionaire. I can't promise these contestants that much success, but I guarantee I can help them make their business dreams realities."

"I'm sure they all look forward to learning from you, so let's meet the contestants," said Joy. "First, let me introduce you to Eve Womack. Eve, come and meet your mentor!"

Blake liked Eve immediately. This woman had done her

homework: she didn't try to shake hands with Blake, but instead waved at her as she chose a seat at the table. When Joy asked Eve about herself, Blake liked her even more because of her bio.

"I used to be a pediatric nurse, until a little boy battling leukemia changed my life. The hospital I worked for was next to an elementary school, and little Julian could see the playground from his room. Every night at bedtime he said his prayers, and he'd finish by saying, 'And I slide down the slide, amen.' We tried to take him out to play once, but he was weak from his treatments and had to keep an IV going, and, well... I went back to school and studied engineering so I could build pediatric recreation centers for kids like him."

"You sound like you already have good ideas, Eve," said Blake, and she meant it. "What are you hoping I can teach you?"

"How to sell my vision, especially to men. When they reject my proposals, I always wonder if one reason is because I'm a woman and engineering is still a man's field," Eve answered in a calm, matter-of-fact voice.

She's not on a self-pity trip. Good. Blake smiled at Eve and said, "Well, welcome, Eve. I'll do all I can to help you." *And yes, I know a thing or two about competing in businesses dominated by men.*

One by one Joy introduced the other contestants, until finally she said, "Our twelfth and final contestant may already be familiar to you for her popular movie roles. Gabby Truitt, come and meet your mentor!"

Blake was troubled by the name Gabby even before its owner sauntered onto the set.

"Hi, all, I'm Gabby Truitt," she grinned, shifting her body from side to side. "I *sooo* want to open my own production company, and this would be such an *awesome* chance to learn and grow."
When she recognized the blonde hair and waifish face and build, she understood what Lang had done. *Twelve weeks of seeing you and your girlfriend four days per week, eh, Lang? It doesn't bother me to see her. As for you, one wrong move and you'll still go to jail.*

"Welcome," Blake said to Gabby, through clenched teeth. Blake thought she could laugh or cry.

Blake smiled widely at the contestants and said, "It's a pleasure to meet you all. Now let me tell you about your first challenge. This week you're going to create a mission statement and a business slogan..."

Chapter Twenty-One

June 3
New York, New York

Filming the introduction of the cast and contestants went well, but it was almost 2 P.M. when they finally stopped for lunch. When they reconvened, Blake was scheduled to conduct her first two private mentoring sessions. The producers had randomly chosen the order in which she'd mentor the contestants. Her first two appointments were with Ray Fisher, an African American with an interest in eco-friendly landscaping, and with Gabby Truitt, who claimed an interest in starting her own film production company.

"I'll call a taxi," Antonio said to Blake as they emerged from the studio into bright summer sunlight that made her envy him his Ray-Bans. "Where do you want to go for lunch?"

"This is New York. You can't walk two blocks without meeting up with a street food vendor. And I'm starving. I'll eat anything that isn't roadkill."

They'd just about walked two blocks, and saw a hot dog cart ahead on the next corner, when Antonio sighed. Blake flashed a worried look at him. "What in the world is wrong?"

"Your friend is back," he muttered, and turned around to face Brett Skeet.

Brett had been hurrying to catch up with them, and he had to come to a sudden stop to avoid colliding with the burly bodyguard. "Whoa. Uh, hi, Blake."

"Hi, Brett. Good-bye, Brett." Blake continued toward the hot dog cart.

"Wait, I really need to talk to you, Blake."

She heard a thump and a grunt, and turned around again. Brett must have tried to dodge Antonio, because now he was doubled over and clutching his stomach, wide-eyed with pain. Antonio stood with fists ready, and curious onlookers were gathering.

"This is turning out to be the most fucked-up day I've had in months." Blake waved at Antonio to relax. "What the hell do you want, Brett?"

"Cha," gasped Brett, finally able to breathe again.

"Say again?" Blake's stomach growled, of the opinion the hot dog cart was much more important than anything Brett Skeet might want to say.

"A job." Brett touched his fingertips to his punched gut and winced. "Jesus, bro, you sure you hit me hard enough?"

"I could do it again if you want," Antonio offered.

"Look up sarcasm in the dictionary, wordsmith." Brett flinched as Antonio raised one hand...and scratched his chin.

Blake bit back a laugh and asked, "Why are you asking *me* for a job? Haven't you messed up my business enough?"

"I quit my real estate job to be with you and hoped we could work together on something." Brett jammed his hands in his slacks pockets, not looking at Blake or Antonio. "I've tried to find something here, but no luck. Please, Blake. I heard you're doing this television thing. Don't they always need extras and stuff like that?"

"You screwed up. Your messiness stalled my Wishman project. How do I know you won't do the same thing again?"

"Let me show you. I'll keep my distance from you. I promise. I just really need a way to get enough money to go back to Miami and pay some of my debt there."

Antonio had lowered his Ray-Bans and was staring at her with arched eyebrows. By now Blake could practically read his mind: "True or not, he's a punk," Antonio would be thinking, "and you shouldn't let him get close to you again."

Blake had learned early to keep her enemies close. She could keep an eye on Brett, she reasoned to herself. He knew a lot about her dealings in their short time together. She didn't want another Sherry wandering the streets. She shifted her footing so that she couldn't see Antonio's arched eyebrows anymore.

Then she said, "Come on, I'll buy you a hot dog. When we go back in the studio, I'll talk to the producers about giving you a job if there's one available."

***

Scheduling conflicts had repeatedly thwarted Blake from meeting with her old friend Robin Love at lunchtime, so Blake had finally made a dinner date with Robin instead. Her mentoring sessions ran longer than planned, making her glad she'd reserved a table for 9 P.M., significantly later than she usually ate her last meal of the day.

It was such a pleasant evening that Blake decided to walk to the restaurant. She'd showered the Lang and Brett cooties off and changed into a cute Gucci black lacquered lace shift dress with square-buckled belt, and black thong sandals. At eight o'clock she set out with Suki for DB Bistro Moderne, a French-American bistro on West Forty-fourth Street.

Robin arrived at the same time Blake and Suki did, and their table was waiting. So was the appetizer of pâté en croûte that Blake had preordered, knowing that she, at least, would be starving by then. A waiter with an authentic French accent took their orders immediately, while they snacked. Blake opted for the Hanger Steak, Robin the Crystal Valley Chicken Breast, and Suki ordered the DB Burger.

"A burger? Really?" Robin grinned at Suki as soon as the waiter left to give their order to the chef. "In a French restaurant, you don't want to be adventurous?"

"I'm part Japanese and part Anglo-Saxon," intoned Suki. "I know exactly nothing about French food."

Blake and Robin laughed. "Girl, one of us better start talking," Blake teased Robin. "We've only got about fifteen years of catching up to do!"

Robin shook her head, and Blake saw a wistfulness on her friend's face that she'd never seen there before. "No, Blake, you only need to catch up with me. You've never stopped being in the news. Just, you shared the spotlight with Lang for a long time." She paused to sip some of her water before adding, "I never liked him."

"When all the other models we hung around with told me to give him a chance, you agreed with them!"

"If a man offers to buy you food, you say yes. That's all I meant. He was such a jerk, though. You never should have started sleeping with him." Robin shook her head again.

"I wish you'd said all that back then. You could have saved me ten years of misery."

"Would you have listened?"

Blake thought about that, then said, "No. I guess not. He was so romantic, when he wasn't being a jerk." She leaned closer to Robin. "But what about you? Why did you stop modeling, and what have you been doing since you quit?"

"I didn't quit. Our agency stopped calling me with jobs. That's the way it is, you know. A few girls, like you, become worldwide sensations. Most, like me, never rise from obscurity." Robin helped herself to some more pâté, while Blake's heart hurt for her.

"I'm so sorry. That isn't fair at all. You were beautiful then. Still are."

"Don't worry, Blake. I moved on. Took me a while to find my niche, but I got there. Now I'm the spokeswoman for a charitable organization that builds and supplies elementary schools in western Africa."

Blake needed to think about that, too, before speaking. Robin had never expressed any interest in children back in their modeling days. The only thing African she was into were the men. "What got you interested in doing that?"

Now that odd wistfulness settled into Robin's facial features again. "Just something to do that is actually positive. I'm done with all the man drama, and being broke. I was homeless just two years ago, Blake."

Dropping her fork, Blake stared at Robin through eyes filling with tears. "Oh, my God, Robin, that's terrible. I don't know what to say, except I'm so very sorry."

Robin reached across the table and took Blake's hand, and Blake gave Robin's a squeeze. *Germs be damned this time,* Blake thought, and wondered if she could get up and give her friend a fierce hug without making a scene.

"It made me stronger, and I vowed that won't happen to me again no matter what I need to do." Robin managed a smile. "You don't know this, but you have always been an inspiration to me. I missed us."

"Me, too," Blake said, her lips forming a smile. She hadn't seen Robin in years, but listening to Robin it was like the absence hurt her more than she could imagine.

Robin stayed silent, as if in her own private thoughts, before she finally spoke. "I hear you're going to be starting a new organization called Mentors & Protégés. To tell the truth, hearing that inspired me to make sure our paths crossed. You're a business genius, and my charity never has enough money for all the needs it's trying to meet. So, I was hoping..."

"If you need anything, I'm here for you now!" Blake knew she was a bit loud because of her excitement for Robin, and didn't care that a few heads turned at nearby tables.

Robin's eyes watered.

"Donations, advertising, you name it. And, Robin?"

"Blake?"

"I don't care what inspired you. I'm glad to have your friendship in my life again."

***

June 4
New York, New York

Blake checked the time on her BlackBerry when she finished her seventh mentoring session, which was with Eve. One o'clock in the afternoon. She was on a pace to finish all the mentoring sessions by lunchtime Friday, when she was scheduled to preside over the first board of directors meeting for Mentors & Protégés.

"Ready for me to call for a taxi?" Antonio asked.

"I sure am. Do you like Greek food? I've got a craving for a gyro wrap." Blake stood and stretched out her back, stiff from five hours of sitting.

"Who doesn't like a good gyro wrap?" Antonio grinned. "Listen, I need to run to the men's room before we catch the cab. Can I get you to stay in here and lock the door until I come back?"

Blake folded her arms across her chest in pretend consternation. "I don't know about that. How will I know it's you?"

"I'll recite the correct secret code."

"And what's that?"

He took off his Ray-Bans and sucked thoughtfully on one earpiece for a bit before answering, "The black bird flies backwards."

"Get out of here, you madman." Blake grinned at Antonio and opened the door for him.

She shut the door and was shaking her head, about to turn the lock, when there was a knock on the door. As she swung it open again she asked, "What did you do, forget your dick?"

"I hope not," said Brett, and grinned at her.

"Oh, shit." Blake tried to slam the door and lock it, but Brett caught the door and held it open about an inch while she pushed against him.

"Come on, Blake, I'm not going to hurt you." Brett grunted

with the effort of keeping the door ajar against Blake's weight. "I just wanted to thank you for getting me a job, that's all."

"Well, you're welcome, but you'd better go before Antonio gets back here."

"I'll be long gone, believe me, but I also wanted to ask if I can take you out to dinner sometime soon, to show my appreciation. Nothing fancy, they don't pay errand-runners well enough for five-star restaurants." Brett smiled at her through the one inch between the door and its frame. "Say you'll think about it, at least."

"I'll think about it."

He let the door shut, and Blake locked it.

When Antonio rapped his knuckles on the door and said "The black bird flies backwards," Blake was still staring at the door, wondering what the hell to think of Brett Skeet.

Chapter Twenty-Two

June 5
New York, New York

At lunchtime Blake was finished with all twelve mentoring sessions and pleased with most of the way her life was progressing. She still needed a solution to her Wishman Spears one-year-to-profitability problem, but that was the only cloud currently on her horizon. It was, however, a pressing cloud, owing to the fact that Thomas Mills was on the board of directors of her Mentors & Protégés, and she'd be seeing him at the first directors meeting that afternoon.

Meanwhile, she had lunch with Margot at the Four Seasons to look forward to. When she and Antonio were inside the taxi, she tried to phone her best friend to tell her they were on the way to pick her up from the hotel where the Mills were staying. After the line rang ten times, Blake disconnected the call and muttered, "That's weird."

"What's up?" Antonio looked up from the ebook he was reading on his smartphone.

"Margot isn't answering my call."

"She's probably in the bathroom. There are bathroom things you can't hurry, and some people don't take their phone to the toilet with them." He paused, then added, "And I wish there were more people like those some people."

Blake couldn't help giggling like a silly schoolgirl. "You don't like hearing the sound of piss pouring into a porcelain throne, Antonio?"

"No, ma'am, I do not. And I like the other bathroom noise even less." His lips turned down in a scowl.

She tried Margot's number again as they neared the hotel, but again got no answer. Antonio's theory that Margot was in the bathroom had comforted Blake the first time Margot didn't answer her phone. Now she couldn't help but worry about her best friend.

They took the elevator to the fourth floor, and Blake knocked on the door of 407. Nobody opened the door. Blake threw an anxious glance at Antonio, then knocked again. And again, the door stayed shut.

Antonio tried turning the handle, and the door opened. "Let me," he murmured, and he stepped into the hotel room, calling, "Hello? Mrs. Mills?"

The room was a shambles, and the air reeked of booze. Blake breathed through her nose as she followed Antonio inside. She noticed that Margot and Thomas were renting a room with two beds, rather than one, and wondered if the couple were at odds with each other. Neither Margot nor Thomas were in the bedroom, but water was running in the bathroom.

For a moment, Antonio hesitated. "We'll both go," he said, and they went to look in the bathroom.

Margot was sprawled in the bathtub with the shower running, a nearly empty bottle of Pearse Lyons single malt whiskey clutched in both hands. She was singing tunelessly, murdering Toni Braxton's "Un-Break My Heart." In the confines of the bathroom, the alcohol smell was so strong that Blake felt tipsy just from the fumes.

Blake stared at Margot, who was oblivious to their presence, for at least a full minute while thinking about what to do. Finally she turned to Antonio and motioned him to step out of the bathroom, and she followed him.

"Order room service. Lots of it. Filling stuff. And coffee, and a pitcher of ice water." She found Margot's suitcases and looked for something casual and comfortable to dress her friend in. "I think we'll be having lunch with Margot here, this time."

Back in the bathroom, Blake shut off the shower, which finally got Margot's attention. "Margot... Honey, what's wrong?"

Margot turned glazed eyes on Blake and moaned, "Oh, Blake. Thomas doesn't love me anymore. He told me so himself, this morning." And then she gave voice to a howling, heart-rending cry.

***

What should have been a joyous occasion for Blake was instead an afternoon of torment. She phoned Suki to take over bodyguard duty two hours early, leaving Margot in Antonio's care.

As the board of directors arrived for the first meeting of

124

Mentors & Protégés, Thomas cornered Blake and asked about her Wishman Spears profitability plans. "That's due July first, you know," he reminded her.

Swallowing a burning desire to ask him why he didn't worry as much about his marriage as he did about Blake's only mistake in more than a decade of real estate development, Blake said with forced calm, "I still have almost a month, Thomas."

"There won't be any extensions," he grumbled. He turned on one heel and took a seat at the table of the conference room, located in the same hotel where his wife lay in a drunken stupor while Antonio tried to revive her.

Blake retreated to the seat at the head of the table, intending to review her notes while she waited for all the board members to arrive. Robin was there. She had practically begged Blake to sit in on the meeting to get a bird's eye view on how this sort of thing worked. Blake was happy to oblige, hoping that Robin may be interested in sitting on her board one day. From the corner of one eye, however, she noticed Robin watching Thomas with wide eyes and slightly open mouth. *Oh, hell, no. You may be lonely, Robin, and Margot's marriage may be in trouble, but I'm not having one friend make bedroom eyes at another friend's husband.*

She got to her feet again and beckoned Robin to step outside the conference room with her. They went for a walk to the women's restroom, Suki trailing after them.

"I know that look, Robin," Blake said, keeping her voice quiet but firm, once they were in the bathroom and she'd made sure they were alone except for the bodyguard. "Forget about it. Thomas Mills is a married man."

Robin chewed her bottom lip, then said, "He must not be happy in his marriage. A happily married man doesn't..."

"Doesn't what?"

"Pat another woman's tush as he walks by, and hand her a business card with his personal cell phone number written on it."

"Thomas..." Blake didn't finish the thought. She wasn't altogether sure what the thought was, really. But she locked gazes with Robin and said, hammering her words, "Let him be, Robin."

"Okay..." Doubt clouded Robin's eyes.

"I mean it. His wife is my best friend."

"I said okay."

They stared at each other until Blake's BlackBerry beeped to alert her that the meeting was due to start in five minutes. Blake nodded and turned to go. "Well. Let's go have a charity-launching meeting."

Suki followed Blake, and Robin followed Suki. Blake wasn't certain, but she thought she heard Robin whisper, "Best friend. That's what you used to call me."

Chapter Twenty-Three

June 10
New York, New York

The twelve beginning contestants of *The Takeover* had completed the first week's challenges, and their work had been evaluated by a panel of marketing experts. Blake had reviewed the mission statements and logos submitted by the contestants, and the evaluations of the marketing gurus. A studio audience had watched film of Blake's mentoring sessions with the contestants, the development by contestants of their mission statements and logos, and the experts giving their analysis of the results.

Now the hour of reckoning had arrived: It was time to choose the first contestant to eliminate due to second-rate performance. In a staff meeting prior to filming Blake's decision and the second week's challenges, the producers and NBC advertising execs discussed who Blake's choice for elimination should be.

"I'm sure you'd like to send your ex-husband's girlfriend home, but the audience reaction to her is extremely favorable," producer Vanessa Reeves told Blake. "She's one of the early front-runners to win."

"Gabby is fun," producer Jerome Harper observed. "Her idea to play against the stereotype of blondes as dumb is really clever, and her logo—a Betty Boop–looking blonde in a Rosie the Riveter pose, with a tattoo of the *Blondes With Brains* BWB logo on her forearm—is attention-getting and amusing. She's definitely a contender."

"I know all that," said Blake, warming her hands with a mug of steaming coffee. It was an unseasonably cool morning. *Thanks for global warming and wild weather, world.* Blake scowled at the Italian dark roast. "Gabby Truitt is not my choice for the first elimination."

"Who is, then?" Vanessa posed the question, but all the ratings- and reviews-minders leaned in toward Blake in breathless anticipation of her answer.

"Spencer Jett."

"You can't be serious!" Some NBC advertising twit slapped his palm to his forehead.

Melodramatic, that. He should be in front of the camera, not behind it, Blake thought at her coffee.

"Our audience rating for him was almost as favorable as Gabby's," the ad twit continued. "He looks a lot like a young Tom Cruise, and he oozes sex appeal. Women want him, and men want to be him. He's got to stay."

"He's an empty-headed clown." Blake looked up from her mug and met their gazes, one by one. Each of her opponents flinched. She, by contrast, did not.

"We don't have another contestant as sweet to look at as Jett is," moaned Jerome, confirming Blake's belief that the man was gay. She didn't care, except that in her experience a liking for dick could be quite distracting. "If Blake sends him home, what will we do for eye candy?"

"Maybe we'll look at the business pros and cons of the challenges the contestants complete, instead of imagining them naked," Blake suggested. She stood and opened the office door, Antonio behind her. "I'm ready to film my decision."

She left without waiting to see if they followed. They'd hired her to be a business coach, not judge of a beauty contest. As one of the world's leading businesswomen, she knew her decision was the right one.

And so she seated herself at the head of the long table on the denlike set, and the twelve contestants gathered around. She looked at the nearest camera operator and asked, "Are we live?"

He shook his head. "We haven't been given the order."

"You're getting it now, on three. One. Two. Three." Blake looked around at the contestants and said, "A week ago I challenged you all to create business mission statements and logos. I reviewed your work, and so did expert marketers. Some of you show promise, and a couple of you even have start-up-ready visions and visuals for your business. One of you, I'm afraid, had nothing original or appealing to offer."

Blake stood and moved to a new addition to the set: a six-foot-tall plush toy that looked like an old-fashioned grandfather clock. "Before everything was computerized, employees would put a card in a clock to stamp the time they started and ended work. They called it punching the clock. I'm sorry, but one of you must punch the clock for the last time." Her eyes roamed the anxious contestants seated around the long table, and she announced, "Spencer Jett, punch out the clock."

Jett sat dazed for several excruciating seconds. Then a few of the other contestants shook hands with him or hugged him, and realization sank in. He got to his feet and trudged to the plush clock, bumped a fist against it, and exited the stage, all while Blake looked on.

She returned to her seat at the table and said, "Now, let's talk about your second week's challenges."

***

"Say, sexy man, haven't I seen you before?"

Brett stood in the queue at a Korean BBQ street food vendor's cart. He didn't recognize the voice, but it must have belonged to the curvaceous, auburn-haired woman in a skintight dress barely longer than her crotch. He found himself salivating for more than lunch, and had to swallow before he asked, "Uh, I think I would have remembered meeting you."

She smirked. "Well, I remember you, foxy fella. You were at the pre-opening party Blake Bertrand had for the Blake Tower, back in Miami in...February, I think it was."

"That's some memory you've got. I wasn't there long, maybe half an hour." He couldn't help himself—he was talking to her boobs, which were in serious danger of escaping the minimal confinement offered by her dress. "To be honest, I crashed that party. I really wanted to meet Blake Bertrand."

"And did you?"

"Yeah. But I blew it with her, eventually."

"Hey, pal, you gonna order something or not? Because if you're not, you should stop holding up the line," grumbled a man two places back from Brett.

"Sorry." Brett turned to the friendly Korean family operating the food cart, ordered and paid for his food, and had a thought. "Want anything?" he asked the auburn lady.

"Just you, thanks." She winked at him.

His little best friend saluted that idea. Moving away from the cart so the line could advance, he said, "Well, after I eat lunch I've gotta go back to work. But maybe I could buy you dinner tonight?"

"That sounds brilliant." She took a notepad and pen out of her purse and scribbled a phone number on a sheet, ripped it off, and tried to hand it to him, but his lunch was making a mess of his hands. Laughing, she tucked the sheet of paper into his pocket...and gave his buddy a gentle nudge. "I'm Sherry, by the way. Don't forget to call me." She walked away, hips swaying mesmerizingly, and vanished in the Midtown crowds.

Eventually, Brett remembered to eat his lunch.

***

Arguing with television producers, eliminating a contestant, mentoring the remaining contestants for their second week's challenge... It all added up to a stressful day, and Blake still had an evening of desperately searching for a solution to the Wishman Spears problem ahead of her. She needed to purge some frustration and worry by working her body. Taking Suki with her, Blake took a taxi to the sports club.

Suki pushed Blake hard. They did strength and flexibility training and aerobic conditioning for an hour, and then Suki put Blake through two and a half hours of combat jujitsu hell. By the time Blake performed acceptably on Suki's "exam time," she felt achy and wobbly all over—but she was in a good mood.

They both took brief showers to remove the sweat and changed into clean clothes because they planned to get takeout for dinner. As they were about to exit the club, however, the voice Blake hated to hear called out, "Blake, you've got to stop following me around. We're divorced now, remember?"

"Ignore him, Boss," Suki recommended, and they stepped out into the New York night.

Lang followed them, and, looking over her shoulder, Blake saw that he had half a dozen burly men around him. She also saw Suki go into a subtle "ready" stance, watching Blake's ex and his henchmen as a cat watches a family of mice.

"We can talk about this, or I can request a restraining order of my own," said Lang.

Suki positioned herself between Lang's posse and Blake. "From what Boss has told me, I knew you're an asshole, but she never mentioned you're also insane."

Lang shook his head. "Not so. After ten years of marriage, I certainly know Blake's handwriting. She's sent me a threatening letter." He held out a hand, and one of his goons took an envelope out of a duffel bag he was carrying. The dude handed the envelope to Lang, who handed it to Suki. "I have the original in my hotel room. This is a copy, but there's no denying it's Blake's writing style."

Keeping the men in view all the while, Suki extracted a sheet of paper from the envelope and scanned it. "This does look like your writing, Boss." She handed it back over her shoulder to Blake.

Hands trembling with baffled rage, Blake squinted at the handwriting in the city's night lights. Incredibly, she was indeed looking at her own handwriting, threatening to hire a hit man to kill Lang for getting his "new whore" on Blake's television show.

"I didn't write this." Though Lang had said it was only a copy, Blake ripped the page to shreds and threw them down on the sidewalk.

"We'll see what a handwriting analysis expert says, if you threaten me again in any way." Lang sneered, then turned to go back inside the sports club.

"Goddamn you, Lang, you want something from me. I know you. What will it take to make you leave me alone?" Blake started to rush after him, but Suki grabbed her and held her back.

"There is nothing," Lang said, looking back at Blake, "that you can say or do to make me happy anymore."

Blake cupped her hands around her mouth and shouted, *"Si tu pito fuera mas chico, solo se vería con microscopio, puto comemierda!"*

One of Lang's goons choked with laughter. Lang's face turned beet-red as he charged toward Blake, snarling, "*What* did you say about my dick?"

He got almost in arm's reach, then Suki moved and Lang soared backward a few feet, tripping two of his henchmen rushing to do battle. Suki struck out with one foot and another goon went down on his knees, fighting to breathe. The other three thought better of trying their luck, but one of them helped Lang stand.

"You're getting served with a restraining order, bitch. And Gabby is going to win your shit show," he spat at her.

"She'll win if she earns it, Lang." Blake touched the scar on her forehead, powerless to stop herself. Her heart raced, and she fought just to make her voice sound cool and collected. "All I care about is making sure you can never fuck with me again."

"Maybe I'll just fuck with everyone you care about, instead." Lang watched Blake with his sooty eyes ablaze as she and Suki climbed into the taxi they'd called for.

"I think he means it, Boss," said Suki as the taxi merged with traffic. "I think he already started, with that senseless attack on Henry."

"I think you're right." Blake wiped her hand against her eyes, brimming with tears now that the crisis was over. "But if it can't be proved, what can I do about it?"

"Well." Suki glanced at Blake, then turned her attention to the passing scenes. "My agency has more than three bodyguards, Boss. Just saying."

Chapter Twenty-Four

June 12
New York, New York

Her day got off to a rotten start when she arrived at the NBC studio to find the security guards and the producers of *The Takeover* waiting for her. "We need to have a serious talk, Blake," said Vanessa. "Let's go to my office."

Blake exchanged glances with Antonio, but followed Vanessa to the office she'd claimed for the duration of *The Takeover* filming. Waiting in her office was a police officer, who stood when they entered the room. Vanessa seated herself behind her desk, Blake and Jerome sat in chairs across from her, and Antonio and the security guards and the police officer remained standing.

The police officer looked at Blake. "Are you Ms. Blake Bertrand?"

Shit, am I about to be arrested? What's going on here? "Yes, I am."

"Ms. Bertrand, it is my duty as an officer of the law to serve you with this restraining order. You are ordered to keep at all times a minimum distance of three hundred feet from Lang Bertrand, except for any exemptions granted on a case-by-case basis by issuing Judge Harrell. In the case of any granted exemptions, police officers must be on the premises for the duration of such time as you are within a proximity normally banned by court order." The officer handed Blake a sheet of paper with the official court letterhead at the top and the judge's signature and seal at the bottom. "I must ask you to leave these premises, pursuant to the restraining order against you. Have a good day, ma'am."

"Wait! This has got to be a mistake." Blake got to her feet and faced the policeman. "I work here. I'm hosting a reality show."

"Judge Harrell is aware of that, ma'am. But as he said, nobody is above the law. Witnesses say you went to the Reebok sports club while Lang Bertrand was there, and you ordered someone in your employ to attack him and his friends." The policeman shrugged. "It's only a temporary restraining order, Ms. Bertrand. There's a hearing scheduled. You can tell your side of the story then—"

"Can I see the judge today?"

"You can go to the courthouse and request to speak with him, but you'd better hurry. He usually leaves early on Fridays."

"Officer, can you wait just a minute or two?" Vanessa pleaded.

"Sure, I suppose so." The policeman leaned against the shut door. *Making sure I don't run and try to hide somewhere in the studio to attack Lang.* The surreal understanding sank in with Blake.

"I hope you can understand, Blake, that if this isn't resolved quickly, it's going to cost NBC dearly in lost time and money. We'd have to start over with a new host, and you'd be considered in breach of your contract with us," Vanessa advised Blake.

"Give the contestants that I was supposed to mentor today my cell phone number, and tell them I'll meet with them over the weekend to coach them," Blake said. "I'm on my way to talk to this judge now, and I expect to be granted an exemption before Wednesday's decision filming."

"We'll send a crew to you this weekend."

"That works." Blake looked to the policeman. "Okay, Officer, I'm ready to go."

***

Judge Harrell agreed to issue an exemption to the temporary restraining order against Blake, but he warned her that it would not be processed and her copy delivered until sometime Monday. Blake yearned to work out her frustrations at the sports club, but she didn't dare risk encountering Lang there. She returned to her apartment in such a foul mood that Antonio actually muttered to Suki, when the martial artist opened the apartment door, "Watch out, she's had a bitch of a day and—"

"And the day has made me a bitch," Blake finished for him, her voice half a growl, and stalked into her bedroom. She put some jazz on the turntable and ran a hot bubble bath for herself, but it didn't help. When she tromped into the kitchen and took out the Jack Daniel's and Coca-Cola, Suki laid a restraining hand on Blake's arm.

Blake threw a punch Suki had taught her, and Suki blocked her with ease and faked a punch of her own. The block that Blake threw up was clumsy and left her off-balance, and a second later she lay facedown on the kitchen floor with Suki holding her still.

"We could work out safer in a park, Boss."

Hysterical laughter and sobs mingled inside Blake and came pouring out of her mouth, waking Matt and bringing Antonio running from the living room. Suki released her hold on Blake and sat back on her heels, waiting for Blake to regain her composure. Meanwhile, Suki told her colleagues, "She'll be all right. Boss just needs to break something or wear herself out trying. I'll handle it."

"I love women, especially my Miranda," Blake heard Matt murmur to Antonio, "but sometimes I think they're all crazy."

"Our whole species is crazy. Men and women just do 'crazy' different from each other," Antonio muttered in reply. If they said anything else about the incident, they were out of Blake's hearing range.

"Get changed, Boss," said Suki, when Blake finally quieted. "While you do that, I'm going to find a good park close by, and we're going to go there, and you're going to try to beat the shit out of me."

"Not possible," Blake whispered.

"You might get lucky. I may trip on something." Suki gave Blake's shoulder a friendly slap, then helped her stand at the same time that she got back on her own feet. It was another of Suki's eerie fluid movements that Blake wondered if she gained from years of martial arts.

Blake changed into one of her glossy, expensive designer jumpsuits and sandals. Suki held a carry-all bag as she tucked her phone into her pocket. "Taxi is on the way," said Suki, and they went to the elevator to ride down to meet their cab.

When the driver asked where they wanted to go, Suki sat up and said, "Battery Park."

"There are a couple of parks closer to the apartment," Blake told the bodyguard.

"I've never been to New York before, and Battery Park is someplace I've heard of all my life. Let's go there." Suki actually looked excited by the idea.

Blake found herself smiling a little. "Okay. Battery Park it is."

The driver pulled into traffic and carried them to the famous collection of cycling, hiking, and skating paths and open areas for throwing Frisbees or playing tag football, among other activities.

It was a fine early summer afternoon, and the beginning of a weekend. Battery Park was filled with people enjoying the outdoors.

Suki opened her carry-all bag and said, "Here. Put these on."

Blake flinched as Suki handed her the pair of high heels she usually kept on her bedside table. "What are you doing with those?"

"Forcing you to wear them…unless you can keep me from laying hands on you." And with that Suki aimed a sweeping kick at Blake's knees and their battle was begun.

They attacked and blocked and evaded until the sun was sinking in the west. Both women were dripping sweat and breathing hard when Suki called, "Time's up." Blake was left gasping while Suki only breathed faster and deeper than usual. Even though Blake knew Suki must have taken it easy on her, she was deliriously proud that the black belt never got a good grip on her.

"Good work." Suki put the high heels back in her bag. "You keep that up, Boss, and in another ten years you might be able to kick my ass." Her blank-faced delivery made Blake laugh, and Suki chuckled along with her.

"I needed this. Thanks, Suki."

"I'm serious. Keep this up." Suki leveled a solemn gaze at Blake. "Someday you're going to decide you don't need bodyguards anymore. You can defend yourself then, if you've taught your body how."

"I will. I promise."

***

Brett stood to hug and kiss Sherry when she walked into the Indian restaurant. This was their third consecutive night of meeting for dinner, and he hoped it would be their third consecutive night of going to her hotel room after. She was a demon in bed, and he couldn't get enough of her. His little buddy stood to greet her, too, as they hugged, and she giggled when she felt his eagerness.

"This place has always had fantastic curry," he advised her as they sat down.

"I look forward to trying it." Sherry took out a paper fan and waved it to cool her bosom. Brett was only too glad to have his attention directed to her generous breasts, and she knew it and winked over the fan at him. "Before we order, though, someone I know is here, and I'd really like you to meet him."

"For you, I'd meet Satan." Brett grinned and started to stand again. "Which table is he at?"

"This one," said a man who'd been sitting in the booth next to theirs all along. "I'm not Satan, but you know someone who thinks I am."

Brett turned and found himself face-to-face with the infamous Lang Bertrand. He threw a disgusted glance at Sherry. "You really want to introduce me to this creep?"

"He's not a creep, Brett. There are two sides to every story," said Sherry, leaning closer and patting Brett's tush in a way that made his best friend jump for joy. "Isn't that something you've learned the hard way? You told me how you were framed at—"

"That's different," Brett snapped. "I don't hit women, but this son of a bitch does."

"Oh, Brett Skeet. You have so much to learn." Lang shook his head. "Some women enjoy a good beating."

Brett blinked, thought fast, said, "I can't see Blake Bertrand as one of those women."

"I tell you what, young man. Have a seat, and I'll do all the talking for a few minutes. Then you think about what I've said, and maybe you'll decide we can do some business together."

He'd never imagined himself listening to what a known wife-beater had to say. But tonight he listened—and found that he believed.

Chapter Twenty-Five

June 13
New York, New York

Blake woke at 4:30 A.M. when her BlackBerry rang. *Oh, my Jesus, please don't let anything be wrong with my mother!* She sat up in bed and punched the Talk button. "Blake here," she blurted.

"You cunt."

She was so unused to being called names in the middle of the night, at least since leaving Lang, that she needed to check the caller ID even though she recognized Margot's voice. Checking confirmed that her best friend was, indeed, cussing her out.

"Margot, what's this—"

"*You* introduced them, Blake. I can't believe how you're betraying me! He's packed his bags and gone to her, and it's all your fault, you fucking bitch!"

From Margot's slurred speech it was obvious she'd been drinking heavily again, but Blake feared she knew what her longtime friend meant, anyway. "Thomas has moved in with another woman? Who?"

"That pixie-faced whore, that's who! Robbie."

"Robin, you mean?"

"I hate you, Blake. Do you hear me? *I hate you Blake.* I never want to see your face or hear your voice again." The line beeped a few tones as Margot tried to press the End Call button, and went silent as she finally succeeded.

"Well, the hits just keep on coming." Blake slid out of bed to get dressed.

***

Late Saturday morning, Blake arrived at a conference room in a hotel for the weekend reality show taping. As she settled in and waited for her first mentoring appointment, the cameraman warned her, "We've only got an hour."

"They're going to have to deal with it." Blake shrugged. "Can you do close-ups and record everything that's said? That should be plenty of material."

"Oh, sure."

"I guess that's all we really need." She arranged some demos on the table, taken from her own business, to illustrate for the contestants what she wanted them to understand.

Her BlackBerry rang again, playing "Big Time" to inform her that the caller was her publicist. Antonio lowered his Ray-Bans to give Blake a quizzical look.

"There's only one way to find out," she told him, and pressed the Talk button. "Hi, Vickie, what's up?"

"Now, this is more like it!" Vickie's voice rang with enthusiasm. "If you're going to get bad publicity, sidewalk fistfights and restraining orders are the sort of bad publicity you should get. I can work with this."

"Shit. You mean that's all over the news?"

"It sure is! Today you're even on the cover of—"

"What are you going to do about it?"

"I'm going to send out press releases telling your side of the story, of course."

"Good. Keep me updated, but I've got to go."

"Why, what's going on?"

"I've got to mentor the show's contestants in a hotel conference room, because Lang has court permission to attend NBC's functions for *The Takeover*, but I don't yet have permission to be there when he is."

"Oh, that's excellent stuff! I'll put in a quote from you about how unfairly the legal system treats women."

Eve Womack stepped into the conference room, and looked as if she thought she should step out again until Blake finished on the phone. Blake waved Eve into a seat as she said, "Gotta go, Vickie," and clicked the call off.

"Is this a bad time?" Eve didn't quite put all her weight on the chair she sat on.

"This hour is your appointment time, so this is a good time for us to talk. But this whole week has been one disaster after another." Blake shook her head. "And as if that's not enough, I've got an ongoing disaster to deal with, so I guess you could say my life is a total mess right now."

"An ongoing disaster? What's wrong?" Eve brushed aside the

tablet she'd brought with her for taking notes, and watched Blake with eyes wide with concern.

"Just a property I can't touch for a year because while I had the flu I trusted someone to file some legal paperwork for me, and they botched it." Blake reached for one of her demonstration materials. "But let's talk about what you need to do for this week's challenge. We've only got an hour, so we should get to work."

"I don't understand, though. Why can't you do anything with your own property, just because of a mistake with some paperwork?"

"To make a long story short, I need some zoning regulations waived or amended to allow my plans for the property to proceed. It's several different things—traffic flow in the area of the building, the building's wiring and so forth need to be modernized, all that sort of stuff." Blake gestured to the materials she wanted Eve to look at. "If you'll look at this—"

"What would happen if you went backward instead of forward?"

Blake stared at Eve, thoroughly confused. *Forward* and *backward* had nothing to do with the demo she was trying to show Eve.

Her bewilderment must have shown in her face, because Eve said, "The wiring and stuff. What if you went retro with it, instead of modernizing?"

Can it really be that simple? "You mean restore it to the way it was when it was built? Make it a historical attraction?"

"Oh, you can do more than that." Eve's smile shone like a star as she pulled her tablet close again and entered search terms. "It isn't just children who love to play. You're talking about the Wishman Spears building, I think, and with that you could create something unique in the world. It could be like a cross between the Smithsonian and a Disney theme park. People could see the whole industrial era come to life there, do hands-on activities—"

"But who would be interested in going somewhere like that?"

"Lots of people! Schools could take field trips there, safety inspectors could hold training seminars to understand from past conditions why today's safety regulations are what they are, labor unions could educate their members and recruit new ones by showing them what industrial work was like before collective bargaining—"

"Eve?"

The woman stopped, her cheeks reddening. "I'm sorry. I didn't mean to sound like I'm telling you how to do your job. I just get an idea and get excited."

"What I was going to say is, you're a genius." Blake hugged Eve tight.

***

All day Blake felt happy and excited for the first time in what seemed like weeks. She couldn't wait to be done with the day's five mentoring sessions, so that she could rush back to her apartment and make phone calls to the people she needed to help her pursue Eve Womack's suggestion.

However, simultaneously all day Blake felt a growing worry about Margot's well-being. By lunchtime she couldn't endure it alone anymore, so she phoned Edith in Miami. When her longtime personal assistant answered her call, Blake asked, "Could you please do me a favor?"

"Sure. What do you need?"

"Would you please go to Margot Mills's house and see if she's okay?"

"I'll try, but if the door is locked I can't get in. Unless she keeps a spare key somewhere, and you know the hiding place."

"I do." She gave directions for finding the Millses' spare house key, and felt much better.

***

When her day's work for *The Takeover* was done, around mid-afternoon, Blake and Antonio returned to her apartment and she got busy contacting architects, engineers, contractors, attorneys, and other experts she needed to talk to about Eve's suggestion for the Wishman Spears. She was in the middle of a three-way call with her New York real estate attorneys, Susan Golden and Peter Britell, when call waiting beeped to alert her that someone was trying to contact her. At the moment she was coaxing the lawyers to translate their legalese into plain English for her, and by the time she felt confident she understood their advice, she forgot to check caller ID to see who tried to reach her.

It was late at night, and Blake was just getting out of the shower, when her phone rang playing "Someone to Watch Over Me." She glanced at the time before pressing the Talk button.

Ten thirty-eight.

My God. Is Edith still at Margot's? "Hi, Edith, how—"

"Blake, Margot is in the hospital." Edith's voice was shaky. "She was unconscious when I found her, and there were empty whiskey bottles and empty medicine bottles and... Blake, she tried to kill herself. They pumped her stomach, and they've got her on suicide watch."

"Jesus." Blake felt icy fingers squeeze her heart. "Thank you so much for going to see about her. Can you do one more favor for me?"

"Do you want to try for plane tickets for tonight, or wait until morning?"

Chapter Twenty-Six

June 14
Miami, Florida

While her red-eye flight from New York to Miami was still in the air, Blake received a text message from Edith: <Margot admitted to University of Miami Hospital, Department of Behavioral Health Services.> Blake immediately phoned for a taxi to meet her, Matt, and Suki at the airport and take them directly to UMH. They arrived at the hospital not long after the patients were served breakfast, and since patients were allowed guests at breakfast and lunch on Sundays, Blake and her bodyguards got trays from the hospital cafeteria and carried their meal to the BHS dining room.

Margot sat, her plate untouched, at a table with one other patient gulping his food as if he hadn't been fed in a week. Blake, Matt, and Suki crowded around the table. Matt and Suki tucked into their food with good appetites, but Blake felt awkward about eating while her best friend sat silent, head bowed, uninterested in the bacon, eggs, and grits in front of her.

Blake eyed her own tray of ham-and-cheese croissants and orange juice, and had an idea. "Hey, hon. Would you rather have my breakfast? I'll be glad to swap."

There was no reaction from Margot, but the other patient at the table looked up, his face alight with hope, and offered, "If you don't want that, I'll eat it."

After pausing to think of a polite reply, Blake said, "I'll keep that in mind." Evidently satisfied, the hearty eater returned his attention to his grits.

Minutes passed without a word from anyone. At last Blake nibbled a ham-and-cheese croissant and said, "This is really good, for hospital food. You should try it." She held an untouched one out to Margot.

Her friend glanced at the food, then slapped it out of Blake's hand. It went flying, coming apart in midair, the ham splashing down in the grits of a patient at a nearby table, one half of the croissant with the cheese stuck to it falling on the floor, and the other half bouncing off the back of a patient's head. The patient promptly dived under the table, screaming, "They're doing it again! Stop them, make them stop!"

"You could have given it to me," sulked the hearty eater at Margot's table. He snatched the other untouched ham-and-cheese croissant off Blake's plate and ran away with it.

Matt watched all the mayhem with slack-jawed alarm. Suki continued serenely eating her Cheerios, except for a pause to whisper to Matt, "Never a dull moment in an insane asylum, it seems."

That whisper got Margot's attention, however. "I am *not* insane," she snarled, and got up from the table and tromped out of the dining room.

Blake abandoned her tray and hurried after Margot. When she heard footsteps moving fast behind her, she knew Matt was following them. Suki, probably, was devouring her cereal and observing life in a psychiatric ward.

Margot plunged into an open door, and Blake found that it was a private bedroom. A television was tuned to some televangelist, but the sound was muted. Margot threw herself on the bed and lay on her side, with her back turned to Blake.

For a minute or maybe two, Blake stood in the doorway looking at her friend. *What can I say to help her?* In all the years she'd known the woman, she'd never seen her so angry and helpless.

If that's all I've got, it's better than nothing. No way am I going to fly from New York to Miami and never even really talk to her.

"You know, Margot, we've known each other twelve years now. I remember you and Thomas hadn't been married long when he introduced us. He hadn't talked you into giving up your flower shop yet. You were outgoing and energetic and enjoying every moment of being alive. No wonder he fell in love with you. So did I, in a different way of course."

She stopped, thinking of Margot as she used to be. A totally different woman than the one who'd just tried to kill herself, and was now outraged at being still alive and rejected by her husband.

"Before you met Thomas, and for almost a whole year after you met him, you had a life of your own and it made you happy. If you were happy without him once, you can be happy without him again. Why don't you start another florist business?"

"Why don't you fuck off," Margot responded, in a shaky voice.

I know that voice. You sound that way when you're feeling something you don't want to. Blake allowed herself a fleeting smile. *So I accomplished something by coming here, thank goodness.*

"There's something I need to give you before I go. I was going to save this until your birthday, and give it to you along with a present, but I think you need it now." Blake opened her purse and took out the note and autograph she got from Amanda Brown, the night she went out with Brett for the first time. "I went to a dinner club one night, and Amanda Brown happened to be performing. I asked her for an autograph for you, and she wrote a note to go with it. I'll just put it on top of the TV."

She laid Amanda Brown's note on the television set, as promised. Then she stepped to the edge of the bed and patted Margot's shoulder, and didn't mind when Margot flinched at her touch. "I love you, lady. If you need anything at all, you tell the staff here to let me know. I'll see you when you're feeling ready to face the world again."

Blake turned around and nodded at Matt. He walked her back to the dining room, where Suki had finished breakfast and sat watching the large flat-screen television with the patients.

"Come on, Suki," Blake said. "You and I can spend the day visiting my mom, and Matt can see his woman while we're back in Miami. We'll fly back to New York in the morning."

***

Jacinta Bertrand was happy to see Blake, but saddened to hear of Margot's suicide attempt. "I won't lie to you, *mija*. When we lost your father, there were times I thought about killing myself. But I had you, and I had my work. Now I look back, and I'm glad I stayed. My daughter makes me proud, and there are people alive today who might not be if I hadn't been their nurse. Your friend will be glad someday that you saved her life."

"I think so too, Mama." Blake squeezed her mother's hand.

They were sitting outside on lawn chairs. Jacinta had just recently ceased needing to wear braces on both legs and her left arm. She'd winced when she lowered herself, with help from her second-shift nurse, into the lawn chair. But now she was watching cottony clouds drift overhead, breathing in the crisp ocean air, so happy she glowed.

Suki was nearby, casually practicing some jujitsu moves she needed to master to earn her fourth-degree black belt. Abruptly she stopped, raised a hand to shade her eyes from the bright afternoon sunlight, and stared down the winding island road. "Boss, are you or your mom expecting company?"

"Not me," Blake said, and stared down the road herself. She couldn't see anything yet, but she wasn't surprised. Suki's senses often seemed to be supernaturally keen.

"Me neither," said Jacinta. She labored to sit up straighter, and the nurse rushed to her side to assist her.

In a matter of seconds, four people came into view around a curve in the road. As they got nearer to Jacinta's condo, Blake realized that two were wearing island security uniforms and two were Miami police officers.

Suki turned her head to look at Blake. "This isn't going to be good news."

"You're probably right."

"Blake? Have you had some kind of trouble?" Jacinta's dark eyes were locked on Blake's face, reading her expressions like a book.

"Lang and I ran into each other in New York. That's all. I can't think of any reason why Miami police would be coming to see me about that, but who knows." Blake shrugged and awaited the arrival of the officers.

"Well...maybe it's about the drunk who hit me." Jacinta chewed her bottom lip, consumed by doubt and worry.

A few minutes later the two security men and the two police officers turned into Jacinta's driveway. They halted there for a minute, carrying on a whispered conversation among themselves. Suki gave them her full attention.

"There's been a fire," the bodyguard told Blake as the four men crossed the lawn to reach them. "One of your Miami properties has burned to the ground, Boss."

"You heard us talking?" one of the police asked Suki, his eyes in danger of popping out of his head.

"She probably reads lips," the other police officer suggested.

"I heard you fine. You"—Suki gestured at the policeman who'd spoken first—"had your back turned to me. I couldn't possibly have been reading lips." She turned her usual blank face to the second officer. "And you decided to be the bad cop, and your friend here will be the good cop."

Blake wanted to scream because yet another disaster had struck her, and she wanted to laugh at the facial expressions of the police officers as they looked at each other in alarm because their plan had been ruined before they ever got started. She shut her eyes, took a deep breath, and forced herself to stay calm. Opening her eyes again she said, "I suppose, from all that, the fire must have been arson. Is that right?"

"Yes, ma'am," the first officer managed, his voice faltering.

The second officer stood up straight and looked down his nose at Blake, evidently determined to take control of the situation. "You had motive to hire someone to burn the place down, Ms. Bertrand. We got an anonymous tip that you're having financial trouble because of that place you bought in New York, that Spears thing. Our informant said your investment partners are threatening to call in their loans to you. Insurance money could be real useful to you right now."

Don't let them intimidate you, Blake told herself. *You're innocent, and you can afford damned good attorneys and investigators to prove it.* "I can prove I'm already making other arrangements to solve that problem."

"Well, then you've got nothing to worry about." The second officer winked at the island security guards, who both sneered appreciatively.

For the first time, Blake realized that she and her mother weren't welcome on the island. She understood now why Suki had started the conversation by unnerving the police and island security, and wondered what else the bodyguard's keen ears had heard them say while they thought themselves out of hearing range.

"You'll need to come with us to the station and give a statement to the detective working this case, ma'am," said the first policeman, finding his courage again.

"Hire an attorney before you talk to them anymore, Boss," Suki advised. "You'd be surprised how many people prefer private security to the police, because some people go into law enforcement to be thugs with a badge to protect them." She was giving the second police officer an icy stare that Blake was grateful wasn't aimed at herself.

"Let's get this over with." Blake got to her feet and bent down to hug and kiss her mom. "Don't worry, Mama, they've got it all wrong. I'll clear this up and see you again before I go back to New

York."

"Be careful, *mija*," Jacinta whispered as a tear rolled down one cheek.

"I'll contact Antonio, Boss," Suki said as she fell into step next to Blake, following the police officers and island security. "He's got a cousin who's a lawyer. They should be able to recommend a good criminal attorney for you." A few seconds later, though Blake hadn't heard anyone say anything, Suki growled, "Because she's got a *right* to an attorney, you prick."

"Criminal?!" Jacinta gasped.

They'd barely climbed aboard the police speedboat when Suki, who had been texting, said, "Get your BlackBerry out and take down this name and number, Boss. Antonio's cousin said the best criminal defense attorney in Florida works for the firm our security agency uses. We happen to have a number to reach him on weekends."

Blake entered the attorney's name and number in her BlackBerry's contacts list, and before the police boat reached the mainland, she was arranging for her new defense attorney to meet her at the station.

***

June 14
New York, New York

Lang Bertrand soaked in his Manhattan hotel room's hot tub, drinking iced vodka and congratulating himself. Sal and Luca had burned down the money-laundering Cuban restaurant in Morningside during Blake's flight from New York to Miami. Making good use of Brett's tales of his time with Blake, Sherry had anonymously phoned Miami police about Blake's financial woes with the Wishman Spears.

And if Blake somehow managed to squirm out of this mess, Lang still had a mission for Brett and schemes for Gabby's participation in Blake's reality television show. Yes, it was a splendid time to be Lang Bertrand, and a miserable time to be Blake.

Chapter Twenty-Seven

June 14
Miami, Florida

Her police escort led Blake into a small room with a wall-mounted video recorder and a table and four chairs, two of which were already occupied. One occupant was a Detective Dixon, a middle-aged man with a shiny bald spot, dressed as if he'd watched too much *Miami Vice* as a child. The other man seated in the room was also middle-aged, but he was a handsome Latino with graying temples and faded jeans. As soon as she stepped into the room, the Latino gentleman stood and pulled out a chair for her.

"I was warned you don't shake hands," he said with a smile as he sat down again. "I'm Enrico Torres with Elliott, Torres, Collins, & Rhodes, and I specialize in criminal defense. Have you been advised of your rights, Ms. Bertrand?"

"Only by my bodyguards." She turned her attention from Torres to Dixon and asked, "Am I under arrest?"

"That hasn't been decided yet, ma'am," Dixon drawled. "Now, where were you—"

"Excuse me, Detective, but my client is under no obligation to answer your questions. Moreover, she has not had an opportunity to consult with her legal counsel about whether it's in her best interest to do so." Torres folded his arms across his chest and fixed a cool stare on Dixon.

"So consult."

"Now, don't take this the wrong way"—Torres flashed a toothy smile at Dixon—"but my client and I would like to talk alone, and somewhere we can be sure we're not spied on." He gestured at the camera.

"We're not well equipped that way, Mr. Torres."

"I didn't imagine you are." Torres leaned back in his chair and looked thoughtful. "You haven't decided whether to charge my client with a crime, and you can't provide facilities for her to talk with me before she chooses whether to answer your questions. Seems to me that Ms. Bertrand here should be free to go, until such time as you arrest her or she and I return at our convenience to speak with you voluntarily."

It took a few seconds for Blake to realize the noise she heard was Dixon grinding his teeth. She looked at Torres and wondered if he was somehow related to Suki, because he had that same blank-faced expression she often wore.

At last Dixon grumbled, "Yeah. I suppose you're right, Torres." He stood, nearly tripped over Torres's outstretched legs on his way to the door, and slammed the door so hard it opened. "I'll need you to stop on your way out and leave us your contact information, Ms. Bertrand. We'll probably want to talk to you soon."

Torres stared at the detective with frank astonishment, widening his eyes and raising his eyebrows. "Really, Dixon. My client is filming a new reality show for NBC, owns properties all over Miami, and has a residence on Fisher Island. If you can't find her when you want to talk to her, it's probably time you retire." He walked side by side with Blake to the front office, where Suki paced like a caged tiger.

"You okay, Boss?" Suki asked.

"She's free to go, for now anyway." Torres consulted his smartphone and said, "I'm in court tomorrow, Ms. Bertrand, but I can see you after hours. Can you come to my office at half past five? We'll order dinner delivered and discuss your case."

Blake frowned. "I can be there, but the producers of *The Takeover* are going to be mighty unhappy about delaying filming."

"With all due respect, Ms. Bertrand, those producers aren't looking at a possible thirty years in prison for first-degree felony arson. If it were me, I'd tell those people they're the least of my worries." He waved to Blake and Suki as he opened the station door. "See you tomorrow at half past five, ma'am."

Blake ran a hand through her hair, knowing she was making a mess of it and, it seemed, her whole life. "Suki, would you do me a favor and call a taxi while I call Vanessa and Vickie?"

"No problem, Boss."

***

June 15
Miami, Florida

At five-fifteen Blake and Suki climbed out of a taxi and knocked on the front door of Elliott, Torres, Collins, & Rhodes. The law firm leased one of the oldest and most distinguished buildings in Coral Gables, a Spanish colonial mission built of cut white stone, with a cobblestone courtyard and a breathtaking view of the Atlantic. Ionic columns flanked the arched door, which was made of some heavy dark wood and etched with elegant patterns that resembled conch shells.

"They must do well to afford this place," Suki murmured as Blake knocked again.

A ruffled-looking pretty young Latina opened the door then. "I'm so sorry, I was on the phone with a client and had to ask him three times to please hold." She offered them a rueful smile and waved them inside. "I'm Mr. Torres's paralegal, Yolanda. He isn't here yet, but he told me to expect you and to make you comfortable. We'll be in this conference room here. It's the most convenient place we've got for a business dinner."

Yolanda showed them into a long, narrow room with a brick fireplace and chandelier light fixtures. A long banquet table dominated the room, surrounded by cushioned chairs that proved to be a fluffy delight to sit in. "Can I bring you anything to drink?"

Suki arched an eyebrow. "How about a pitcher of margaritas?"

It took Yolanda a few seconds to decide Suki must be joking. She gave a nervous giggle and said, "I'm afraid we're nonalcoholic here. Would you like a soda?"

"Maybe a pitcher of ice water instead, and some glasses?" Blake suggested.

"I'll be right back with that." Yolanda vanished from the door.

Before she returned, Mr. Torres entered with his phone pressed to his ear. He murmured greetings to them as he settled into a chair, and a look of relief passed over his handsome face as he sank into the cushions. "Yeah, I'll have to get back to you on that," he told whoever he was on the phone with. "Got to consult with a new client now, though. *Bueno.*"

Yolanda breezed into the room carrying a platter with a pitcher of ice water and half a dozen glasses on it. As she carefully set the platter on the table, Torres asked, "Is Kenton still here, by chance?"

Kenton? Why is that name familiar? Blake stared at her hands, folded together on the table, and tried to answer her own question.

"Yes, sir, but I saw him packing up for the night. Do you want me to catch him?"

"Please do. I need to consult with him." Torres looked at Blake and explained, "I defended your ex-husband on a DWI several years ago, and I need to make sure that representing you won't be looked at as a conflict of interest for any reason. Kenton Rhodes is one of the best in all the Eastern states at procedural questions like that."

Even as Torres finished explaining, the man who must be Kenton Rhodes entered the room. Tall, long strapping legs, and a tailored gray suit and lavender tie.

About the time she finished staring at his tie, she realized he was staring at her too, gray-faced as if he were looking at a ghost. When she raised her gaze to his face, she understood why. His light brown skin, his curly black hair, those eyeglasses exactly like the ones worn by the actor who played Amy Winehouses's boyfriend in the music video for "You Know I'm No Good"… She knew that face from literally hundreds of photographs taken by her private detective.

This is the man who adopted my son.

"Kenton?" Torres waved a hand in front of the man's face, and at last the man looked at his law partner. "What do you say? Any problem with me representing Ms. Bertrand, do you think?"

"I…I'm sorry, I was distracted." Kenton Rhodes seated himself in the other chair next to Torres. He listened intently as Torres explained about having once defended Lang Bertrand from a DWI charge, but at the same time he pulled a phone out of his pants pocket, tapped a few keys, and glanced at Blake again before putting the phone away again.

"So?" Torres finished his explanation for a second time and regarded Kenton curiously. "What's the verdict?"

"No problem with you representing her. If the case ends up involving Lang as well as Blake, though, you'll either need to represent both of them or work in partnership with Lang's attorney. Otherwise, if Lang went to prison and Blake walked, Lang could accuse you of selling him out."

Torres nodded. "Got it. Okay, man, go on home to your boy. Tell him Uncle Rico said hi."

"You bet." Kenton Rhodes stood up, and Blake noticed that he was taller than six feet, maybe even six-four, with longer legs and broader shoulders than average.

She watched the man her son called "dad" go, hesitating just a moment in the door to look back at her again before disappearing down the corridor. It took her a few breaths to realize that Torres was asking what sort of food she'd like delivered.

***

Blake couldn't tell Torres much about the property she was suspected of burning down. She'd asked Charles to round up all the information about the place and the deal for it that he could find. That amounted to a file consisting of a single note: acquired by Lang Bertrand, January 2008.

"You and Lang often did business separately, while married?" Torres asked, as Yolanda typed essential information from the conversation into a file on her laptop.

"We had such different interests, it just made sense. I wanted a ripple effect—transform key properties, and thereby transform the surrounding communities. He wanted to be the biggest fish in every pond." Blake shrugged. "Our finances were combined, but our business projects were mostly separated."

Torres nodded. "Since the restaurant was awarded to you in your divorce, have you had any dealings with the grounds or management?"

"I didn't even know it was mine. Lang and I had a lot of property to be divided between us when we divorced. Slightly more than a billion dollars' worth. Charles and I haven't finished going through the settlement, recording what's mine and what's Lang's."

"Now, if we can just prove that, and/or prove you were elsewhere when the restaurant burned down, the district attorney won't bother you anymore." Torres asked more questions as they ate the Chinese food they'd ordered, working out what his strategy for clearing Blake's name should be.

It was late when Blake and Suki emerged from the old Spanish building, and when Blake powered on her BlackBerry, she discovered several messages waiting for her. Vickie and Vanessa both wanted updates, of course, as did Edith and Blake's mom.

There was also a text message from Kenton Rhodes. <Got your number from office computer database. We should meet. You know why.>

Chapter Twenty-Eight

June 15
Miami, Florida

"**W**ait for me," Blake told the taxi driver, when she pulled into a parking space at the Hialeah apartment complex, where Kenton Rhodes lived with Blake's son. "I don't think I'll be long."

"As long as I'm paid for my time, you can take all night," the driver replied. The woman turned on the cab's interior lights and picked up a newspaper to read while waiting.

<I'm in the playground, on the swings,> Kenton texted Blake.

Since the bodyguard had better night vision, Suki preceded Blake into the apartment complex playground. There were stars out, but no moon.

True to his word, Kenton sat in a swing. He wasn't swinging, just gently rocking back and forth. After getting home from work he'd changed into long khaki shorts and a basketball T-shirt. He was wearing those eyeglasses Blake couldn't help thinking of as nerdily sexy. In fact, even with only dim starlight to see him by, she found herself admiring the well-defined muscles of his arms and legs and the scholarly aura he presented even in casual clothes.

"Hi, Ms. Bertrand," Kenton said, dragging his feet to bring the rocking swing to a stop. "I know it's late. I promise not to keep you out long."

"It's okay." Blake settled into the swing next to his. Suki, meanwhile, climbed the slide as if gravity meant nothing to her, and seated herself cross-legged at the top.

Kenton took his smartphone out of his shorts pocket and tapped a few keys, then showed the display to Blake. A photograph of Lionel holding his French horn grinned at her. "This is my kid," Kenton said, and after Blake nodded he studied the boy's face. "You know, Ms. Bertrand, I've seen your face for years, but until today I never noticed how much my son's face looks like yours."

"Please call me Blake." *I know he wants to know, but how the hell do I tell him? All these years I've planned to contact Lionel when he's eighteen, but I never imagined talking to the man who raised him...*

"You came to the All State Band concert." Kenton still looked at his picture of Lionel. "You saw my boy. We all got a good look at him during his solo." Now Kenton turned his head and leveled his thoughtful gaze at Blake's face again. "He's who you came to see, isn't he?"

Blake nodded again. It hurt to return Kenton's gaze, so she looked at her feet instead. She wore her usual Gucci sandals, and her sandaled feet next to Kenton's on the sandy Miami soil made her think of romantic moonlit walks on the beach. *You're done with all that, girl, remember? Lang and Brett are proof you've got no sense about relationships.*

"I know you've got every right to tell me to mind my own business," said Kenton, "but I need to ask you this, and I hope you'll answer and tell me the truth. Are you Lionel's birth mother?"

Ah, there it is. Blake shut her eyes and whispered, "Yes."

Neither of them said anything more, for how long Blake couldn't be sure. She opened her eyes again eventually, and found Kenton watching her. A patient compassion mellowed his face. Blake realized that Kenton was waiting for anything else she might be willing to tell him, but he'd ask no more questions.

She stared at her feet again, because if she kept looking at him watching her with such kindness she'd probably cry. "I was raped. I was so afraid that if I kept my baby I'd remember that terror and pain every time I looked at my child. That's why I gave him up." *If I admit the rest, will he do something like get a restraining order against me?* She took a breath and braved the confession. "I've regretted that ever since."

"That's understandable. Lionel is a great kid." Kenton reached out and patted Blake's shoulder. "Whoever the oxygen-wasting sack of shit is that raped you, I promise your son is nothing like him."

Blake couldn't hold back the tears anymore. She buried her face in her hands and moaned, and felt strong arms fold around her. Kenton held her until she was all cried out, and for the first time since she was a little girl, Blake didn't care that a man saw her crying.

"Thank you," she whispered, when she pulled away from him. She didn't want to, but she knew it had to be done.

"No, thank you." Kenton smiled, and Blake noticed his eyes were shining with tears too. "My wife and I were so happy together with him."

Blake remembered Johnny Capps telling her, a few years ago, that Lionel's adoptive parents had divorced. *She's who Lionel will always think of, when he thinks of the word "mom." Not me.* Tears threatened to spill from her eyes again, and she stood up and looked across the playground at the parking lot, seeing if the taxi was still there. It was.

"Can I contact him when he's eighteen? I've always wanted to do that." Blake hesitated, then added, "I have a lot to offer him, and I'd like to."

"Sure." Kenton stood too, and stretched from feet to fingertips of his upraised arms. "And thank you for telling me. He's asked about his biological parents, but I didn't know anything to tell him. Now I do."

Panic swept through Blake, and she whirled to fix her stare on Kenton. "Don't tell him he's a rape baby, Kenton. I beg you."

Kenton regarded her for a few breaths, head tilted to one side. At last he took off his eyeglasses and said, "I don't think I'd do the boy any favors if I pretended such things don't happen. But I'll wait until he's older to tell him that part, at least. Or you can tell him. For now, I'll just let him know I found out that his birth mother is a smart, successful businesswoman who looks forward to meeting him in a few more years."

Blake felt torn, but Kenton made a valid point. She nodded and said, "I guess I'll be in contact in about four more years, then."

As she followed Suki back toward the waiting taxi, she heard Kenton call after her, "We'll look forward to that day, Blake."

***

June 16
Miami, Florida

She spent a nervous day in her condo on Fisher Island, hoping for a progress report from Torres. Preferably one with good news.

Just before 4 P.M., she got her wish. Her BlackBerry rang, and the caller ID told her it was Torres calling. No sooner had she pressed the Talk button than Torres started speaking.

"Blake, hi, Yolanda has been a busy girl today, and it's paid off. Four people who traveled first class with you from New York to Miami recognized you as Blake Bertrand. That puts you airborne when the restaurant fire started, so the district attorney will have to agree you can't have started the fire yourself. We also examined your financial records all the way back to your divorce, and we didn't find any mysterious payouts or withdrawals that could mean you hired an arsonist. I'm going to talk to the DA before office hours close for the day, and you should be free to go back to New York as soon as you like."

"That's excellent news, Mr. Torres." Blake felt muscles she didn't even know she had begin relaxing.

An hour later, Blake and Suki and Matt were at the airport buying tickets for the next flight to New York, and Vanessa was hastily making out a schedule for filming the rest of *The Takeover*. The Delta was somewhere over Tennessee when Blake remembered Kenton Rhodes holding her while she cried, and she wished she could tell the pilot to turn around.

***

June 17
New York, New York

Back in New York, Blake still had some mentoring sessions to finish. Vanessa's plan called for those to be done Wednesday, along with filming Blake presenting the third week's challenge. The second week's elimination was still being decided. Thursday would be the only day the contestants received to work on their second challenge, which was to research competitors in the business each was interested in opening and identify some beneficial way to make their own product different. Friday Blake would eliminate a second contestant and mentor the remaining ten. *The Takeover* would then be back on schedule.

One of her second week's leftover mentoring sessions was with Gabby Truitt, Lang's girlfriend. Per the randomly selected order, Gabby's appointment was the last. Blake welcomed the girl into her office and explained the revised schedule Vanessa had put together. Unlike everyone else, Gabby protested.

"We're supposed to have from Wednesday through Sunday to do each week's challenge! This is too much to do in only one day. I don't think it's fair that some of us get one day to do this research shit, while other people have had since Wednesday of last week. Just because you went to Florida and got arrested—"

I expected someone to say something about that. I should have known it would be Gabby. Lang has probably been "coaching" her on what to say to me. Blake remembered some times when Lang had coached her, and found herself pitying the girl sitting across the desk from her. *She doesn't seem so bad. Young and too easy to manipulate, like I used to be, that's all.*

Blake waved for the cameraman to stop recording, and forced herself to stay calm. "I wasn't arrested, Gabby. I was questioned and let go."

"Yeah, whatever. It still isn't fair for some people to have a week and other people a day."

Blake motioned to the cameraman to start recording again. "You're right. It's not fair. But guess what? Things go wrong sometimes in business, and sometimes your partners have unexpected obstacles or even abandon you. A successful entrepreneur tries to foresee complications and plan for them, and always climbs back on if the horse throws them."

"Maybe that's easy if you've been in business awhile and know what can go wrong. But when you're new—"

"When you're new, you watch what your competition is doing and learn from their mistakes as much as possible, so you make fewer of your own. You should have been learning all you could from the most successful production companies before I gave you an assignment to do that."

Gabby's mouth was curved downward in a pout worthy of a two-year-old. Blake took a breath and said, "Now, listen, here's what I'd suggest you do..."

***

June 19
New York, New York

After the filming of Blake's announcement that Brittany Nelson was the second contestant she'd decided to eliminate, Blake conducted four mentoring sessions before noon. She was exhausted and ravenously hungry. Rather than go out for lunch, she asked Antonio to go get something from one of the street food vendors and they'd eat in her office.

"What's the password I should listen for this time?" She heaved herself out of her chair and realized her butt was numb from so much sitting. *Hang in there, tush, you've got six more hours of sitting to do today.*

After a moment's thought, Antonio said, "If a bear market shits on Wall Street—"

"Oh, get out of my office." Blake laughed in spite of herself. "And stop hanging around Matt so much. Your sense of humor is getting to be like his."

He tipped his Ray-Bans to her and swept out of her office. Blake shut and locked the door behind him. She began doing some stretches to work the stiffness out of her muscles. As she started feeling better, someone knocked on her door.

"Password?" she called, grabbing her toes and holding for ten seconds.

"I didn't know there was one," said Brett's voice.

"Well, there is when my bodyguard is away." She stood straight and tried to think of a polite way to ask the question, but she was too weary from the day's frantic pace. "What do you want, Brett?"

"I was just thinking you've had a hell of a week, so maybe tonight is a good time for me to take you out to dinner to thank you for my job."

She hesitated to answer, giving the idea some thought. By dinnertime she'd be ready to collapse into bed, but then again a relaxing meal with... Well, she wasn't sure she could call Brett a "friend," but he at least understood what it's like to be under police suspicion. It was true, what he said—it had been a hell of a week.

"Okay. Where should I meet you, and when?"

"Do you like clam rolls?"

"I don't know, but I like most seafood." *I'd kill for clam rolls.* It was one of her favorite foods. Her father used to take the family to a spot at City Island where they made the best ones outside of Massachusetts.

"Well, how about Littleneck? It's a New England clam shack in Brooklyn. Say, eight o'clock?"

Blake did some quick calculating. She'd finish the mentoring sessions at seven, and Friday night traffic in the city would mean an hour was just enough time to travel from the studio to the restaurant by taxi. Technically Antonio's shift should end at three, and Suki's should begin then. If she asked Suki to bring a change of clothes, she could be reasonably fresh for dinner.

"I'll meet you there."

"Sweet! I'll see you later."

My bodyguards are going to hate this.

Chapter Twenty-Nine

June 19
New York, New York

Littleneck was a small, glass-doored place easily mistaken for any other greasy diner until a person got near enough to read the words "clams" and "lobsters" on the windows. Brett was waiting for them outside, wearing a baseball cap for protection from the rain that had been falling for a half hour.

"My dad is originally from Boston, and he loves this place," Brett confided as he opened the door for Blake and Suki. "He says this is the real thing, clam rolls just like you get in Maine and Massachusetts and all. I say he's right."

Judging by the aromas in the air, Blake didn't doubt the food was delicious. Scents of garlic and tartar sauce and greasy french fries and beer made a tantalizing mix that got Blake's tummy growling to be fed.

They started with bowls of clam chowder, followed by Blake's memorable experience of clam rolls. Buttered, toasted, top-split hot dog buns held hot, tender giant fried clams. On the side were homemade pickled cucumbers, and Brett also sprung for an order of fluffy french fries shared among the three of them.

She was too enraptured by the food to make conversation, so it wasn't until they'd cleaned their plates that she leaned back in her chair and murmured, "Thank you, Brett, that was heavenly."

He smiled and said, "I'm glad. You needed some heaven after all the hell you've been through lately."

Blake slanted a glance at Suki, and asked, "What was it like for you, your first time being questioned by the police?" Blake recalled a time when Brett shared he was arrested for robbery as a teen.

With his head bowed, Brett said in a hushed voice, "Terrifying, even though I'd done exactly what I was accused of." He looked up, meeting her gaze, and added, "Second time, I was pissed, because I hadn't done the shit they said I did, but they refused to believe me because I'd fucked up once and admitted it."

"Now I know how you must have felt. Both times."

He shrugged. "Well, that's life as a person of color, isn't it. Listen, let's not ruin a good night by talking about the shit legal system. What do you say we go for a walk, or maybe go watch a movie on that big old TV of yours? I've got a Netflix account we can use to download something."

"A movie sounds good." She grinned. "Something funny, or maybe action with lots of righteous ass-kicking."

"You've got it." He laid down a generous tip on their table, and wrapped an arm around her shoulders as they went out to the street to hail a cab. She flinched at first, then enjoyed the comfort of his arm around her. It felt good.

Later, as they sat on her sofa watching *Midnight in Paris* Brett turned his attention from the movie to study Blake's face and posture for a minute. "Girl, you're wound up tight as a spring."

She flashed a small smile at him and said, "Yeah, well, I guess a few days of hell aren't totally erased by one yummy dinner. I didn't expect you to be sitting here...again."

"Tell me why you hate me."

"I can't because I don't."

He slid closer to her and began rubbing her shoulders, his strong hands soon massaging all the tension out of her muscles. As she relaxed under his attentions, he leaned in and whispered in her ear, "We could have more than one dinner tonight, if you know what I mean."

Instantly she tensed up again. "I don't think that would be a good idea."

"I don't either," put in Suki, blank-faced and cross-legged in a recliner.

"I'm not saying let's be a couple again. I know I screwed that up. But we were good in bed together, and that's a great way to get rid of stress." Brett turned his hands palms-up in surrender. "Up to you, Blake, but I still care about you, and I hate seeing you unhappy."

They watched the rest of the movie in silence. Near the end Matt drifted into the living room, rubbing sleep out of his eyes. He noticed Brett, looked at Suki, and she shrugged.

"I'm going to need more coffee," Matt muttered, and turned back to the kitchen.

When the movie ended, Brett stood and put his cap on. Blake

walked with him to the door, and he spread his arms for a hug. She moved into his embrace and thought, *If I close my eyes I can pretend he's Kenton Rhodes.*

Blake knew she shouldn't yield to temptation, but she couldn't help herself. "Don't go."

"You sure?"

She nodded. "I just need a quick shower first. It was a long, rough day."

He grinned. "Showering together could be fun."

"Oh, Jesus," Matt muttered as he walked past them with a steaming cup of coffee and seated himself in the other recliner.

"Something about nailing somebody to a tree on your mind, Matt?" Suki still had no facial expression.

Blake took Brett's hand in hers and led him into her bedroom, under the disapproving stare of Matt and the practiced blank face of Suki. Blake mixed the hot and cold water to exactly the temperature she craved, and turned around to find Brett already stripped naked and very much in the mood. He helped her out of her clothes and lifted her into the shower. They soaped and scrubbed each other, with pauses for nibblings and sucklings in strategic locations. She let herself abandon every worry. Brett wasn't everything, but he definitely knew how to make a woman feel like one.

He kissed her, his tongue playing hide and seek with hers, and just as she caught him he slid a hand between her legs and stroked her love button with an expert finger. She groaned, and he picked her up and held her straddling his hips. They merged in the stinging spray, and Brett had to lean against the shower wall as Blake's pelvis took on a will of its own and hammered him for what seemed an eternity.

Finally she was finished, and he set her down gently on her feet again. They were both gasping for breath.

"God, that was amazing," Blake managed at last.

He laughed and pulled her into his arms again. "It's fine if you just call me Brett."

***

Sometime in the night, Blake woke from a strange dream of people shooting at her with lasers. Her bladder nagged her to empty it, so she slid out of bed and stumbled into the bathroom.

It was when she emerged and stepped toward the bed that she noticed a dim red aura coming from her open closet. She investigated, pushing hangers of garments aside, and found a palm-sized silvery gadget with a lens glowing bright red.

A camera. Her heart froze, and for a moment or two she felt like she was choking. *Goddamn you, Brett Skeet.*

She picked up her bathrobe which she'd last left draped over the chair at her desk, slid into it, and pushed her feet into her slippers. Padding into the living room, she showed the camera to Matt. "Go ahead and tell me I'm a fool. I deserve it."

Matt shook his head. "No, Ms. Bertrand. You're not a fool. Just a rich lady, and that means a lot of people are gonna want to take advantage of you."

He took the camera from her, inspected it, then flipped open a panel and tapped out a little plastic-looking card. "Without this, no harm done."

Then Matt stood and strode into Blake's bedroom, and shook Brett's shoulder to wake him. "Put your clothes on and get out," he barked as soon as Brett opened his eyes.

"What? Something wrong?" Brett sat up in bed, blinking against the light from the hallway streaming through the open bedroom door.

"Yeah, you." Matt dropped the camera on Brett's lap. "I'm giving you two minutes to get your sorry ass out of Ms. Bertrand's apartment, or I'll put you out by force."

Incredibly, Brett tried to hand the camera back to Matt. "This isn't mine."

Matt seized Brett by a handful of hair and hauled him yelping out of the bed. "I wasn't fucking joking, man. Put your damn clothes on and get out. You can take your camera with you. But Ms. Bertrand keeps this." He showed the memory card to Brett for a moment before dropping it in his jeans pocket.

Brett scowled, but didn't say a word as he rushed into his briefs and pants. He grabbed his shirt and shoes and camera and ran out of the apartment, slamming the door behind him.

Blake went into the kitchen and made herself a Jack and Coke and drank it down. "Well, Brett Skeet," she muttered to herself, "you're no Kenton Rhodes, that's for damn sure. Hell, he probably isn't as great as I've imagined, either."

***

June 20
New York, New York

She slept late, waking up just in time for lunch. That turned out to be a couple of bacon and egg biscuits Antonio had brought from McDonald's. Not as healthy as she usually liked, but, damn it, she deserved some self-indulgence today.

In keeping with that thought, after she ate her microwaved Mc-brunch and washed it down with some coffee laced with plenty of cream, she went out on the veranda and pressed her BlackBerry's speed-dial number for Uncle Thorne. He answered just before her call would have gone to voicemail, sounding still drowsy himself.

"Hi there, girl. Are you okay? You're not having any more problems about that fire, are you?"

"No. That was awful, though, but by itself I think I could handle it. Just..." Blake watched the Saturday comings and goings of New Yorkers, no less busy than on a weekday.

"Just?" Uncle Thorne asked, prompting her.

"There's just been so *much* to handle, lately." Blake found herself baring her heart to Uncle Thorne: the race to make a one-year profitability plan for the Wishman Spears, Margot's suicide attempt, Brett's attempts first to possess her and then to sell her out, Lang's mind games with the restraining order and getting his girlfriend on the reality show, being questioned about the arson at the restaurant, everything.

"Whew. Girl, you need a vacation," Uncle Thorne suggested, when at last she'd told him everything.

"I agree, but I can't take one because of the damned TV show." Blake wondered what it must be like to be anonymous, like so many of the people going about their weekend activities ten stories below her.

"Maybe not, but there's another possibility, you know."

"Yeah, what's that?"

"Well, your Mentors & Protégés is launching Monday, isn't it? You've got hiking with that Internet genius Mark Summers for auction, and a guitar lesson with me, and a bunch of stuff like that. How about putting yourself up for auction, and have a day you'd never have if it's you calling all the shots?"

Blake felt a smile sneak onto her lips. "Uncle Thorne, you're a *genius*."

He chuckled and responded, "Now that's something I don't often hear. But I have my moments."

"I love you. Thanks for letting me vent and for giving me an idea for getting away from it all for a day."

"Love you back, girl. Call me anytime, you know that."

When they ended the call, Blake promptly put herself up for auction. She fought the urge to specify what she and the winning bidder would do together, instead listing simply "an afternoon with Blake Bertrand." *It's a day away from everything. This may be one helluva adventure.*

She changed into a jumpsuit for her jujitsu lesson from Suki, grinning with anticipation. Monday couldn't come soon enough.

Chapter Thirty

June 22
New York, New York

Blake wasn't surprised when Brett called in sick from work at *The Takeover* Monday morning. *No doubt he's busy working a new scam. I feel bad for whomever he's conning, but that's never again going to be me.*

The website to raise funds for her Mentors & Protégés activities, dreamittolife.org, opened for auction bids at 8 A.M. EST. All day, whenever she had a minute free from reality television duties, Blake monitored the progress of the first auctions.

Hiking with Mark Summers, the first premium package, Blake priced to open at $10,000. By noon the bidding was already at $60,800.

A Lesson With Former Santana Guitarist started at $500, but by noon the highest bid had climbed to $8,300. She made a mental note to look up the leading bidder on the Internet. He was in Maroon 5, unless she was mistaken.

Dinner With Manley and Melinda Yates was a package she expected to appeal to business leaders and tech fans alike, so she'd assigned an opening price of $5,000. As of noon, the top bid was $23,200 and certain to climb some more.

A soccer ball autographed by David Leckam had fetched a high bid, so far, of $1,700. U2's Bono had donated an autographed guitar that he'd actually used extensively on the band's latest record and tour, and that was going for a cool $2,500, undoubtedly with more to come. Lady Gaga offered one of her most outrageous music video costumes, and bids for it had already soared to $19,100. No celebrity item was going for less than $1,000.

As for *An Afternoon With Blake Bertrand*, she'd settled on an opening price of $500 for that, too. She was astonished to find that by noon someone was already bidding $33,000. Even as she watched, an anonymous bidder offered $35,000 to spend a few hours with her. For a moment she worried that the anonymous bidder might be Lang, but she quickly dismissed that fear. He was obeying the letter of the restraining order, if not its spirit. Not even Lang would be audacious enough to believe the issuing judge would grant him an exception because he won an afternoon with her in an auction.

Whoever the anonymous bidder for a few hours with her might be, Blake was thrilled. *Halfway through the first day of auctions, my Mentors & Protégés has already raised more than $100,000! I can go ahead and announce the official launch!* She texted Vickie to do just that.

<On it. And way to go!,> Vickie texted in reply.

***

Vanessa and Jerome visited Blake's NBC studio office as she and Antonio were getting ready to leave for the night. "Blake," said Vanessa, flashing a broad smile, "Jerome and I have been discussing the remaining contestants, and we were wondering if you've got any thoughts yet on who you'll choose as the winner."

"Not really. I haven't even announced the third elimination, and after that there's still nine contestants left." Blake didn't sit down again, but she leaned against her desk and studied first Vanessa's face and then Jerome's. *What are these two up to now?*

Jerome seemed to be trying to hide behind Vanessa, but he surprised Blake by speaking next. "Don't you think one or two stand out from the pack, though?"

Blake glanced at Antonio. His eyebrows were arched, visible in spite of his Ray-Bans. *At least I'm not alone in thinking this is a weird conversation to be having so early in the competition.*

"Of course a few people have been especially impressive so far," Blake conceded.

"If you had to name four who you think have the best chance of winning, who would you say?" Vanessa's piercing gaze reminded Blake of a predator judging the right moment to snatch its prey.

Blake shook her head. "There's every chance the four best now aren't going to be the four best by the end."

"For the sake of argument, tell us who you think the best four are now, then."

She considered for a minute, her head bowed so that their watchful faces wouldn't distract her. "Ray Fisher is working hard on every assignment. Vin Guevara is brilliant. Eve Womack is both." After hesitating a moment, she finished, "Gabby Truitt never seems to be exerting herself or thinking outside the box, but somehow she keeps coming up with the goods. So, those are the four who've done the best so far."

Vanessa and Jerome exchanged happy grins. "That's good, your thoughts are similar to ours. And Jerome and I are thinking that Gabby should win."

Blake stood up straight, taken by surprise. "Why?"

"As you say, she comes up with the goods for every assignment. She's also got charisma, and the others don't." Vanessa folded her arms across her chest. Almost behind her, Jerome nodded agreement.

"I also said that may change by the end of the competition. Starting a business is a lot of hard work. It takes months of planning and preparations to do it well. These contestants have only twelve weeks. Some are going to burn out before the end, watch and see."

"Maybe you should give Gabby a little extra help if she needs it, to make sure she wins."

"Absolutely not." Blake slung her purse over her shoulder. "The winner will be the person who has most earned it. Now, if you'll excuse me, I need to go for the night."

Blake marched out of her office with Antonio close behind her. *Why can't I just have a good day anymore? For every good thing that happens, lately, at least two bad things happen.*

Antonio glanced at Blake's face as they waited for their taxi back to the apartment to arrive. "Should I call Suki and warn her you're in the mood to kick the shit out of somebody?"

She made a face. "Please don't. When Suki thinks I'm in a bad mood, she works me until I hurt all over for a week."

***

As if her thoughts were a premonition, Blake entered her apartment to find two men in black suits sitting on her sofa, waiting for her. Suki sat in one of the recliners, dressed for jujitsu, staring at the visitors. "Hi, Boss," said Suki, when Blake stood in the doorway. "These two guys from the FBI want to talk to you."

"Oh, hell. What can it be this time?" Blake flung her purse down by the door and stood by the giant flat-screen TV, her gaze locked with those of the agents.

The agents looked at each other for a moment. What that accomplished, Blake couldn't guess, because they were both wearing shades. Both turned their heads to look at her again, in perfect unison, and the slightly taller one said, "Ma'am, is it possible we could talk to you in private?"

"It's possible," Suki answered for Blake. "But it won't happen. We're here to protect Blake Bertrand. Even from the FBI, if you try to hurt her."

They looked at each other again as Antonio moved to stand between Blake and the agents. The taller one spoke. "Let's just be direct, then. Ms. Bertrand, Miami police have requested FBI assistance in investigating the fire that burned down your Cuban restaurant. Do you have any idea why?"

"No. And I don't know why you'd want to talk to me about it, anyway. My attorney already proved I was airborne when the fire started, and that I haven't made any financial transactions that could be payment to an arsonist." She eyed the recliner that stood empty, weary and wondering if she'd somehow be at a disadvantage if she sat down.

"Your Cuban restaurant was engaged in money laundering for the Mafia," said the shorter agent.

Blake's legs felt rubbery all of a sudden. She leaned against the wall. "I don't have anything to do with the Mafia!"

"Well, ma'am, I'm afraid that's just not true." The shorter agent crossed his legs and studied her through his shades. "Our investigation already shows that a number of properties purchased and maintained by you and your ex-husband laundered money for the Mafia."

"It must have been Lang's doing." Blake didn't resist as Antonio helped her into the empty recliner. He then positioned himself behind her. She felt a wild urge to giggle as she imagined Antonio and his Ray-Bans having a staring match with the FBI agents in their shades.

"Can you prove you had nothing to do with it?" inquired the taller agent.

"I thought the burden of proof is on the prosecution, because the defense is innocent until proven guilty," countered Suki.

The agents shot shaded looks at Suki, in unison, and again Blake felt a crazed need to giggle. She bowed her head over her knees and clamped her hands over her face to stifle the impulse.

"That's true, ma'am, but even early in the investigation the evidence isn't looking good for your employer, here."

"Well, Boss will just have to hope her attorney can call your evidence into question. And yes, she does have an attorney, so maybe you should speak with him." Suki continued staring at them, her expression cold and unmoved as a statue's. Being without shades clearly didn't faze her.

"May we have your attorney's name and number, Ms. Bertrand?" The taller agent pulled an ink pen and a mini notepad out of his jacket pocket and waited to make notes of the information.

Blake consulted her BlackBerry for the contact info of Enrico Torres, and the agent dutifully scribbled the name and number. The agent then read them back to her to confirm he'd got everything correct. He tucked pen and pad away, stood, and said, "I'm sure we'll talk again soon."

The shorter agent stood, too, and threw up a salute at Blake as he followed his partner out of the apartment. Blake stared at her BlackBerry, her stomach caught in the grip of an icy fist. "I guess I'd better call my attorney, too."

She dialed Torres's number and wished her life was a nightmare she could wake up from.

Chapter Thirty-One

June 23
New York, New York

In the morning Blake found herself all over the news. There was the announcement of her charity's first program. With the success of her launch, she decided to add a local grant program for Black female college grads who wanted to start their own businesses. Along with this good news, unfortunately, there was also a disclosure that Blake Bertrand and her ex-husband, Lang Bertrand, were being investigated by the FBI for alleged Mafia dealings.

Before she even arrived at the NBC studio for the day's work on *The Takeover*, her BlackBerry rang with the caller ID showing that J-Lo wanted to talk to her. She took a deep breath and pressed the Talk button.

"Good morning, this is Blake Bertrand speaking."

"Hi, Blake, Jennifer's publicist here." There was a brief silence, filled with an awkwardness that hurt Blake's ear worse than a scream. "Uh, first, congratulations on all the money you raised for charity yesterday."

"I couldn't have done it without you and Jen. Jennifer's work as spokeswoman has been superb, and donating some of her time for auction was a tremendous help too."

"Yeah. About that... Listen, I know you're having a rough time, but I've got to know. This stuff about you working for the Mafia, is it true?"

"No. I give you my word, that's got to be something Lang was doing in secret. This crap is as much a surprise to me as it is to everyone else."

There was silence again for a moment or two, and then the publicist said, "Okay. I believe you, Blake. We'll stick with you...unless it gets so bad we're in danger of going down with you. I hope you understand."

"Of course." Her call waiting beeped, and Blake said, "Thanks for asking me before deciding what to do. I'd better take this call, though, it may be my attorney."

"Sure. Good luck." The publicist clicked off.

Much to Blake's astonishment, caller ID said her next caller was Kenton Rhodes. She pressed Talk and said, "This is Blake."

"Hi, Kenton Rhodes here. I'd say good morning, but I have a feeling it isn't."

She gave voice to a mirthless laugh. "You're so right about that."

"I'm calling to let you know that Torres and I discussed the new development last night. You see, usually when our firm has a case that's going through the federal courts instead of Florida's, I'm the attorney who handles it. But I can't represent you, because... Well, you know why, I hope."

"Yeah. I get it." Blake felt stinging tears welling up in her eyes. "Thanks for letting me know. I'll start looking for a new attorney."

"Wait! I wasn't done yet." Kenton talked faster. "I'm going to call a good friend of mine from law school. She's one of Florida's best federal criminal defense attorneys. I'll ask her to partner with Torres on representing you." He hesitated and added, "If that's okay with you, that is."

"Oh, Kenton, it's more than okay! I don't know how I'll ever be able to thank you enough for this." A tear spilled from her right eye as the taxi stopped at the NBC studio, but now it was a warm and gentle tear of relief.

"I'm glad to help. Listen, I've got to get going, and I'm sure you do too, but I'll be sending you something later. It's a little video of Lionel that I made last night. He's putting together a jazz rock band, and they sound really good."

Blake smiled. "I can't wait to see it. Thanks, Kenton."

"My pleasure. Keep your chin up." He clicked off, and Blake went into the studio actually feeling like her luck was turning around at last.

***

That feeling was reinforced during her lunch break, when Blake finally looked to see who the winner of the auction for an afternoon with her turned out to be. It was the person who'd chosen to bid anonymously, but now that the auction had ended, the bidder's identity was revealed: Her afternoon would be spent with Tanaya Steele, a singer and actress who was a current sensation on the pop charts, heartbroken by her father's death, and desperately needing something that brought pleasure to her life. Tanaya's feel-good music had certainly done that. But it had definitely been a while since she indulged in anything but jazz.

"I can't believe my luck," Blake confided to Antonio. "Tanaya Steele just paid $72,000 to spend an afternoon with me! I'd pay that much to spend an afternoon with her!"

Antonio lowered his Ray-Bans. "You might want to call her and schedule the meeting. She's waited all night and all morning to hear from you, already."

"Jesus, you're right." Blake tried to tap Tanaya Steele's phone number into her BlackBerry, but her fingers were trembling with excitement. "Here, could you put the number in for me as I read it out?"

Antonio dialed the number for her, and as he handed the BlackBerry back to Blake, she heard Tanaya Steele's unmistakable voice say, "Tanaya Steele talkin', but who am I talkin' to?"

Blake swallowed hard and managed, "Tanaya Steele, this is Blake Bertrand. Is this a good time to schedule our afternoon?"

"You bet it is! I'm between jobs for the next couple of weeks, so girl, just choose a day and time and place. I'll be there."

Thinking fast, Blake realized the current week was filled with too many obligations. "Next week sometime? Except for Wednesday, name your preference and I can make it happen."

"How about Friday? I'm hoping you'll feel like dinner when the afternoon ends."

"Sounds good! What would you like to do?"

"Let's go shopping. This is the only chance I'll ever get to buy clothes with one of the world's most beautiful women to give me advice."

"You flatter me, but you're on. Saks Fifth Avenue to start with sound okay to you? About one o'clock?"

"Girl, it's a date. I'll see you there and then!"

Blake pressed End Call, feeling giddy. *Shopping and dinner with Tanaya Steele! Things really are finally getting better for me!*

***

June 26
New York, New York

Wednesday she'd eliminated Nathan Moore from competition in The Takeover, and she'd hustled to do all the mentoring sessions with the remaining nine contestants by noon Friday. At two o'clock she was due to attend the first post-launch board of directors meeting of Mentors & Protégés. She and Antonio ate take-away seafood pad thai from Red Egg for lunch, Blake reviewing her notes for the meeting and Antonio watching the people in Times Square.

"Hey, Blake. Sorry to interrupt, but I've been wondering something."

She looked up from the Docs2Go file she'd been studying on her BlackBerry. "What's that?"

Antonio's eyes were unreadable behind his Ray-Bans. "Have you seen or heard anything out of Brett Skeet this week?"

Blake shook her head. "No, only that he's called out sick every day."

"That's odd." Antonio finished off his meal and tossed the empty carton in a nearby street corner garbage can.

"You think so? I figured he's just working some new scam and can't be bothered to show up for errand-boy wages."

Shaking his head, Antonio said, "Not like his type. Con artists who've found a better gig either quit a low-paying job or do a disappearing act. They don't keep calling in sick unless they're trying to hang onto the job until something better comes along."

"Well, he'd better be at work Monday or have a doctor call to confirm he's not able to come to work yet. NBC won't hold his job open forever. Just too many other people who'd be glad to get it."

Blake finished her lunch, tossed her empty carton in the garbage, and she and Antonio walked to the hotel room where she'd rented a conference room for the meeting. Thomas Mills sat at the conference table, Robin Love by his side. He beckoned Blake to him as soon as she entered the room, and she forced herself not to smile.

"Since we have a few minutes before the meeting starts, I just thought I'd ask," Thomas said. "Have you got a plan to make the Wishman Spears profitable in a year?"

For answer, Blake dropped a thick manila envelope on the table in front of Thomas with a thunk that echoed in the room. "All the details are there, plus six months' worth of advance booking requests for when it's open for business. I sent copies to the other investment partners yesterday by overnight mail. You can spend the weekend discussing among yourselves."

"Hi, Blake," said Robin.

"Weird acoustics in this room," said Blake. "Sometimes it's like you hear someone talking when there's nobody there."

Robin bit her lip to keep from crying as Blake began speaking to the board of directors. Blake felt a pang of remorse, but she told herself, *I told her to stay away from Margot's husband. She made her choice, and she can live with the consequences.*

***

After the meeting ended, Blake found two voicemails waiting for her: one from her bank and one from attorney Enrico Torres. She entered her password to listen to the message, wondering what it could be about. *My bank never calls me. They just email me.*

"Ms. Bertrand, we regret to inform you that the FBI has requested that a hold be placed on all transactions you request, until further notice. If you need more information, please call back at—"

She almost dropped the BlackBerry in her haste to close that message and listen to the one from Torres. "Hi, Blake, Rico Torres here. I'm sorry to tell you this, but this morning my partner on your FBI case tried to deposit the retainer check you mailed to her. Her bank informed her that there's a freeze on all your accounts and assets—"

"Fucking hell."

One week of good luck, and now there's line of people waiting their turn to screw me over. Again. When will this shit ever end?

Chapter Thirty-Two

June 27
New York, New York

Blake sat at her desk after breakfast, her wallet removed from her purse, counting her cash. She'd always kept a few thousand dollars in currency handy, just in case of emergencies. Not enough to pay the next month's rent for her New York penthouse apartment, though. Only six thousand dollars stood between Blake Bertrand and a homeless shelter.

In New York, six thousand dollars didn't last long at all. Blake had felt helpless before, but never about money.

Antonio knocked on her door, although it was standing open. She looked up and asked, "Hi, Antonio, what's up?"

"I just talked to Blitz Security. You've been a great customer, so they'll let you run a tab for a month while you try to straighten out the FBI."

"Well, a month isn't long, but at least it's something." She stared at the wad of Benjamins in her hand and murmured, "It's looking like that month may be spent sharing a cardboard box in an alley. That's my biggest worry, just now."

"You've got some rich and famous friends. Why not ask for some help?"

"I'd sooner take a dive off the veranda."

"That's foolish, Ms. Bertrand. Most people in this country are just living from one week to the next, one paycheck to the next. Do you think they never ask for help?" He shook his head. "Here you've started a charity, and you don't even know the meaning of the word."

Antonio turned around and walked away, leaving Blake lost in thought. *Jesus, he's right. There are places in the world where I could live for years on six thousand dollars. Hell, there are places in this country where I'd be good for a few months. Worrying about how to pay rent is new to me, but it's how most people live.* For a while, she had no idea how long, she sat gawking at her handful of cash as if it were a revelation...which she supposed it was. *Nobody should ever be in serious danger of homelessness. Why do we let this shit happen?*

Finally she picked up her BlackBerry and speed-dialed Uncle Thorne. *I've got to get myself out of this mess first. Then I can work on changing things.* When Uncle Thorne answered with a sleepy "Heyyyy, Blake," she began explaining.

***

July 1
New York, New York

Thanks to Western Union and Uncle Thorne, Blake had enough money for rent, food, and taxis for July and August. Her six-month lease expired then, and her own and her mother's Fisher Island condos were prepaid through the end of the year. No, her life was not ideal, but at least she no longer faced homelessness. Too many other Americans couldn't say the same...as she now realized.

Brett Skeet had returned to work on Monday, both eyes a vomit-colored mix of yellows and greens and his right arm in a sling. Someone had obviously given him one hell of a beating. Blake knew how that felt, thanks to Lang. In spite of everything, she wanted to tell Brett that he had her sympathy, even share tips she'd learned for relieving pain and speeding healing. Regretfully, she reached the conclusion that she couldn't risk feeling so much pity for him that she gave him access to her again. So, although it took all her willpower to resist, she didn't speak to him.

However, after filming of the fourth elimination on Wednesday, in which Blake told Miguel Lopez to punch out the clock, Vanessa and Jerome requested a private meeting with her. As soon as the door to Vanessa's office was shut, Blake warned them, "If you're repeating your suggestion that I plan for Gabby Truitt to win, I'm still determined to award the win to whoever deserves it most."

"No, no, that's not it at all!" In spite of his protest, Jerome seemed to be trying to melt into his chair.

"We just wanted to give you a heads-up about Brett Skeet," explained Vanessa. "First he was absent all week, last week. Maybe it's not his fault someone obviously beat the shit out of him, but still without him we were short-staffed. Yesterday, though, he did something unforgivable. We're firing him this afternoon. You asked us to give him a job, so we thought you'd like to know we can't keep him anymore, and why."

Blake bowed her head, consumed by pity for Brett and angry at herself for feeling that way. "What did he do yesterday?"

Jerome leaned closer to her and whispered, "He told an advertising rep to go fuck himself."

"Not just any advertiser, either. One of the top companies buying ad time during broadcast of *The Takeover*," clarified Vanessa.

"FedEx," Jerome added.

She ran a hand through her hair, needing the release of frustration. "I appreciate the warning. But maybe I should tell him, since I'm the reason he's been working here at all."

Vanessa and Jerome exchanged glances, giving the idea consideration. Finally Vanessa said, "Yes, do that. I don't mind being spared the hassle, that's for sure."

Blake nodded, got to her feet, and with Antonio following her, she left Vanessa's office in search of Brett. She found him in the studio break room, sharing a table with Gabby Truitt. That startled Blake for a moment, but even more surprising was that Brett was eating what appeared to be a peanut butter and jelly sandwich. *He's economizing. Shit, this is going to suck elephant turds.*

She stood in the doorway and waited for Brett and Gabby to notice her presence. They were whispering to each other, but Blake couldn't make out any of the words. She wished Suki were there. The martial artist had such keen ears. They seemed supernatural.

"Hi, Brett. I need to talk to you." She tried to look him in the eyes, but she just couldn't do it. "Will you come to my office when you're done with your sandwich?"

"I can talk now." Brett popped the last bite into his mouth and followed Blake and Antonio into Blake's office.

Blake shut her eyes and took a couple of deep breaths, bracing herself. She wasn't braced yet when Brett asked, "Am I fired?"

"I know the timing couldn't be worse, and I'm so sorry about that. But, yeah, Vanessa said something happened yesterday, and this was her decision."

"Thank God!" Brett stood with an ear-to-ear grin on his face.

Blake wondered if she'd been slipped a hallucinogen somehow. "What?"

"This is exactly what I wanted," Brett explained, hesitating at Blake's office door.

"I don't understand—" Blake started, but Brett interrupted.

"Watch out for Lang, Blake. He's doing everything he can think of to fuck you up." Brett pointed to his slowly healing black eyes. "I disappointed him when I didn't bring him video of us having sex."

"Oh. Jesus." Blake's mind was a whirling chaotic mess. "How—"

Brett interrupted again. "I need to vanish for a while, but I've heard him talking to some people. So trust me just this one last time, Blake, and have some kind of expert take a look at your accountant's books. If they do it right, you should have Lang by the balls."

He opened the door and sprinted out of the studio. Blake had to run to catch up with him. "Wait, Brett!"

Bouncing on his toes, Brett stopped, but he kept nervously looking around. "I really need to go, Blake."

She took a thousand dollars out of her wallet and handed it to him. "I'm trusting you one last time."

He flipped a wave at her and got lost in the crowded downtown streets. Blake turned to go back to the studio and found Antonio watching her.

"Was I an idiot just now?" Blake tucked her wallet back into her purse, stomach churning as she awaited the insightful bodyguard's answer.

"No." Antonio swept his Ray-Bans off so she could see the sincerity in his eyes. "That dude doesn't tell the truth often, but this was one of the times he did."

"I wonder how I can afford an expert to look at my accountant's books." Blake puzzled over that as she returned to her office and waited for her first mentoring session of the week to begin.

***

July 3
New York, New York

Saks Fifth Avenue occupied a whole city block across from the Rockefeller Center and stood a proud ten stories high, with flags mounted by many of the windows. Blake always thought its exterior looked deceptively like an office building.

Inside, however, was a whole other world of opulence. Which, for the first time in her adult life, Blake could not afford.

Tanaya Steele stood near the information booth on the Fiftieth Street side of the ground floor. Blake almost didn't recognize her as the pop diva darling she was known for, because Tanaya was dressed in jeans, casual blouse, sneakers, and an Italian silk scarf wrapped elegantly around her head. She looked, in other words, like a middle-class woman ready for a once-in-a-lifetime shopping splurge in one of the world's most famous department stores.

"Hey, girl, you look fabulous as always!" Tanaya threw her arms around Blake in an enthusiastic greeting.

Blake returned the hug with equal enthusiasm, but felt obligated to be honest immediately. "Thanks, but the way things have been going lately, I can't afford to spend much money today. In fact"—she eyed her Gucci clothes and shook her head—"I may have to sell off my whole wardrobe to keep myself in groceries soon."

"I've heard about all the shit happening to you. It's criminal the way everybody is doing you lately, Blake, but you gotta keep your head up. The best revenge is keeping your dignity intact." Tanaya clasped Blake's hand and led her through the ground floor's maze of cosmetics salespeople and perfume spritzers. Suki actually had to walk fast to keep up with them. "Today, just forget all that, and if you want anything, I'll be glad to get it for you."

"I couldn't—"

"Stop me? No, you couldn't. Glad you know it." Tanaya threw a wink over her shoulder at Blake.

For the next three hours they explored every one of the ten floors of Saks, and soon Tanaya decreed a rule: anything wearable that either of them looked at longer than five seconds must be tried on. Blake found herself remembering her modeling days, when she and Robin and a few other girls who enjoyed each other's company used to spend time off together shopping for bargain-but-stylish clothes, furniture, even groceries. She'd forgotten how much fun it was to be with another woman.

That thought brought back other memories that made Blake blush. She moved behind a packed rack of blouses and hoped Tanaya didn't notice Blake's red face and wonder what Blake could be thinking.

When Tanaya suggested they go browse the lingerie boutique two blocks farther down Fifth Avenue, Blake eyed her bag of Saks goodies that Tanaya had bought for her and shook her head. "Let's do something else. Please. I'm afraid you'd spend more money on me, and I don't even have anybody to wear lingerie for."

"Now we've got to go there, Blake. It's when you're single that you ought to get new lingerie. You got to love yourself, so other folks can see you're worth loving." Tanaya hooked an arm through Blake's and escorted her out of Saks and down the street. Suki followed them, blank-faced as always.

Two hours later Blake was the proud new owner of an Agent Provocateur bathrobe made entirely of white lace, a diaphanous rose pink silk bra, and knickers hand-crafted by Carine Gilson. Tanaya had treated herself to an elegant jade-green-and-black silk kimono and feathery lace bra and thong. "Talk about loving yourself," Tanaya said as the cashier bagged Blake's sexy new garments. "If you don't love yourself in those, you just can't love at all!"

Blake blushed again, with nowhere to hide. Tanaya chuckled and clapped Blake's shoulder. "Come on, five hours of shopping has got me a little hungry and a lot thirsty. Let's go hit someplace with a good bar."

"I don't have a preference." Blake thought how that statement could be interpreted, and blushed hotter than ever.

"I'll take you to Otto's pizzeria. That's my favorite place to go unrecognized and drink great wine and eat great pizza." Tanaya beckoned Blake to follow her, and hailed a passing cab.

Within an hour, they were seated at a table in a cheery Italian restaurant, drinking a red wine that cost $200 per bottle. Blake had a potent buzz by the time the waiter delivered their pizza, topped with asparagus and goat cheese. She'd trusted Tanaya's recommendation, and she didn't regret it. This was the most delicious pizza she'd eaten in her whole life, and it saddened her to think that probably nothing like it could be found in Miami.

About nine o'clock in the evening, Tanaya refilled their wineglasses and said, "I've had a wonderful time today, Blake. You're worth every penny I paid to meet you."

"Thanks." Blake smiled, and didn't know what else to say. Drunk and getting sleepy, her shyness of being with someone like Tanaya was coming back.

"I don't really want it to end. Why don't we get a hotel room and have a sleepover? It will be like we're a couple of teenage girls. We can try on clothes and drink and snack and stay up all night if we feel like it."

Blake chuckled. She had never done a sleepover like most teenage girls. "I don't know about staying up all night—I'm half asleep already from all the wine. But it sounds fun."

"Well, all right then, I'll call for a room." Tanaya took out her phone and dialed information, requested transfer to her favorite hotel in Manhattan, and arranged for a room to be waiting for them.

Suki halted outside the hotel room and said, "Enjoy the sleepover, Boss. If you need me, I'll be in the hallway."

"Aren't you joining us?" Blake wished she'd thought to ask Tanaya for a second room, for Suki.

"No, I'll just call Matt and tell him he's taking my shift tomorrow because I'm taking his tonight. Third-shift bodyguards are used to entertaining themselves while the boss sleeps." Suki shrugged and seated herself cross-legged by the hotel room door.

Drunk as she was, at first Blake wasn't sure what seemed strange about the hotel room. It was luxurious, as everything about her day with Tanaya had been. Thick carpet was gentle on her feet, which ached from walking around all day. A basket of gourmet chocolates, cheeses, and crackers awaited them, along with a bucket of chilled champagne. In the bathroom was a hot tub as well as shower, and the towels and washcloths were decadently soft.

And there was only one bed, she finally realized as she sat on it to kick off her shoes. Tanaya sat next to her and said, "Why don't we show off our new clothes for each other?"

Blake's heart raced. She met Tanaya's eyes and asked, "Even the lingerie?"

"Especially the lingerie," answered Tanaya, and she cupped Blake's face in her cool, dark, neatly manicured hands and touched her lips to Blake's.

For a moment Blake didn't respond, shocked into paralysis. Memories of fooling around with other models in her younger years filled her head. That had been fun, undeniably, but also...unfulfilling. She'd always thought that meant she was purely heterosexual.

Now, as Tanaya traced Blake's lips with the tip of her warm, wet tongue, all the nerve endings in Blake's nipples and that magic spot between her legs shrieked for more, More, MORE. She grabbed Tanaya's hips and caught her idol's tongue with her own, and moaned ecstatically when Tanaya dropped her hands to Blake's breasts and circled her thumbs around Blake's nipples.

"Have you ever been with a woman before?" purred Tanaya, beginning to slide Blake's blouse off.

"When I was a model some of the girls and I played around," Blake whispered, shivering a little as the air conditioning touched her chest and back, bare except for a bra that Tanaya was already unhooking. "It wasn't like...*this.*" At the last word, Tanaya whisked Blake's bra off and gave her left nipple a suckling kiss.

"Oh yeah? Why not?" Tanaya turned her attention to Blake's right nipple, and the love button between Blake's legs got hard and sore with need.

"We didn't know what we were doing," Blake gasped.

Tanaya raised her eyes to Blake's and gave a hushed laugh. And then she laid Blake back on the fluffy covers and pressed her breasts together and sucked both nipples at once, hard—at the same time her hand brushed Blake's hot zone.

Blake hoped third-shift bodyguards were used to listening to their boss scream.

***

She awakened to Suki standing over her, looking embarrassed. "I'm sorry, Boss. When she left just now, I thought you must be up and ready to go."

"What?" Blake sat up, realized she was naked, and pulled the covers up to her neck. "Tanaya is gone?"

Suki nodded, then mumbled, "Uh, you want to sleep some more?"

A sadness filled Blake's chest, so overfull she thought her heart was trying to burst. "No. I'll get dressed."

Going through the clothes Tanaya bought for her when she was back in her penthouse apartment, Blake found a note from Tanaya scribbled on hotel stationery: "Fun day and fun sleepover! Wishing you best of luck, Blake. –Tanaya"

Love 'em and leave 'em—not just for men anymore, Blake thought, and smiled.

Chapter Thirty-Three

July 5
New York, New York

While the rest of the country had celebrated Independence Day on Saturday, Blake spent the day listening to jazz records on her turntable and drinking Jack and Coke. Before night she'd fallen asleep on her bed, at least twice as drunk as the night before and lost in a melancholy she felt through to the core of her bones.

Sunday morning she was awakened by a hammering on the apartment door echoed by the hammering in her head. *Matt or one of the others will handle it*, she promised herself, and pulled the covers over her head to try to mute the noise.

It was a futile effort. As soon as the knocking stopped, the voice of Margot Mills lifted in a shout that bounced around in the apartment walls and Blake's skull. "Blake Bertrand! I haven't slept in two nights and it's your fault, so you'd better get your ass out of bed and talk to me!"

Blake added the pillow to the padding protecting her ears from the cruel world outside. That, too, was in vain. Margot yanked the pillow away in one direction and the covers in another.

"You know I'm old enough to be your mother, and right now I'm tempted to whip your butt," Margot said, much too loud. Blake could've sworn her best friend's words were nails she was banging into Blake's head.

"Go away," Blake moaned, reaching for her other pillow.

"Oh, no you don't." Margot raced around the bed and snatched away the second pillow, as well. "Now, just you sit up and listen to me."

Blake looked at Antonio and Matt, standing in her doorway and watching the performance with matching grins. "Make her stop."

"No, ma'am," said Matt. "I never tangle with a woman in a

mood like that."

"Me neither," agreed Antonio.

"Why did I have to hear from your Uncle Thorne that you've got no money?" Margot dumped pillows and covers in a heap on the floor and glared at Blake, her hands on her hips.

"I thought you were in the hospital." Blake's thoughts crawled through a swampland of hangover, and after a time she remembered and added, "And I thought you might hate me."

"You saved my life." Margot's face softened and she sat at Blake's feet and reached for Blake's nearer hand. "I was angry at you. Hell, I was angry at the whole world. But I could never hate you, Blake."

Blake shook her head and mumbled, "Even if I thought we were okay, you've got your own troubles to deal with."

"And you have troubles you can't deal with alone." Margot squeezed Blake's hand. "Besides, since getting out of the hospital Wednesday, I've been fine. I've even filed for divorce. When Edith told me you've laid off everyone who worked for you, I thought I'd have a heart attack."

"I would have welcomed one when the FBI froze all my assets." Blake stared at her bare knees. Her legs needed shaving in the worst way, and she wondered if she could do it when she felt like someone had beat her from head to toe with a baseball bat.

"Well, they're going to have to unfreeze them, because I know my Blake wouldn't screw around with the Mafia." Margot gave Blake's hand another squeeze, then released it to shrug her purse off her shoulder. "Now, first, how much do you need for rent?"

"Uncle Thorne sent me some money. I'm okay."

"Define okay."

"I've got the rent for this place paid until the lease expires. I can eat, as long as it's nothing fancy. I already have a ticket back to Miami and a moving company hired to take all my stuff back to Fisher Island. Mom and I have our condos paid through December."

"You didn't say anything about an attorney. Or your mom's nurses and physical therapy. Or maybe even a detective to prove you're innocent."

"Uncle Thorne couldn't afford all that."

"Well, honey, Thomas owes me half of all the millions he's earned during our marriage. I can afford all that and more."

Margot took out her checkbook and poised a pen over it. "Name an amount, or I'll just guess."

***

August 18
New York, New York

Weeks passed. Much happened in that time, and yet time seemed to crawl.

One week at a time, Blake eliminated six more contestants from *The Takeover*: Sierra Willis, Chase Painter, Eric Schroeder, Vin Guevara, Danny Sun, and Ray Fisher each in turn punched out the clock. Each week, Vanessa and Jerome urged Blake to name Gabby Truitt as the winner at the show's end. Barbara Santers contacted Blake, asking her to appear on *The Scene* the day after broadcast of the final episode of *The Takeover*, so that Santers could make a one-time return to the show to interview Blake. It was Blake's pleasure to say yes to the invitation, because it meant a lifelong dream would actually come true.

Kenton Rhodes sent Blake at least one video per week of Lionel's jazz band rehearsing, and shared with her the boy's desire to start performing in public venues and Kenton's reluctance to let him begin living the show business life so young. Blake didn't share with Kenton how each video made her heart ache to be a mother to her son, and how each conversation made her yearn to feel Kenton's arms around her again.

Acting on the tip Brett Skeet had given her, attorney Enrico Torres and his consulting partner Stephanie Chesser hired a forensic accountant to examine the copy of the Bertrand bookkeeping that Blake got as part of her divorce. Within a few days of being hired, the forensic accountant reported that the Bertrand books were "cooked to a crisp." He added that an expert could easily decipher how Lang had concealed his work for the Mafia from Blake throughout their marriage, including paying their shared accountant to keep an accurate set of records for Lang and present carefully doctored records to Blake. Torres and Chesser provided a partial copy of the forensic accountant's final report to the FBI, who promised to do as requested and announce a formal public declaration that Blake Bertrand was no longer suspected of any wrongdoing.

She was still waiting for that, and for the rest of her money to be taken off hold. Meanwhile, she had only this last week of filming, and then she could prepare for her move back to Miami. She wasn't sorry that she'd be leaving New York. Miami was home, where her courageous mother Jacinta no longer needed a cane to climb stairs or walk long distances, where Margot was building a new life, where her son Lionel was growing up fast, and where Kenton loved her in her dreams and in the waking world had just declared himself a candidate for the U.S. House of Representatives.

On this Tuesday afternoon, Blake sat in a meeting with Vanessa, Jerome, and some NBC executives and representatives of major advertisers, comparing how Gabby Truitt and Eve Womack had performed on the final challenge of *The Takeover*. "*Entertainment Weekly, Wall Street Journal*, and *TMZ* have all predicted Gabby to win," observed one of the advertising reps.

"They should fire their fortune tellers," Blake replied. "Gabby hasn't earned the win."

"How can you say that? Their final projects were equally well done," Vanessa protested.

"In some other universe, maybe, but not in this one." Blake sat up straight and met each person's gaze in turn. "Eve's marketing strategy for her pediatric recreation center is simply brilliant. She made a TV commercial that moves viewers to both tears and laughter, and her proposal to hospital management makes such a good argument for the business value of adding a pediatric rec center that I can't imagine anyone saying no to her. Gabby's TV commercial is cute but a half hour later viewers can't tell you the name of her company, and her proposal to movie studios doesn't really convince me that they should use her production company rather than anyone else's."

"Viewers consistently rate Gabby higher for likability than Eve," Jerome mentioned, and then withdrew inside his shell.

"I suppose that would be paramount in importance, if they both wanted to live their lives on film stages. This show is about who's the most promising entrepreneur. Or at least, that's what I was told when I was asked to host it. I never would have agreed to do this if I'd been told it's only about who viewers would rather go out for drinks with."

Nobody spoke. Blake nodded, more to herself than anyone else. "Tomorrow I declare Eve Womack winner of *The Takeover*. I suggest you all get used to the idea." She stood, as did Antonio, and since it was then half past four o'clock, she returned to her apartment early.

***

Lights. Cameras. Action:

Seated at the long conference table on the set of *The Takeover*, Blake faced Gabby Truitt and Eve Womack for the last time. Both women were jittery with anticipation, Eve frequently flexing her hands and Gabby bouncing one foot on the floor at rapid speed.

"As always, your work on this challenge was reviewed by experts. In this case, professional marketing agencies rated your promotional strategies and materials by the same criteria they use for their own employees. They also brought in test viewers for your TV commercials, and panels whose members were recruited from the professions you'd need to sell your business to in competition with rival businesses. You were both considered to have done good work."

Blake stood before she said, "In business, being good isn't enough. You've got to convince the world you're the best."

She moved to stand by the plush clock, and looked back at the two anxious women still sitting at the table. "Two-thirds of the marketing agencies, test viewers, and panels of professionals agreed on one of you as the winner. And I agree with their reasoning. So...Gabby Truitt, punch out the clock. Eve Womack, congratulations on being the first winner of The Takeover."

Melodrama:

"This is a joke, right?" Gabby continued to sit at the table, looking around with a dazed expression on her face. Meanwhile, Eve's family and significant other rushed onto the stage to hug and cheer for her.

Nobody replied to her, so Gabby shouted, "I was promised I'd win!"

Vanessa flapped an urgent hand at the director, who motioned the cameraman to cut the recording. "Now, Gabby, we talked about this—"

"You Promised!" Gabby burst into a flood of tears and choking sobs, and ran off the stage.

Blake felt a knot rise in her throat. She marched toward Vanessa and demanded, "Was she telling the truth? Did you promise her she'd win?"

"We thought we could persuade you," said Jerome, behind Vanessa. He cowered as Vanessa whirled around and leveled a piercing glare at him.

"So this is reality TV," Blake said, looking at another camera that appeared to be still recording. "But whose reality is it?"

She walked off the stage and tried to find Gabby, Matt following her. But Gabby and Lang were nowhere to be found.

Chapter Thirty-Four

August 20
New York, New York

The next day Blake made it on the cover of the local New York City newspaper again. This time it was all about a secret she wanted to keep. One that she had planned to hold near and dear until the time was right, or at least until the dust had settled with her financial and legal drama. "Blake A Flake? Secret Son." She kept her eyes glued to the page as she absorbed every icky, sticky line of lies.

Well, I'll be damned, Blake said to herself. She slammed the paper down in her lap. She was in the car on her way to the airport to catch a plane back to Miami. It took every bit of strength she had not to tell the driver to turn back around. She couldn't leave this mess behind in New York. She picked up the phone.

"Vickie, what the hell is going on? Why didn't you call or even warn me about this hot-ass mess on the cover of the *Daily News!?* I pay you good money to keep me informed and keep shit like this off the radar—"

As Blake belted into Vickie, she noticed Vickie didn't have much to say at all.

"Vickie? You have no right to be speechless right now. You can't be more shocked than I am," Blake said, totally bewildered. Then her stomach sank. "Did you leak this? Did you sell me out?"

"Blake," Vickie finally said with a sigh. "I did it for your own good. Your brand and name are going down. I'm sorry. This gives you a chance to control the story, tell your side. You can be the mom who makes it right, and repent for your sins. Tons of women will support you. After all, you were raped, and a victim of domestic violence."

Blake put the phone down, took a deep breath, and brought it back to her ears. She still hadn't responded to Vickie. She had no idea how much Vickie knew, but she knew far more than she had let on. *But how?* Blake wondered.

She picked the phone back up. "You're fired," Blake said, coolly, and hung up.

Now, she was left to pick up the pieces. "Driver, please go faster, I don't want to miss my plane," Blake said as she slipped her shades back on. Then she thought about Lionel.

On the flight, it dawned on her that maybe she did need to take control and leave her fate out of others' hands. Everyone had made a decision or *tried* to make a decision for her, from Vanessa to Vickie, and she wasn't having it anymore. Let the shit hit the fan, she thought. It was about time she shed any and all drama, and started again.

***

August 21
Miami, Florida

While in Miami, she made another major decision. She let Suki and Antonio go. It wasn't easy because she had grown attached, especially to Suki, but there was always a danger in letting people get so close you can't do without them. Blake thought if she was going to be open about her life and face it head on—the good and the bad—she had to do it alone. Blake was at a point where a growing fearlessness was taking over, and she was starting to not give a toot. The only thing she cared about was Lionel and getting back on top.

She also had some business to clean up. Robin. The word in town was that Robin had moved in with Thomas in a condo in Miami Beach. Her plan was to knock some sense into Robin, and hope she could persuade her to leave Thomas. As much as Margot seemed sure to divorce him, she just didn't think it was right that Robin got away with the kit and kaboodle. As long as Robin and Thomas were together, she could never get rid of the guilt she'd carry around, even if Margot had forgiven her.

She sent Robin a text. <Let's meet. 2pm today at Orchid?>

Orchid was a quaint Thai restaurant, discreet and out of the way from prying eyes. Blake held her breath waiting for Robin to respond. She felt a deep desperation to make this work, and thought about even paying Robin. But no, she thought again.

<Will we be alone?> Blake read the text.

<Yes, just want to talk,> Blake texted back.

<K>

Blake took that last text as a yes, and she called Orchid to make the reservation, which was only two hours away. It seemed like an eternity.

***

Blake waited for fifteen minutes until Robin arrived. When she did, it looked like Thomas was sparing no expense to keep her maintained. Prada bag, check. Gucci heels, check. Versace shades and a fitted Chanel dress topped her confident look as she glided into the room. Blake beckoned the waiter to get Robin's attention. Within seconds, Robin was walking toward the table.

"Hey," Robin quipped as she slipped off her shades.

"Hey," Blake said dryly.

"You look nice." Robin half-smiled at Blake. "New York seemed to do you some good. Beautiful Herrera dress. Is that the new Birkin?"

Blake nodded, looking bored. "You almost seemed surprised. You know I always take care of myself despite what you've been hearing."

Robin cleared her throat. "Well, I don't know how bad things really are."

Blake signaled to the waiter, a tall, slender man with short, wispy hair. "Are you ladies ready to order?" he asked.

Blake eyed the menu over once. "I'll just have a glass of wine. Make that two."

Robin held her hand up. "I'll pass on the wine, please. Sparkling water is fine."

Blake gave Robin a one-eyed look. "You pass up alcohol. Free alcohol?"

"Well, what can I say? Thomas has made me into a honest woman."

Blake clenched her teeth. She knew his name was coming up somehow. But she'd wanted to be the one to bring it up. She was the one who called the meeting. "Speaking of..." Blake began. "When is that going to end? You know it will never work, Robin."

Robin pressed her lips together and hissed. "You're just jealous, Blake. All that access, and the best you can do is a bunch of old steel buildings that are worth nothing in this market. You couldn't even keep a man. So don't tell me about what can't work. You obviously have no clue."

Blake raised an eyebrow. She was glad they were in public

because she wanted to pummel her fists into Robin with her pompous, arrogant attitude. Blake knew from years of training in the boardroom how to deal with anxiety-ridden people who wanted to project their feelings of inadequacy on her. So, in her steadiest, calmest tone, she said, "I owe what I have to no one. I know tricks and secrets to survival you can only imagine. I'm what you aspire to be on your best days. I always have been. You took Thomas because you wanted some of this life. And now you got it. Soon, he will leave you. If he can leave a wife after twenty years, you're nothing more than a weekend jaunt." Blake looked at her watch. "And it's Sunday."

Robin looked down at her empty plate. The waiter came just in time with their drinks. Robin sipped hers slowly as she seemingly battled with what to say next.

"So, Robin, why don't we make it easy for everyone. Leave Thomas. I'm sure he will give you a nice allowance. And certainly he won't fight to keep you. Find someone who will actually want to do more than fuck you. You're not his first stray while he's been with Margot, and that makes you anything but special." Blake swirled the wine in her glass as she studied Robin, whose confident swagger suddenly seemed to fade.

"Are you just jealous that if I take one of your most lucrative investors, you'll have to start going through me to get to him?" Robin smirked.

That caught Blake off guard. She was surprised at Robin's remark, but she had a point. Blake wasn't about to let her know it. "I've made Thomas more money in the last five years than he's made in twenty-five years in the business. So leave the big talk for the players. Okay?"

Robin pressed her lips together so hard Blake could see every line around her mouth.

"You can never be me, even if you buy up all of the East Coast, start another charity, or stay with Thomas...it'll never happen." Robin's shoulders slumped. "I don't know why I thought you'd be on my side."

"*Your* side?"

"I was your best friend. Now there's this Margot woman. Thomas is my way of, yes, having the life I was supposed to have. The one you got with *other* people's money—you call *investors*."

"Fuck you, Robin," Blake said in a slow, cool manner.

Robin rolled her eyes. "Thomas is handling that just fine. I'm pregnant."

Blake nearly dropped her drink.

"And it *is* Thomas's," Robin quipped, sitting up straight. "We're moving in together. So much for weekend jaunts. I'll be in his life forever. No matter who likes it or not," Robin said, with an almost juvenile-little-girl tone in her snap back.

Blake stood up and shook her head in pity. "You just have no idea how this life works. When you get to this level nothing, not even a whore with your baby, is going to make you choose her over millions. Thomas will never leave Margot. Even if he does, he will never leave her. In time, you'll know exactly what I mean."

Blake dropped a fifty-dollar bill on the table and adjusted her Birkin bag in the crux of her arm, and left Robin behind.

Chapter Thirty-Five

August 30
Miami, Florida

"So what now? Why did you bother going to New York City? Your business is all out in the street now. Have you ever thought how it would affect Lionel when he becomes a man?" Jacinta asked as they sat on the balcony of her condo.

Blake hadn't told her mother about Kenton yet. It was almost too good to be true, and a tiny part of her still had a hard time believing it. "I met Lionel's adoptive father."

Jacinta glared at Blake. "And you didn't tell me?!"

"I'm telling you now." Blake ran down how she met Kenton while Jacinta kept her ears glued to every word. "He sends me videos of Lionel now. I don't have to sneak around anymore."

Jacinta just shook her head as she took it all in. "Well, how does that man know you're Lionel's mother?"

"Remember, I had an open adoption. I did that so Lionel can be free to contact me when he was ready."

Jacinta's worried eyes grew calmer. "I trust you. If you feel so strongly that this is right, then it may good for you to do. In fact," she said, raising a finger, "I know it is. When can I see him?"

Tears gathered at the corner of Blake's eyes. "I'll arrange for us to go to Kenton's. Not now, but eventually I'll tell the whole story. But for now, I'm telling him I'm his mother and I love him."

***

That night, Blake and her mom visited Kenton and Lionel. Kenton had picked up a few boxes of pizza and fried calamari.

"Where is he?" Blake asked Kenton after making a quick introduction between her mother and him. Jacinta waited in the living room as they spoke.

"He's still upstairs," Kenton said. "I told him he would have an important visitor. Not who, but I think he's expecting something big. He's ready."

Blake stood frozen, her shoulders and neck feeling tight and painful. Almost as if reading her mind, Kenton put both arms around her. He squeezed her gently and said, "A child will always love their parent. It's called unconditional love, Blake. Welcome it."

Blake thanked him with her yes, and walked back to the living room to wait for Lionel. *Unconditional love.* What was that, she thought. She couldn't remember a time when nothing came without conditions; she expected them.

"He's coming," Blake said to Jacinta. Jacinta put her hand to her heart as they both turned to look at Lionel coming down the steps.

Blake stood. He looked just like her father. Tall, with a long, lanky body; thick, curly hair that he wore loose; and light brown skin. Blake fell to her knees.

Lionel stood before her in an awkward stance, and a face filled with questions and a tinge of impatience. She took him into her embrace. He was stiff, but obliged. Jacinta and Kenton stood quietly to the side.

"I'm your mother," Blake said, looking up at him. She hadn't thought of any fancy words to pepper her revelation. She just wanted to say it.

Lionel stood there. He looked to Kenton for approval. Kenton put his hand on his shoulder and said, "So you officially have two parents you're stuck with."

Lionel finally broke a smile. "Mom? You're my mom?"

Blake nodded as the floodgates of tears gushed out. "And I love you. I want to be in your life, Lionel. If you will have me," she said. She braced herself for a swirl of questions.

"I love you, too," he said in that pure innocence only a child could have, and an unconditional sense of love she never experienced before came over her. *So this is what it feels like.*

She rose and grabbed him into her arms again. They stood together, holding each other.

Jacinta joined in the hug, and Blake said, "This is your grandmother. My mother."

Lionel nodded, rubbing his eyes from sleep or tears. "Hi," he said, swaying his body from side to side.

Jacinta grabbed him and pulled him toward her, almost taking him off balance. Blake and Kenton laughed. So did Lionel.

"These are for you. It's in your blood," Jacinta said, handing

Lionel a small box of Blake's father's CDs and raw, uncut jazz tunes. "Your granddaddy would have loved to see this day. You have generations of gifted, talented men behind you."

Kenton sat on the couch with his feet kicked up on the leather ottoman, letting the two women own the moment, but Blake wondered if he didn't feel a bit left out. Pizza for all and several Jazz CDs later spelled the end to one of the most memorable nights of Blake's life.

Chapter Thirty-Six

September 2
Miami, FL

Kenton met Blake for dinner at a quiet, tucked away restaurant that didn't have a name or an awning. There was no phone number listed. It was exclusive and private—exactly what they needed.

"So how many women have you brought to this little hideout?" Blake said, smiling and nursing her glass of red wine. They sat outside in the garden area staring at the shiny, black lagoon in front of them.

Kenton looked into her eyes. "I figured with all the press and such that you didn't want any more attention. And no, I haven't brought anyone else here. It just opened." He smiled back.

Blake smirked coolly. "So glad things went well the other night. I wasn't sure how it was gonna go down."

"Neither was I, honestly. Lionel did well. I'm proud of him, and you...and your mom."

Blake laughed. "She thought she would never see the day when Lionel and I reunited. I'm glad she did," Blake said, gazing back at Kenton. "And thank you, for making this work."

"Ahh, no big deal. Plus, if it means I get to see you more, I'll do *anything*," he said, arching a brow.

"Well, you can start with telling me why are we alone tonight? Dinner? Fancy restaurant?"

"Because I want to be with you. Or get to know you better," he said, self-correcting.

"I like both answers."

"I want you to know that this isn't about Lionel," Kenton said, loosening the collar of his perfectly pressed, buttoned white shirt. He leaned his back against the chair. "This is about me and you. If we had met under other circumstances, I would still feel the same. You?"

Blake's eyes scanned his handsome features, the broadness of his shoulders, his thick, bushy eyebrows that shaped dark, deep-set eyes. She stopped at his lips, and slightly parted hers at the thought of kissing them.

"Blake?" he said, breaking her concentration.

"Our connection isn't all about Lionel. I know."

"It isn't. When I first laid eyes on you, I just knew it. Damn, if I had met you at an after-work bar, I would have kicked it to you there. Anywhere."

They laughed.

"When should I tell Lionel everything? You think he can handle the full truth about his father?"

"I don't know, Blake," Kenton said, shrugging. "I know the boy, but he's growing up and it may hit him pretty heavy. I say do it when it feels right. That can be anytime. I'm sure he has questions too."

"I wish I didn't have to let him down. I don't know who his father is, there's nothing I can really say besides how it happened."

"Blake, you gotta let the gates fall open. Everyone knows. Do you want him to find out some other way about the rape?"

"I don't," Blake said, her heart beating fast.

Kenton reached for her hand. "You'll make a great mom. You have so much to teach him that I can't. Take it one day at a time."

Blake nodded, holding back tears.

"And there's another thing. I've thought long and hard on this, Blake. I don't plan to be lawyer my whole life. I have plans to run for the Senate. Lionel knows this already, and he's okay with being in the limelight for a minute. And if you're in our lives, you would be too."

Blake laughed and reached for her wine. "I'm no stranger to that." She could only imagine how her background and dramas could hurt his chances, but she didn't want to defeat his dream. "I'm fine with that, since we don't know where this is all going. *Us*, I mean."

"I know where I want *us* to go." He looked at Blake intently, his eyes saying more than words could. Their plates sat cold, but the words heated up. "I want you in my life."

"Senator, though?"

"Don't worry, I don't plan on running for president later," he said, picking up his fork.

"I'm fine with being Blake's mom, even you and I exploring

what we've got here. I'm feeling you as much as you're feeling me, Kenton. But I'm not so sure about playing the good girlfriend if you're running for office." Blake shook her head in refusal.

"Listen to me," he whispered in her ear. The diamonds in her ear tickled his lips. He moved them to the side and kissed her lobes.

"I'm listening," she purred.

"I do good as a lawyer, but as Senator, I will have relationships that can last a lifetime. It's legacy making."

Blake liked the sound of it, but she wasn't used to being a part of anyone else's dreams. She was a lone soul in the world. But she too felt that need to change.

"Kenton, I think it's great what you're doing. But think carefully. I'm not exactly political material. I have some dirty laundry."

"Don't we all?" he said, low and heavy.

Their eyes locked, and Blake felt *that* conversation was for later. Kenton intrigued her, and she liked that.

"I can win this election coming up in a few years. You just have to promise you'll stand by me."

Blake nodded; she was always up for a challenge. Kenton leaned in and touched her soft, glossy lips with his.

Chapter Thirty-Seven

September 21
Miami, Florida

Weeks passed and Blake hadn't thought for one minute to return to New York. She had Charles to take care of the financials, and an expert legal team on call to handle her case via phone or email. Her life in Miami had gotten wrapped up quickly with Kenton and dealing with the Margot-Thomas drama. *It just never seems to end*, she thought as her eyes glided over a distraught text from Margot.

<Come over. You won't believe this.>

It didn't take long before Blake found herself in the driver seat of her black Lamborghini heading over to Margot's. Her brain spun with what could be next. She was pretty sure Margot knew about the pregnancy, and was hoping that Thomas did the right thing and told her. There was no way she was going to keep being the bearer of bad news in Margot's life.

Blake ascended the winding driveway of Margot's lavish home, parking right in the front next to the Margot's white Mercedes. She lightly dabbed her lips with a peach-colored lipstick in the mirror, hopped out of her car, and took a deep breath as she walked up the steps.

"Honey!" Margot said, before she could even ring the bell. Margot wrapped her arms around her.

Blake let her body fall into Margot's embrace and inhaled the sweet rose-scented perfume she wore. Whimpers followed.

"Why are you crying? You were just smiling from ear to ear," Blake said, lowering her head to look into Margot's tiny brown eyes. She took Margot's hand as she led her friend into the private den.

"What is going on?" Blake said in a demanding but kind tone.

"It's Thomas." Margot grabbed a napkin that sat on a glass table between them.

Blake listened.

"He wants to come back. He doesn't want to divorce."

The tears kept flowing from Margot's eyes as she continued. "She's pregnant and he wants us to raise the baby."

Blake's stomach plummeted to her stilettos. "What? Huh?"

"I'm done with him! How can he have the audacity to do this! To get a whore pregnant and expect me to raise the baby? Is he insane?" Margot said, squeezing the tissue for dear life between her dainty hands.

"Breathe, Margot. Think through this. Are you sure you want to divorce Thomas?"

"Yes, yes, oh, hell yes!" Margot raged. "What else can I do? I have to show him I mean business. He has ruined our lives."

Blake looked intently at Margot, who seemed more hurt than angry. No matter how many times Margot said yes, just by the sheer look of lost in her eyes, she could tell her best friend was not ready to throw away twenty years. She was hurt, and hurt was okay.

"Sounds to me like you are holding all the cards, Margot. I wouldn't fret. Thomas is putty in your hands now."

Just then, Margot's eyes transfixed on Blake's relaxed face. "What do you mean?" she asked, wiping her face dry.

Blake stood up, folded her arms against her chest, and paced the room, thinking. She stopped near the sun-drenched bay window. "If Thomas wants to come back," Blake said, "he's probably willing to do what you want to make this all go away. Does it matter to you why he's coming back?"

"I bet it's to keep his money. He can't afford to pay me in a divorce settlement and take care of that wench with his baby."

"Let's face it, Thomas probably could. I'm sure he's coming back because he genuinely wants to be with you. Sometimes a man has to hit a wall before he can look back to appreciate what he had. You and Thomas always wanted a child. Robin wants money. She couldn't care less about the baby. Work something out."

Margot looked up at Blake. "Are you saying pay Robin off?"

"You said it, not me." Blake grinned.

"Oh, no, I'm divorcing that scum bucket," Margot said, pointing in the air. Her eyes burst into tears again.

"Margot." Blake held her shoulders. "You don't have to prove anything to me. I won't judge you if you stay with him. No one will."

Margot shook her head. "I'm just so embarrassed. He hurt me more than he could ever know." She took another tissue. "But I do love that man. We have over twenty years together. He has been there for me even when I hurt him the most." She smiled to herself. "I haven't exactly been the perfect little angel wife."

Blake smiled with her eyes about the time Margot told her about an affair she had had with her masseuse, Lau, a thick, muscled Malaysian man who was twenty-five years her junior. Thomas found out and fired him, but not before Thomas beat him to a pulp. Things were never the same, but they made it work. Blake was convinced that this was an unusual marriage of love and convenience that Thomas and Margot unconsciously worked out between them.

"Make a deal with Robin. Have Thomas talk to her. I guarantee you she will hand over that baby faster than a Serena Williams serve."

Margot sighed deeply. "I would love my own child, but I would be happy with any child, especially one born from Thomas. Maybe in some strange way this is a gift?" Margot asked, her eyebrows raised.

"Maybe," Blake said, sitting back down across from her. "Don't let Robin win. Thomas and you belong together. I see this working out for everyone. Are you willing to see that Robin has some kind of monthly allowance?"

"For what?"

"I'm just saying women like that tend to get ideas. Maybe write her a nice check. I'm sure she knows some secrets by now you don't want told."

"Well, I hope Thomas wasn't that stupid."

"Anything's possible. But I always believe every woman should leave a situation stronger, better, no matter what it is. Though I may not talk to Robin anyway, I did have a friendship with her, and I don't want to see her discarded or out on the streets because of this. You will need Robin on your side for this to work."

Margot nodded. "True. We're gonna handle it like real women. I knew what I was signing up for years ago when I married Thomas. Scratch that, when we started dating. Wives all over in my shoes know we have to deal with a lot to enjoy this lifestyle. I'm not willing to give up my life for anyone. I won't be a victim to anyone's bad decisions."

"You control your own destiny," Blake added. "We all do," thinking of her own woes.

"I also plan to keep pursuing my own ideas, maybe even start my own business."

"That's right, Margot. Tell Thomas. Tell him what you need. Demand it. Like you said, you both made mistakes." Blake rose and headed to the door. "If you need anything, let me know, but I know you can handle this."

Blake walked out into the shiny Sunday afternoon with the brightest smile she had all day. She wasn't so sure what she was happy about. Maybe it was because she helped instead of destroy Margot's marriage or that love and companionship still reigned at the end of the day. Margot and Thomas were, to her, the Black power couple trying to make it work in the hectic, crazy life they all shared. It kept the light burning in her own heart. It wasn't about who was right or wrong. It was about winning. Today, Margot was her hero.

Chapter Thirty-Eight

September 22
Miami, FL

U p the next morning as she puttered around her Miami Beach home, Blake felt a familiar restlessness rising in her chest. She helped Margot, hell, maybe even Robin with a nice fat check, but was she helping herself enough? The idea she had for Margot was pretty genius, she thought. Just having the guts to suggest it without Margot cursing her out a second time was a risk. Blake held the warm cup of tea in her hand, and an old name from her past came to mind.

Jake Jones. He was a private investigator she hired many years ago to find some dirt on a competing real estate firm that had sabotaged a few of her early purchases in Harlem. He was able to dig up the clandestine second life of Mark Spencer, one of the managing directors that Blake threatened to expose. Mark backed down, and slowly Blake began building her portfolio to turn abandoned, burnt-out brownstones in Harlem into valuable family homes. It was something Mark and his agency never did, only buying and holding, never fixing. Blake was credited as one of the first buyers to make Harlem the real estate hot pot it turned into during the early 2000s.

Blake's cell phone was at the far wing of the house, and she took a few steps downstairs to her office, flanked in gorgeous, clean lines of steel blue and silver. Her sturdy, shiny steel-colored desk was neatly arranged with a phone, MacBook, and a few pens. She never did business here, only in emergencies.

"Jake, this is Blake Bertrand. It has been forever, but I need a favor. Call me, if uh, this is you," she said, hanging up the office phone in hesitation. She wasn't even sure if this old number worked, and beat herself up for a few seconds for giving her full name. What if it wasn't Jake, and a freak stranger who would call her back?

But before she could even let that thought settle in, her office phone rang.

"Long time," said Jake in his light, quippy voice. "I've been keeping tabs on you," he teased.

"I'm sure you have," Blake laughed, relieved to hear from him. "It can't be any better than what these tabloids are pulling out their asses."

"Congratulations on everything you've been doing. Forget those fuckers, they deserve to die."

Blake gulped. She remembered Jake being quite the eccentric, and scary. She was glad to know some of the old Jake was still there. "Speaking of fuckers..."

"I know you need something," he interrupted. "I'll do anything, and if I can't my guys will."

Blake gulped again, but inside she felt excited. Jake could really do anything she wanted. That was good to know. "Well, I don't need anything that can get your hands too dirty, and I hope I never will. But you know I got a case, right?"

"Yup."

"I need it to disappear. My lawyers got my financial papers to the FBI that cleared me, but they are sweeping it under the rug. There has been no public declaration of my innocence, making me look like I'm still a criminal," Blake said, breathless. She took a pause. "They are screwing me over, probably embarrassed that they screwed up this investigation looking at me, when all the resources should have gone to investigating Lang—"

"Blake, they hate you. Everybody hates everyone in this world," Jake philosophized. "You're young, successful, gorgeous, and they want to stop you from getting to that next level. Don't let them."

"Exactly, I can forget this and move on like nothing happened, standing judged by others for the rest of my life. Or you can do something for me."

"All ears."

"Dig some dirt up on the DA handling my case. That *fucker* has more dirt in his life than a Dyson. If he can't do his job, I'll have to make him do his job, and do it right."

"Send me the deets now," Jake commanded. "I like this one."

"Me, too," Blake grinned. "Email address still the same?"

"Indeed."

Blake pulled up her computer and sent Jake the DA's name and anything else about him.

Jake replied three hours later.

***

September 28
Miami, Florida

Blake and Kenton sat in his living room to catch the evening news. Lionel was in his room doing homework, which Blake thought was just fine. She didn't want him to see what was coming up.

"I can't wait to see what that DA has to say about all this. What an asshole," hissed Kenton as he shook his head.

Blake melted into his arms. She didn't reveal that she already knew what the district attorney had to say. She learned to always keep some things to herself. Blake smiled as she sipped her glass of red wine. Actually, she hadn't said a word for the last ten minutes they had been together. He knew she was tense, and she hoped he wouldn't press her. If he did, she'd have to lie.

"Here it is," Kenton said, turning up the news.

Blake put her drink down. Jake had assured her all was taken care of. As the DA spoke, a slim grin ran across Blake's lips.

"—So, I stand here now to say that we have closed the case against Blake Bertrand. She is innocent, the charges have been dropped. We will now proceed with the further investigation of other persons of interest—"

Blake clapped, and so did Kenton. "Hear, hear," Kenton said, holding up his glass of wine and handing Blake's to her. "Congratulations. You are finally a free woman."

They both clinked their glasses to a quick toast. "Well, I figured it was about time they made this public declaration. I can go on with my life."

"How long will it take for them to unfreeze your assets?"

"Oh, it's done already." Blake slipped, then clenched her jaw. *Oops,* she thought.

"How? He just made the declaration today. I'm sure there's some paperwork?"

Blake didn't answer, and brought her glass to her lips.

Kenton lowered his eyes on her, arching his right brow. "What did you do?"

"Nothing anyone else in my shoes wouldn't do. Let's just say all is well. It was just this public declaration that had to be done.

I'm fine. All is fine. Okay?" Blake said, looking at him sternly. She hadn't had to answer to a man since being married, and she was in no mood to start today. No way, she thought, she was going to tell Kenton about Jake, or that he discovered that the DA led a second life picking up male prostitutes. Jake took explicit photos, showed it to the DA, and gave him twenty-four hours to confess or he would send them to the local newspapers, and TV stations. It didn't take but a second for the DA to comply and wipe Blake clean like a whistle.

If I only knew that was all I had to do, Blake said to herself as she shook her head.

"So you ain't gonna tell me?" Kenton still eyed her curiously, inching closer to her.

She inched back. "Nope," she said, picking up her bag. She gave him a light kiss on the lips. "I'm gonna say good-bye to Lionel. Then," she said, brushing his neck with her fingers," when I see you tomorrow, you'll forget these silly questions, and I'll forget to answer them. Okay?"

He nodded and looked at her like a puppy in distress. "Good," she said, planting another kiss on his lips. This one was decidedly more intense than the first. She wanted to stay, in his bed, but she wasn't quite ready yet.

"Good night, Lionel, I'll see you next weekend," Blake, said, creeping her son's bedroom door open. She walked in and hugged him tightly.

Lionel looked up, tight coils of hair covering his head. He put his pen down, hugged her back. Each time his hug got a little tighter. He smiled widely and nodded, "Good night, Mommy," he said, and turned back to his book.

Mommy. Blake's heart warmed as she closed the door softly and stood there like she never wanted to leave.

Chapter Thirty-Nine

October 5
Miami, Florida

"Will your phone ever stop ringing?" Margot laughed as she sat in Blake's Miami Beach office.

"What can I say? The world is happy that I am back in business. But it sure as hell wasn't without a cost." Blake put her phone back in her bag, but no sooner had she done that when a text message came through. She reminded herself to check it later. She had been receiving a flurry of texts, too, from old and prospective clients. Everyone was ready to do business with her again.

"I lost money. Time is money in this business," Blake said, leaning back on her chair. "But that means nothing to me. I'm glad to have my name back, and all. However, I did have some time to think. I need to reinvent myself. I don't want to be in this business forever. You see, the wolves come at the door every so often, and I am tired of fighting the wolves—"

"Not you, Blake," Margot said, shaking her head playfully. "Ms. Queen of Fixing. You are more than equipped to handle this."

Blake stayed silent and rested her chin in her hands. "Maybe, but does that mean I should keep doing this? I can use those skills in anything. Damn it, instead of buying up the real estate on a Caribbean island, maybe I just want to lie on the island?! Can I lie on the island sipping a Mai Tai on the beach, Margot?"

Margot laughed at Blake, who smiled sarcastically imagining herself lounging on a beach chair. "Well, honey. Come to think of it, you don't take vacations. You are the hardest-working woman I know. So, what's the plan, then?"

"I don't know yet. I may finish up this Wishman Spears deal now and think about that later. Margot, since we haven't spoken, there is a lot of stuff you missed." Blake looked over Margot's shoulder and signaled to her assistant to hold any calls. "I have a son." Blake filled Margot in on Lionel, his recitals, visiting him in secret, and her "growing" friendship with Kenton.

Margot's mouth hung open the entire time.

"I want to get to know Lionel, like a mother, and—Kenton too."

"So you're a mommy?" Margot smiled warmly.

"Not a real mommy, but a mother. I want to be a real mommy."

"You are, dear." Margot touched her hand. "You are."

"I fought to keep my empire together for me, and for Lionel. This is my legacy for my son. I won't let anyone rip that away from me."

"And Kenton?"

Blake blushed.

"Ooh, girl, did you sleep with him?"

"Not yet," Blake gushed. "He is handsome, kind, sexy, and the adoptive father of my son. I mean, I couldn't make this up! The powers that be brought us together somehow for some reason."

"Well, the reason is obviously for you to be back in Lionel's life."

"Right, I just didn't expect a man to come with the package, you know?"

Margot sighed. "You got a two-for-one deal. Not many women would complain."

"You know my track record with men. Brett? Lang? Not good," Blake, turning down the corners of her mouth. "*Bad.*"

"This is different," Margot said, raising her chin. "Maybe this is your chance to fix those wrongs. I say give the man some!"

Blake laughed out loud, as Margot sat straight-faced. She was serious.

"And you and Thomas?" Blake asked.

Margot waved her hand like she was batting a fly. "That chick took that check quicker than a crackhead taking a five-dollar bill."

Blake eyes widened, and she said, "I'm not gonna ask how much."

"She was cheaper than I thought."

"Hmm." Blake nodded, surprised that Robin didn't push for more.

"We have an agreement that we can raise the child, no visitations. She was more than willing to comply. But I'm not surprised, I knew she was a coldhearted bitch."

"I'm proud of you, Margot. Has Thomas moved back in yet?"

"We're working on it," she said, slowly. Then her eyes lit up. "I hired an interior designer for the baby's room."

"I can't wait to see it," Blake said, hearing her phone buzz again for another message.

***

Later, Blake and Kenton were walking on the lawn surrounding her home under the warm evening glow of the moon.

"Dinner was bad, as in good," Kenton grinned as they climbed the steps to go back inside. "How did you know I love seafood?"

"What Black man doesn't," Blake laughed, her hair slightly damp from the humidity. She tucked it behind her ear.

"I love it when you do that. Let me help." He tucked the hair on the other side behind her ear, tracing his fingers down the nape of her neck, until his hands gripped her in an embrace.

She took a deep breath.

"I can fall in love with you, Ms. Bertrand," Kenton whispered in her ear.

She hit him playfully, swinging her head back. "I thought you already were!"

He kept a serious face. "I am."

"Am?"

"I love you," he said, his eyes watering slightly. "Sorry, don't want to overwhelm you."

"Too late for that." Blake said against his lips, inhaling his vanilla-scented cologne.

"I love you," he whispered repeatedly in her ear.

She walked Kenton inside her home, and still holding each other, they giggled like school kids as they misstepped to the bedroom.

Blake closed the door and laid Kenton down. She slipped off her turquoise silk maxi dress to reveal nothing but skin underneath. There was just enough light in the room to touch her curves. She stood there letting Kenton's eyes canvass her taut, fit body. She completely owned the moment, and his lips formed a smile. Finally, he unbuttoned his shirt and tossed his clothes to the side.

Blake studied the gift that saluted her, and finally climbed into bed with him. She led his hands to her breasts. He kneaded her nipples between his fingers and brought them to his mouth. "Mmmm," he moaned like a child digging into a moist chocolate cake. Blake collapsed on her back, and Kenton lowered his long, lean body on top of hers. His lips lingered around the edges of her neck and shoulders. He took his time inching down to her breasts, closing his mouth over her hardened nipples. He moved down to her soft stomach and inner thighs, brushing his tongue against her moistness. Then he mounted her thighs around his shoulders and lost himself between them.

Blake pressed her hips into him, feeling her insides soften and melt in his mouth. She gently grabbed his head with one hand. "Don't stop, don't stop," she begged him until she erupted with the kind of pleasure she only had in her dreams.

"Jezzzus," she called out as he filled her up, sliding inside her with a thrust that landed perfectly. Their bodies slick with sweat, the mangled mix of his cologne and sweat in the air, Kenton rocked her with a gentle steadiness. He didn't want it to end, and neither did she. They kissed as he moved inside her, holding his body up with his hands and burying his hips into her. He didn't take his eyes off Blake for a second as she gripped his muscled shoulders. A tattoo on his upper arm, with a symbol that looked like a weapon of sorts with the words "God's Angel," stared back at her.

Overwhelmed, Blake was. She didn't know what to expect from Kenton anymore. But one thing she was sure of. He was no angel in the bedroom.

Chapter Forty

The following month, Blake headed back to New York. She brought her mother with her for company. She still was getting used to flying alone without Suki and the rest of her team. She missed them.

In the living room of her condo, she watched her mom finish a light work of Pilates.

"Two months ago, I couldn't lift my leg to get in the shower. Check me out now?" Her mother put her arms out and did a slow turn.

Blake clapped from across the room as she handed a towel to her mom, who was no Pilates expert. But she was still relieved to see her perform the subtle moves the physical therapist recommended.

They sat at the dining table, and Blake made her mom a plate of smoked salmon, fried eggs, and toast. Blake was skipping a full breakfast this morning.

"You know, *mija*, you should think of doing the Pilates," Jacinta said, chewing on a piece of toast. "You don't sweat."

Blake laughed and said, "I like sweating when I work out. In fact, I'm going for a run in the park after I finish this banana."

"Eww, and you come back all sweaty and stinky?" Jacinta held her nose.

Blake rolled her eyes. "Sweat detoxifies the body."

"Well, I'm clean, I don't need detox. You kids come up with the craziest things." Jacinta cut into a delicate slice of smoked salmon as she spoke, and as wrong as her mom was, she was just happy she was there.

Ten minutes later Blake was out the door, on a jog she hadn't done in months. She was determined to get her stride back. With Kenton and Lionel in her life practically full time, she needed to keep her space and meet her own needs when she could.

She ran about a quarter mile, inhaling the crisp cool air and whisking past the trees, strollers, and pedestrians, who mostly seemed to be going in the opposite direction. She recognized no one. Years ago when she started jogging, she'd look forward to the familiar faces on her path. It told her she was on schedule and part of something that was improving her life. *I have to do this more often*, Blake told herself, slowing down her pace when she heard her name called from behind. She stopped, wiped the sweat from her forehead, and spun around.

"Think you're the only one who cares about looking good these days?" Lang said, dressed in gray sweats.

Blake began running again. She wanted to disappear from Lang's sight, but he strode right alongside her.

"Can we talk?" he asked, looking at her in between breaths. His hair was matted from sweat already, and it had only been a few minutes.

"Hell to the fucking no," Blake said, calmly, changing directions, hoping he would get the hint. He disappeared. Blake hopped back on her usual route that led to her apartment. She dug in her fanny pack for her phone to call and check on her mother, when she realized she forgot it.

"Oh, damn, shit!" Blake shouted. She had only gone without her phone twice in the last seven years. "Shit!" Her runner's high diminished as her long, graceful strides turned into sputtered steps. She took a few swigs of her water, looked around, and decided to walk home. It was only fifteen minutes away, she thought. The crinkly leaves beneath her feet made her smile, and she relaxed into her new walking pace.

As she approached the Ramble that led to the side of the park closest to her apartment, Lang appeared. He blocked her path.

She took a step back, jaw and fists clenched. A metallic taste grew in her mouth. *One two three. What would Suki do? One two three.* She thought that there was no way she could muster up in seconds what took Suki years to master or go toe-to-toe with a two hundred–pound man.

Lang stared at her with hollow, cold eyes. His nostrils flared with each hefty breath.

Blake whirled around to run back, but he grabbed her by the neck and stopped her breath.

"Bitch, I've been wanting you all to myself. You think you can get rid of me, do you?" Lang stared into her eyes.

Blake still couldn't breathe. Her hands grasped at his around her neck, scratching him so hard, he bled. He let her go and pushed her to the ground, but Blake wasn't giving up. She remembered a move Suki had taught her about the correct way to stand after a fall with the least chance of getting hit. She put her foot on the ground, the other knee down, and lifted her arm to guard against Lang's wing at her head with his foot. She lifted her hips up and threw the hardest kick she could get out into Lang's knee. With Lang bent over in pain, she put her arms up for defense.

Lang pulled out a knife, grabbed her, and traced it down the bridge of her nose. "After I'm done with you, you'll never want to look in the mirror again, bitch," he said, spit gathering at the corners of his lips. He threw her to the ground and climbed on top.

Tears flowed from Blake's eyes as she lay frozen. With her free hands, she dove her fingers straight into Lang's eyes, remembering that Suki had told her to "think of digging dirt." The pain caused Lang to drop the knife as he brought his hands to his face. She got up to run, but he grabbed her by the leg and pounced on her again, busting her lip open.

"I still see you got that fight in you. But what if I told you something that would make you wish you were dead?"

Blake's face was matted with blood, and her body was pressed into the dirt by his weight. Her heart raced as she thought about what to do.

He grinded his hips into her and whispered in her ear, "Lionel."

Blake cried out. "Don't you fuck with him!"

Lang pressed his lips into her ear. "Remember that night I took you in the dark? When am I gonna see my son, bitch?!"

Blake didn't know what came over her, but she wrapped her legs around Lang. With all her might, she managed to flip them both over. She rolled off him, but he reached for her again. Kicking him in the face, she rose on her feet. She wasn't running anymore, she thought. "You raped me! It was you?!" Blake felt her mind draw black. Everything turned off. Lang, hobbling back and forth with his bloody face. She in the woods, with her world crashing down on her.

Lang charged at Blake until they both rolled on the ground. He pinned her down, and as she kicked and spat at him, he pulled out the knife again and swung it at her. She moved her face quickly enough, grabbed a loose rock, and smashed his head. He rolled over in pain, still calling toward her. Blake still crying, saw a gun.

Blake found another rock and pounded it into Lang's head until he stopped moving.

She looked up at the sky, fell on her knees, and screamed the loudest she could from her soul.

Chapter Forty-One

November 10
New York, New York

Blake lay in the hospital, wrapped from head to toe. She was being cared for in the psychiatric section. When she looked up from her bed, she saw all the people who mattered to her. Kenton, her mother, Lionel, Margot—even Suki.

"I wanna die," Blake cried, her body in such pain she could barely move a muscle.

"Honey, no," Margot said. She put her hand on Blake's forehead. "You will be fine, Blake. What happened to you shouldn't have happened to anyone. You will get past this, we all will."

"I wanted to kill his ass, but you beat me to it, Boss," Suki said, straight-faced as everyone shifted their feet at the iciness in her voice.

Blake managed a grunt of acknowledgment, then it dawned on her. No one could really look at her, not even her mother.

"He's dead?" Blake said in a low, tired voice. "I killed someone?"

Kenton leaned in close to her. "Don't speak. We are taking care of everything. Don't try to remember anything. No charges will be filed."

"Charges?" Blake said, looking alarmed. She looked at Jacinta, who sat in a corner of the room, rocking her body back and forth while she said the rosary in Spanish.

Everyone's eyes landed on Blake.

"Lang passed away a few hours ago," Kenton said, plainly.

"Lionel," Blake said, feeling the full impact of the moment as she brushed her son's face with her hand.
She closed her eyes again, as if she wanted to disappear and never return. "I didn't know what else to do."

"That's why it's self-defense. You were protecting yourself."
Blake felt empty. Dead inside herself. Something told her that

Lang had taken enough from her, and he had almost taken her with him. She was still alive, her second chance to make things right in her life again.

"God forgive me," Blake cried out. "Please forgive me!"
Lionel sat quietly, looking at Blake. She stared at him, searching for words.

"Do you want him to leave?" Kenton asked.

"No, he can be here. He should know what happened."

"Lionel," Blake said, doing her best to sit up in the bed with Kenton's help. "Lang was your father. I'm sorry," she said, reading the saddened look on his face. She took a deep swallow. "Lang raped me many years ago, and you were born. You are my greatest gift, and I hope you—"

"I forgive you, Mommy. I couldn't let anyone hurt you like he did. I hate him," Lionel said, his eyes swollen.

She laid his head on her chest. "It's okay. Feel what you feel. I'm here for you," she said, brushing his hair with her hands as he cried. "I love you."

"I love you, too," he said.

Kenton and Margot left the room, followed by Suki, who laid a bouquet of flowers from the team on Blake's nightstand. Blake smiled at her warmly.

Now she and Lionel were left alone. Blake held him for at least fifteen minutes, and when she looked down, he had fallen asleep on her chest. For the first time in a while, she felt free and loved unconditionally.

***

November 12
Miami, Florida

When Blake checked out of the hospital, she boarded the next available flight to Miami.

As she watched the city get smaller and smaller from the ascending plane, her stomach sank. With her mother seated next to her, she wondered what Jacinta was thinking. She hadn't said many words and kept her rosary to her chest. She knew her mother was praying for her. She didn't exactly expect a pat on the back for what she did, but she wanted something.

"I'm sorry," she said to Jacinta, who sat with her red-colored rosary dangling between her fingers. "I ask God to forgive me every day."

Jacinta patted Blake's hands. "I am praying for myself."

Blake tilted her head to the side. "What?"

"I wish you had killed him earlier. I wish he was never born. I wish I could have seen you kill that *hijo de la granputa!*"

A few passengers turned to look at them.

Blake didn't know whether to laugh or cry. She put her arms around her mother, feeling her fragile head landing on her shoulders, her soft, gray curls tumbling down the side of her face. Jacinta's body shook. "You almost died, *mija*. You almost died," she wept.

A flight attendant walked by and handed Blake a napkin for Jacinta. "Scared of flying, eh." She half-smiled at Blake.

Blake nodded. She had thought Jacinta's silence was all about her, when her mother probably had gone through just as much pain as she did. Instead of being comforted by her mother's words assuring her that her soul would be rescued from damnation after a thousand Hail Marys, she comforted her mother and let the warmth of her mother's body heal her.

***

Several hours later, after Blake dropped her mom off at her condo, she went home. There was no one there but Kenton.

"How are you?" he said, standing at her door in loose linen slacks and a white shirt. "Or is that a dumb question?"

"Dumb," Blake muttered as he took her bags and she flopped her body on the couch.

He sat beside her. "Are you going to be okay?"

The sounds of Miles Davis's "So What" vibrated through the walls from the next room. *He must have gotten his hands on my jazz collection, one of Daddy's favorites.* But Blake couldn't bring herself to mention it. She let the ebbs and flows of the jazz melody calm and soothe her.

"You know," Kenton said, moving closer, his breath against her. "You don't have to be strong for me."

Blake rubbed her head, hoping that the sleep that awaited her didn't come with any more nightmares.

"I'm okay, I said. Don't you get it? I don't have time to spend in a mental hospital or go over this a hundred times. I got shit I have to do."

Kenton kissed her forehead gently. "Let me make love to you."

He turned her face to his and landed a kiss on her mouth.

She felt her body loosen. "I'm not in the mood," she said, but she was. She wanted nothing more.

"I don't believe you." He smiled.

"Kenton," she said, smiling, "I don't know how to relax sometimes. I can't. I killed a man."

Kenton rose and walked to the kitchen, reappearing in seconds with two glasses of wine. "Here," he said. "Wine is for things you have to accept. You have to accept what happened and *how* it happened."

Blake gulped the wine down. Kenton handed her his glass and said, "And this too shall pass."

She took a long, satisfying sip. "People may forgive, but they won't forget."

"What matters is that you forgive yourself. Fuck, people."

Blake held in her urge to laugh. She had never heard Kenton curse. She nodded in agreement and sipped again. She knew that she held the power switch to turn this all around, but not today.

"You weren't charged with anything. All the witnesses who saw the attack vouched that you fought for your life. Successfully, I might add."

"I'm sure there's some karma somewhere for my ass."

"Blake, you did the right thing. Trust me."

"What about you? I know this won't help your campaign at all."

"This will be old news by next week when they find something else. Okay?" He swept a few strands of hair away from her eyes. "If you keep looking guilty, people will treat you that way. Celebrate, Blake. You're an inspiration."

"How?"

Kenton pulled out a few letters. "These were sitting in the mailbox. Can't be more than a few days old. I'm thinking this is fan mail." He smiled.

Blake opened the letters. They were from women thanking her for her courage. It was like the cloud over her began to float away. "This one," she said, reading it closely, "is an invitation to speak at the Global Women Against Violence Summit next year."

He laughed. "Did you check your email yet?"

Blake's eyes darted to her phone, and she opened her email to find that it was jam-packed with invitations and emails of support. Her jaw dropped.

"Now, can you see the other side of this? Don't create a jail for yourself, when the rest of the world has already set you free."

Blake closed the email. "I'll have Edith get to these in the morning," she said, looking at the ground, humbled by what she read. "Among other things. God knows how much unfinished business there is. Wishman Spears." She looked up at the ceiling. "That'll be my last building."

"Blake?" Kenton looked up at her face. "How about we just focus on now, getting now right?"

"Now hasn't been right for a long time," Blake said, shaking her head back and forth. "And I don't know how to fix it anymore. I don't think I want to."

"Come with me." Kenton took her by the hand to the bedroom as Miles's periodic lifts in tension seemed to fit Kenton's unhurried, easy way about it all. There, he laid her on the bed and crawled next to her. Cocooned by his full-bodied embrace, Blake felt protected. He held the space for her to be herself—messy, vulnerable, and loved. Tears streamed down her nose, cheeks, and lips like water let out from a dam. Each tear came from the pit of her stomach and the deep anguish she hadn't been able to let flow till now. She imagined each tear bringing her to a better understanding of her own self, not washing away, but blessing the good and bad of her past. Right then, a thin silver beam of light came through a slit in the curtains and penetrated the darkness. It was just enough to see.

EPILOGUE

Blake stood in front of the towering Wishman Spears building with her team, including Thomas. She was snug in the middle with a pair of scissors about to cut her last ribbon, when a reporter asked, "Ms. Bertrand, what's next for you?"

Blake looked at the passersby and small group of investors who stood before her with TV cameras and newspaper reporters. "I have some plans, which I will reveal when the time is right. Now is the time to celebrate the opening of one of the most beautiful pieces of real estate the city has ever seen!" With that, Blake clipped the ribbon to signify that Wishman Spears was finally open for business.

This was what Blake lived for, but the truth was, she had other plans already mapped out. She was moving quietly out of Miami with Kenton to create a real family for Lionel, and support Kenton's run for Senator. She thought it was an excellent way to give back, and if she had to vote for a Senator, it would be for Kenton Rhodes. Blake knew that he had lived under her spotlight for over a year, and she was okay with putting the shoe on the other foot.

"You never looked better in McQueens," Margot said to Blake.

Blake kicked her foot back playfully. She was wearing the six-inch McQueen sandals she kept by her bed. "And I never felt better than I do today, except the day Lionel came back into my life."

"Are you ready to play the Senator's wife?" whispered Margot in her ear.

Blake laughed, for she didn't exactly imagine herself being anybody's anything. "We're not getting married. I just agreed to go with him, and see what I can do."

"Knowing you, Blake, you will find yourself into something. Big."

"True," Blake laughed. "But right now I'm just excited. I've got two awesome men in my life that care about me. I'm just finally glad I let them do that."

"It can be pretty hard for girls like us when our lives lose control." Margot winked as she held Anna, Thomas's lovely daughter that they had both easily adopted from an eager Robin.

"It's that craziness that little miracles seep through." Blake lovingly eyed little Anna. "Sometimes I wonder why I worried so much."